THIS ANGELIC LAND

THIS
ANGELIC
LAND

Aris Janigian

WEST OF WEST BOOKS
LOS ANGELES

Cover Art by Lou Beach

Cover and Book Design by Lausten Cossutta Design

Printing and Binding by McNaughton & Gunn, Inc.
Saline, MI

Orders, inquiries and correspondence should be addressed to:
West of West Books
137 North Larchmont Boulevard, #653
Los Angeles, CA 90004
For web orders, inquiries or correspondence go to:
www.thisangelicland.com

Distributed by:
Small Press Distribution
1341 7th Street
Berkeley, CA 94710
spdbooks.org

For my brother, Eric Janigian

"And so the Princes fade from earth,
scarce seen by souls of men
But tho' obscur'd, this is the form
of the Angelic land."
              from William Blake's
              America—a Prophecy

PROLOGUE

AT THE HEART OF A STORY like this, The Kurd told me, there should be love—a man and woman, or friends, two people, anyway, who, amid the destruction, find in each other what may be worth dying for, what may even require it. As the city burns, imagine them at the kitchen table with cups of coffee, an atom of intimacy in a galaxy of waste. Watching the ashes drift, they might still speak of another life in another place, certain that if such goodness between two people were possible then all was not lost, even if all might be destroyed.

Forget that it wasn't 1915, 1934, or 1984. Forget that we were hardly on death marches or stuffed into cattle cars or terror-bound to a chair—no, just the opposite, we were cock-walking pilgrims, each from a different country and caste, supercharged with will. Yes, we were a melancholy distance away from all that was familiar, at an outpost far from home; but each toted his or her best, the very most finely spun and handsomely hewn. There we showed, bartered, bought, and sold, to better store up for the long journey ahead on the magic lantern-lighted road.

Only in the middle of that sojourn we were forced to stop, such was the commotion over the high fence, stop and stoop and peer through peepholes. In black and white, the monochrome color of the plainest of dreams, several police, batons cocked, surrounded a man prone on the ground with his head vaguely raised. Then the man rose, and a policeman struck him, and the man went down, and then rose again and the policeman struck him again, and again, and with each strike the man rose rather than fell, until another policeman, appalled, put out a hand. "Stop."

Suddenly, the man, like some cornered and wounded buffalo, lunged, and at the vile sight of his unlikely power they lunged back, his buffalo-sized body absorbing blow after baton blow. Groping in the darkness as though for a life rope, he fell to his knees like a supplicant. What must he do, *melt into the ground* before they would relent? He did melt to the ground, and one of the hyenas put a foot to his nape, and they struck his prostrate bulk. They were striking him for anything now, not because he was resisting them, but because he was there, because it simply struck their fancy. A tort of blows landed at each rung of his body, and when he jumped from pain they struck him for that too. Finally, convinced he was subdued, the hyenas cuffed his hands and lashed them to his ankles behind his back and dragged him facedown to the side of the street, where he was left to his debased self. And the hyenas loped back and forth, taking notes, dispatching reports, contented with their quarry.

What was done was done, except for a man hiding in the shadows, who at that moment had turned his camera on and now had in hand an accounting, a moving negative a mere minute long. With no floodlight or fanfare or marketing budget, in a matter of days this shortest-of-shorts dumbstruck the world. We watched it, endlessly studied it, tried to find a way to stamp it with reason, with purpose; but it continued to mystify, spooling upon its own tortured body, its own sadomasochistic logic.

Twelve persons were charged to put its meaning to rest. They watched and listened for three weeks, and frame for frame tried to fix the meaning of the *moving negative*; they accepted arguments, retorts, theories, and counter-theories about what was in the hyenas' minds during each frame—what frame of mind accompanied the frame, how did the hyenas' action comport with the hyena handbook, why did the buffalo lunge at one of them, why, once surrounded, did the buffalo not submit?

They listened to experts and counter-experts, and bystanders who told of what we had not seen:

1. The encounter that night had begun on the freeway, with the buffalo trying to outrun the hyenas for eight miles at an ungodly speed.

2. In the vehicle, three men rode alongside the beast. When orders were given to heel, only the beast demurred. His stare blank, his limbs inarticulate, sweat dripping from his brow.

3. Whipped up and frothing, the beast grabbed his arse and to provoke the hyenas shook it brazenly.

4. Forthwith, it was surmised the beast had eaten crystalline, a hellish substance, and that this was what had unleashed in him such a formidable force. Upon this surmise, the entire pack, even those hyenas of two minds, were galvanized.

5. With stun guns, twice he'd been struck. But rather than wreaking havoc upon his flesh, the guns' hundred thousand mortifying volts by all appearance did multiply it.

6. The best science has it that no man not possessed by a malevolent force could prove so refractory to such stuns, be so impervious to pain.

7. As the malefactor was struck, emanating from his throat were grunts and reports of otherworldly import. Note: these diabolical cries rose even over the vulture's terrific thunder.

8. Even when subdued, handcuffed, nearly snuffed, the beast's spirit, animated by unknowns, was lambent still.

9. Of the beating, true, one of the hyenas had opined he'd never had a hand in anything akin; it reminded him, he averred, of *a hard ball game*, part of the good ol' American pastime, during which he had *hit a home run*.

10. There were spectators to this "sport." Some watched frozen in horror, others rallied the hyenas on, yet others pleaded for the hyenas not to mortally wound him.

11. Hospital pictures revealed that from the beating his face had lost its features. Blood-red, ochre, and plum-colored bruises, tumescent and everywhere split; it looked like something that from inhumation had begun to putrefy.

12. One eye from distension was sealed shut, and from a baton blow that had severed his face from ear to chin, a new eye was opened.

13. Before it was sewn shut, there were those who deposed: along the round of the iris was inscribed, *novue ordo seclorum.* "A new world has begun."

And the jury went into a room to deliberate. There, with the information they were handed, they elevated and elaborated, parsed the pure from the impure, the subtle part from the gross, and within a matter of days returned with their verdict: not guilty. How? How! It was as though the beating was leger-demain, that your eyes perhaps were cataract, your reasoning sublimated, from dereliction deprived, or that what you saw was a base version of the real, that the *deluxe, superlit* version existed elsewhere, where only those twelve people had in *lux*-ury stood.

Sensing the fulminate taking shape, civic leaders and clergy rose to prayer, imploring, flapping, squawking, one by one, run-ning the sky the way crows do before a storm; but no sooner had they come than space was emptied of them, of sense itself. The city had turned into a sense vacuum, and in a matter of hours into this vital negativity, this perfect black body, particles began to collide and form a kind of supernova. It was just about dusk when you felt it from the heavens with an appalling force hit.

In a section of the city there was thunder, lightning, a gale strong enough to bust open the cages and set loose a horde: they flooded into the streets throwing bottles and rocks, overturning garbage cans, and screaming from rage. Then they began striking at cars with bats and bars and jumping up and down. And then we saw, from a peephole in the sky this time, a big truck lumber like a lost elephant into an intersection and dumbly stop. Within seconds they had swung up and lifted from right out of his seat the driver, a sad, waif-like figure. They dragged him into a clear-ing, where he cowered and looked confused, because never, even on TV, even in the movies, had he seen anything like this. They screeched and hollered and spat at him and jumped up and down, and threw him to the ground, and one of them held his head down with a foot, and the others kicked and struck him, and he wondered—as he wobbled to his feet like a newborn calf, lost his balance and fell, and tried to find his feet again—what was going on, and they stood over him, kicking and striking, aping each other, and then a man with an **X** on his chest hurled a canister at his head, and then another man, at point-blank range, did a trick with a brick, busting it on the scrawny calf's skull, whereupon his body collapsed to the asphalt and went limp. We saw the bloody mop of his newborn head; his innocent body curled up unconscious. We saw the bricklayer do a little jig.

PART 1

I WAS PUTTERING AROUND my Manhattan apartment, still working through jet lag, when the riots in LA began. I had just returned from Beirut, where I had filmed my first feature length documentary, whose subtitle, *The Burden and Promise of Memory*, could just as well serve as the title for what I've decided to embark on here.

My parents, my aunt, and my cousin lived in Hollywood, and not so far away, in Mid-Wilshire, were my brother Adam and my good friend Sasha. For three days I sat at the edge of my seat, with the TV remote in one hand and the telephone in the other, ringing my brother up nearly every hour, following his "eyes on the ground" through the helter-skelter path the riots cut.

My name is Eric Derderian. My family were refugees from the Lebanese Civil War, and yes, there was a dark irony in the fact that they were now reliving the horrors we had crossed half the world to escape. Yes, I was worried about them, but along-side the worry, I confess, was a vague satisfaction in watching LA get precisely what I believed it deserved for the very reasons I had left it.

But that satisfaction would quickly dim, as the riots spread, and my brother's voice grew from astonished to bewildered to alarmed to grim. As most of America watched a city collapse upon itself like a building rigged for demolition. Before the smoke had cleared, literally, I was boarding a red-eye flight from JFK to LAX. I knew, roughly, what I would find in Los Angeles, but I was hardly prepared for what I wouldn't.

For its sheer destructive force, the so-called Rodney King riots were unprecedented in U.S. history. The legendary Watts

7

riots of 1965 couldn't hold a candle to them. Hardly any section of Los Angeles went unscathed, and whole neighborhoods were eviscerated. In the tersest of terms, fifty-five people were killed, thousands injured, and ten thousand businesses destroyed, at a cost of over a billion dollars. But behind each number, as they say, is a story, and as I sit in my studio apartment in Manhattan, almost exactly six months to the day after the riots ended, having completed that documentary project on Beirut, I will try to tell that story. Even though it is one that I will likely never stop writing, I am driven to begin, and to do the best I can from the bits and pieces I have in hand.

Around 7:00 p.m. on the first day of the riots, our little cousin, Hovig, the gangster, rang Adam up.

"Are you tuned into this shit?" Hovig asked.

Adam said, "What are you laughing about? They're rioting out there."

"Bro, this is nothing. I'm telling you..."

"Telling me what? Is this an occasion for laughter? People getting beaten to death?"

"When'd you start talking like that? 'Occasion for laughter' Did that old man teach you that shit? The Wizard—bro, is he from fucking Oz or what?"

"Ease up on The Wizard or I'll rip your earring out with my teeth."

"Keep your head down, bro."

"Pull your pants up."

Adam had brought a case of tequila home for tasting because they'd raised his regular pour a buck a bottle and he needed a sub. He had a cheap tequila-tasting buzz going, which made him a little edgy.

Adam asked, "Did you see what they did, to this guy in the truck?"

"Bro, remember Lebanon. The shit we went through in Beirut. Worse. That's the word, bro, on the street. Protests motests, bro—the *sevs* (blacks) are out for it."

"Out for what?"

On the ground, cars neverminded the traffic lights, stop

8

signs, the roads themselves, weaving, pausing, and darting through the throng.

"Where the fuck are the police?"

Hovig answered, "Protecting their turf."

"Their turf is our fucking turf!"

"That's the big illusion you all live in, you and your martini crowd."

"Please, don't start in with that."

"Wait and see who you call, bro, when the shit hits the fan."

"Hold on," Adam said, his attention tacking to the TV.

> TED
> We're switching now to Trish Eliason,
> who is reporting live from Parker
> Center.
>
> [Trish, an all-American brown-haired beauty,
> is standing microphone in hand in front of a
> mob. The mob is chanting that the LA police are
> "Racist," that LA's top cop is "A Criminal."]

Adam told Hovig, "They're down there at Parker Center."

"Let it burn, bro. Those cops don't mean nothing to us. They take care of their own— *Yahudis*, movie stars, rich spoiled white punks like your partner, Nick, dick, the guy who's fucking you blind. But don't worry, bro, I've got our family covered. If they come around here, we'll kill them, bro."

"What are you talking about? Jesus."

"Bro, watch your mouth. Hey, we're the first Christians."

"Later."

"Hey, Adam."

"What, Hovig?"

"I love you, bro. You're my blood."

"Love you too. Be careful. Think about your Mom."

> TRISH
> All colors are represented here tonight,
> Ted. Nobody seems to have gone untouched

by the verdicts. For the most part, this
is an orderly demonstration, but there
is considerable tension in the air.

                    TED
For some of us, Trish, who were here
during the riots of '65, this brings
back terrible memories. This is a very
unwelcome reminder of those events.
We are covering this from downtown Los
Angeles, approximately, now, four hours
since the verdict "not guilty" was
handed down in Simi Valley today.

                   TRISH
                (knowingly)
I think that is just what's at issue
here tonight, Ted. People have told me
that, in their minds, guilty was the
only possible verdict any reasonable
person could render. We can only wonder
what Rodney King is thinking at this
moment.

                    TED
We understand that he is sequestered
in his apartment, refusing to speak to
reporters. Trish, I'm wondering if we
can get the input of some people who are
there now, in their words what they are
feeling right now. Obviously there is a
lot of anger and frustration, but we'd
like to have it in their words.

[Trish gently taps a man on the back.
He turns around, and then two other black men
turn with him.]

                   TRISH
Sir, would you care to tell us what
brought you here, what's going on in the
minds of the people here tonight, what
exactly are you protesting?

                PROTESTER 1
What do you mean, *What*? That bullshit in
Simi Valley is what.

                    TRISH
We just would like to get your
impression...

                  PROTESTER 2
Who their right minds can say them cops
didn't mean to do what they did? This
is no justice. This is injustice, this
is what you call violence, not just
against the Rodney King, but the black
community.

                  PROTESTER 1
And we here to make sure the LAPD knows
that we sick and tired of being treated
like animals and that we going to take
justice into our own hands.

                  PROTESTER 3
Say black man can't get no justice
through system, he's gonna get it
another way. We're not gonna roll over
and play dead no more. This ain't even
the beginning. The city of LA ain't seen
nothin' yet. We ain't gonna let up till
the whole world knows how we feels. The
city, the cops, newspapers, the whole
city gets blame, the whole city is
racist. That ain't no impression, that's
the truth!

                    TRISH
The verdict has obviously opened up deep
wounds in the community, Ted.

                     TED
For those of you just joining us, we are
broadcasting live from Parker Center,
where protesters have gathered to openly
protest the Simi Valley verdict. The
station management has told us that we
will stay with the action as long as is
necessary tonight.

[And, then, suddenly, what looks like a fire.]

                    TRISH
Hundreds of people have brought their

                     II

opinions to the doorstep of the LAPD,
and are…

                    TED
What is that, Trish?

[Trish, holding the microphone tensely,
turns around.]

                   TRISH
From here it looks… it looks like the
kiosk. Yes. I think you can see it in
back of me. [stepping aside] I believe
that is the kiosk. The kiosk here at
Parker Center is on fire. Things are
escalating very swiftly here, Ted. I am
not sure we can say for certain now that
things will not escalate.

                    TED
                 (concerned)
We have to ask, we've moved beyond a
certain decorum here, folks. Do you feel
safe there, Trish?

                   TRISH
We're fine here, Ted, though the mood
here is very tense, indeed.

                    TED
Trish?

                   TRISH
Yes, Ted?

                    TED
We have a source here who confirms that
windows have been smashed at the Times
building.

The phone rang again. Adam picked it up.

"What's going on out there?" It was Sasha, the museum
curator.

"I don't know. I think, I just heard, the *LA Times* building was attacked."

She gasped, "Oh my god. I need to get out of the house. I need to debrief. Can you please debrief with me? Please!"

"Hold on."

TED

```
...no doubt now that the riot seems to
have come downtown, folks. What we
prayed, hoped would stay isolated to one
area seems to have spread. Once again,
we just received a report that the LA
Times building has been the focus of a
group of protesters, and that the build-
ing has been attacked.
```

Sasha said, "PLEASE!"

"M" WAS NEARLY EMPTY when Adam walked in. Brad and Chris, his two mid-week barkeeps, both actors in real life who relied on big tips to support their astral aspirations, stood at the far end chatting with a couple of regulars, Lucas and Lucia. Brad came over with a toothpick in his mouth. He flipped a napkin in front of Adam, and Adam asked for a martini.

"Olives on the side?"

"Thanks."

"Hey Lucas, Lucia."

Hunched over his drink, Lucas ticked his head. Lucia smiled shyly.

"Can you believe what's going down out there?" Adam said.

"Yah," he said.

"So sad," she said.

Lucas was a middle-aged Hungarian writer/director hoping to break into the industry; Lucia was a black-haired, blue-eyed, twenty-two-year-old beauty from Poland who looked sixteen. They were lovers, but for the longest time everyone had assumed she was his assistant.

Sasha walked in. Over a black turtleneck she had thrown

a long black coat. Her face, even at a distance, showed abject shock, like she'd just been made to confront some dark feature of her personality in therapy.

"Lord," she said, shaking her head.

"Sit. Relax."

"How can you say that?" she said. "Relax? Did you see what they did to that man in the truck! Oh my god." She reached for Adam's arm as though he might fall off the barstool. "Does this remind you of Lebanon? Does it feel like that to you?"

"Not really. Not yet."

"I thought you were Armenian," Brad said. "Didn't know you were a Lebanoner."

"It's Lebanese, Brad, not Lebanoner."

"Excuuuse me."

"Martini, please," Sasha told Brad. "Gin."

She fumbled for a cigarette from her purse. Pretty, sophisticated, super-opinionated, Iranian, and basically good-hearted, she was also insanely, almost diabolically high strung, so he let her puff her puffs to settle down.

"Where exactly is Florence and Normandie?"

Brad mixed the drink and poured it into a glass. "Just around the corner, really."

"What corner?"

He pushed the drink forward.

"To be honest, I don't know. Anybody know?"

Her fingers were so jittery that an ounce of her gin splashed out of her glass before she got it to her lips.

Dabbing at her blouse with a napkin, she asked, "Across the freeway. The 10 freeway?"

Adam regularly traveled Normandie, but Florence? Shit. Could've been the Italian one for all he knew.

Back to the trucker, "I can't believe he didn't run!" Sasha said.

Adam said, "Going after a cop, a judge, I don't know. But a truck driver? These people are innocent. Just taking stuff from here to there."

"He just sat, like he expected they were coming. The way he just got out of the truck. Almost politely."

"I know."

She said, "To not at least try to lock your door? Don't trucks have locks?"

"Like he panicked... froze... I don't know what he was thinking. Maybe he figured he was cornered."

"THAT'S MY WHOLE POINT! How can a man be cornered in a truck! I mean, just keep going! Ohhh!" she lamented the trucker's imbecility.

"Like the Lamb of God he gave himself up," Lucas came out of nowhere to tell them.

Sasha shuddered and rolled her eyes theatrically. She hated Lucas, whom she believed was sexually exploiting lovely Lucia.

"I don't think so," Sasha said.

Adam said, "They're no geniuses, these truck drivers. All that time on the road, that alone messes with your brain."

Sasha said, "Are these African-American men angry at the verdicts? Are these gangs out there or what? I mean, or is it something else?"

"Yeah," Brad said, "they were probably all jonesing to the hilt."

"What do they do down there?"

"Ice. Crystal meth. It's a mind snapper."

"Absurd," Sasha said. "There were hundreds of people out there, maybe thousands. It wasn't about crystal meth! Why are you moving your mouth when I talk, Brad?"

"Nothing," he said.

"It's annoying."

It was an acting technique he'd picked up the week before that he was practicing, watching the mouth move so closely you could actually guess what a person would next say.

Sasha continued, "Is this about inner-city poverty? Social injustice? Are these people righting a social wrong?"

"W-owe," Brad went.

She said, "Where is this rage coming from?"

"Where is *that* coming from," Brad said. "You sound like this JC teacher I had. Sociology or something."

Adam said, "Maybe you're getting a little overly analytical at this point."

"Think so. Aren't these obvious questions: Race,

disenfranchisement; what are the operative concepts here?"

Adam said, "I imagine all of the above. What do your artists have to say?"

"I just talked to one, Sally Stroke, up in Silverlake. You saw her show."

"The hacked-up mannequins. Was that real blood, by the way?" The stuff was smeared all over their plastic bodies, even pooled at their plastic feet.

"Her own."

Adam said, "No shit." He had thought maybe she'd fetched it from a blood bank.

"Wasn't that an incredible show?"

Adam shrugged his shoulders, as if to say, "not really."

"You liked that show when you saw it. You changed your mind in a month?" She looked hurt.

"I guess I needed time to digest."

"No. Definitely you changed your mind."

Adam excused himself to the bathroom.

He'd already been to probably thirty gallery openings with her. Wine and cheese and crackers and Perrier and people exchanging phone numbers, and the artists themselves looking strikingly artistic, but hardly anyone paying attention to the art. The reason for this was obvious: anything that wasn't moving, that wasn't engineered for instant change, transformation, difference, was hard to focus on. The very idea of something being the same now as it would be ten minutes from now already bored everyone stiff. Adam's conclusion was that Sally had gone over the top for shock value. Forget about faith, hope, love; the struggle wasn't even a struggle *for* anything anymore; it was a struggle *against* something, mainly boredom.

Brad and Sasha were in the middle of it when Adam returned.

"I just look at all this as a chance to see a part of reality," Brad was telling her. "Why get all involved?"

"You see," Sasha said, "this is what… what…" she was searching for the right word. "…What *hurts* me about LA. This attitude. The melee out there *is* yours, I have news for you."

Adam ordered another martini.

"*Mellay*. Kind of the opposite of mellow." Brad reached for the vermouth and said, "I don't think artists should be involved in society *per se*. As an actor, you have to be on the outside looking in."

Sasha, who believed that art was about uncovering the conceits and prejudices and power relations that *disenfranchised* or *marginalized* gays, lesbians, women, African-Americans, Chicanas, transsexuals, transvestites, and others, raised her voice to a near shriek. "But where's your politics?"

Brad shook the drink, poured it into a fresh glass, and scooted it in front of Adam. Coolly, he said, "Totally not political. That's where I'm at with my politics. Anarchist."

"In *what* sense? The Berkman sense?"

"*In my sense*. What anarchism is. Nobody's sense but my own."

Jason stepped up to the little group with his hands raised, a gesture of surrender.

Lucas said, "Even biggest democrat is anarchist in his heart."

Lucia giggled. He turned to kiss her, giggling himself. Thirty years apart, they were like two urchins.

Sasha pressed Brad: "So what is happening out there is anarchy, nothing more?"

Brad said, "Whatever. Why are you getting personal?"

"What do you mean, 'Personal.' In what way?"

Lucas laughed. "Vatever. So 'merican, this speech."

Sasha had had enough of Lucas. "Okay already. Can you let us converse in peace?"

Lucia whispered something in Lucas' ear, probably an admonition. He nodded, okay, okay.

Sasha shook her head as though dazed. The gesture shoved Brad's ego into a corner. "Hey," he threw up his hands. "Chill. I mean, how am I supposed to know what it is? I just told you my philosophy, not what was behind all this *mellay*."

"Did you hooch it up before work today?" Adam asked him.

He cocked his head back, hesitating, and said "Nooo…"

Jason said, "I'll tell you what it is. You want to know what it is, I'll tell you what it is."

Chuckling sarcastically, Sasha said, "Am I asking too much?"

"Thing is, all I'm saying, there's no 'big philosophy' out there." Brad polished the counter with a rag. "I mean, everybody is doing his own thing. Why is this so difficult for you to get?"

"Hello," Jason said, and clutched Brad's arm, "Can I respond to this? Can I finish here? I don't know why people can't listen to other people. That's a problem: Listening."

"Go ahead, man," Adam said, "we're listening."

"Like I was saying, people are what they are because of what they *were*."

"You mean like in reincarnation, dude?" Brad asked.

Jason ran his fingers through his jet-black hair, sighed, and said, "Yes, like reincarnation."

Brad said, "I believe in that. I believe in reincarnation."

"BUT YOU'RE AN ANARCHIST!" Sasha dropped her head in defeat.

Jason said, "Be honest, everything you guys have said, I don't even know what it means. If you empty your mind, you won't know what it means either. It'll just sound like a bird song, or a cat meowing. The question is: who are you? You know, what did you do in your past life? Karma. That's the question."

Sasha came back: "Are you trying to tell me that this is all about past lives now. Is this why LA drives me crazy?"

"Choose not to believe it, but everything is…"

Sasha cut him off "So it's no use worrying ourselves about it. What's going to happen is going to happen? Let's party!"

"I won't go there," Jason said. "Sarcasm is the worst kind of energy. But to answer your question: in a way, yes. And in a way, no. Maybe *your* karma makes you change the situation. Maybe it doesn't. To know what's really going on, you have to know how all the karma in the world adds up. That's enlighten-ment. And hey, you guys are okay—hey, *I'm* okay—but none of us is the Buddha."

"Some philosophy." She put "philosophy" in quotation marks with her fingers.

"People thinking philosophy: That's a problem. Get rid of

your ego, and your philosophy goes with it."

Two groups of three had come through the door. The bartenders nodded to one another and went to attend to them.

Sasha said, "Sometimes I feel like…I don't know what. Like there's no way to get anywhere anymore. So many discourses."

Adam took her home and hugged her good night, her skinny little curator's body vaguely trembling beneath her jet-black outfit. When he let go, she reached back for his hand, like she bore news she hadn't the courage up until that second to deliver.

"You remind me of your brother," she said, and then instantly amended herself, "but different."

"That makes perfect sense."

"I miss him." It was an admission. An intimate admission. The rioting and her fear together had brought her feelings into focus. "Oh how I do miss all of New York right now!"

The other thing was, she hadn't slept with anyone in six months. Her standing as director of a high-profile non-profit museum, she had assumed, would lend her a degree of power and desirability, a kind of artistic power-broker seductiveness. In New York, to be seated on some artistic thing gave you sex appeal; in LA it didn't.

"I can't see anything like this happening in New York. It just couldn't."

"You're probably right. We'll talk tomorrow. Call me first thing."

Adam kissed her once more and told her good night.

He understood all too well what she was feeling, above and beyond what had happened that night. It was the bigger feeling of solid, even blessed ground suddenly crumbling beneath one's feet. His first experience with this had been just after his sixteenth birthday, a luxurious, softly flickering seventy-five-degree day, when he had lit out for the beach in Dad's 1972 Datsun. He took Sunset Boulevard, passing the strip joints and guitar shops and Mexican restaurants, and then the boutiques and Tower Records and that crazy Book Soup (why not Book Stew or Book Salad?). All along the way homes trimmed the relaxed hills as delightfully as Christmas ornaments. He glided through Beverly Hills, where on either side of the wide road the trees glittered, and down the grassy median joggers logged their miles. *How strangely blinkered we live,* (he wrote in his notebook, years later), *we at the brink.* Indeed, a mix of innocence and impudence, an unsustainable combination, was in fact sustained in Los Angeles, and by nothing short, it sometimes seemed to Adam, of holy grace.

And after seven years living in the city he was beginning to feel it, allowing himself to feel it; weight-free and giddy he slid down the last hill toward the ocean, its protean effervescence almost a state of mind, like the infinite play of God's mind.

When he hit Pacific Coast Highway, he cut south, parked at Venice, flipped his sandals off and made for the dazzling shore. The water's rhythmic churning at his feet, the lapping wind and crying gulls, all of it made for an exquisite commotion. In the perfect privacy of his thoughts the other beachcombers, half a dozen or so, seemed almost virtual, like holograms. He came from somewhere else, but what did it matter from where, everyone was from somewhere else—even, in a way, people born in LA. Its locus was fundamentally immaterial, almost like consciousness, not a thing but a happening. Though all this—and its meaning would become clear to him only years later—what he felt then was simple freedom from his bombed-out past in Lebanon. Venice said it all—the simple fact of its name, appropriated without shame, without parody. Only *these Americans*, as Mom called them, would dare, dare steal the name of a world-class city-state for a patch of coastal dirt cut into here and there with "canals" that were little more than dead-end ditches. As a young boy in Lebanon Adam had always admired America for its principles, industry, and power, but it had taken living in LA for him to absorb the tectonic power of its playfulness. The power to invent required the power to ignore and forget. That was the secret, what made *these Americans* so different.

In a way, he had been American all along. Different from the start: Grandmother had told Adam as much. He felt it in the tremendous ebb and flow of his emotions. As far back as he could remember, *they* had stuffed him into a school uniform and suit, bound him to a desk and church pew, all in order to organize, maybe even galvanize his makeup. It wouldn't have worked.

Lebanon would have cast him off as a mistake, and he probably would have destroyed himself there. "What's wrong with that boy," they would have said. That tremendous ebb and flow was synchronized with the tremendous ebb and flow of the city he had landed in. Adam was no longer on the outside wondering how to make himself normal, but rather on the inside, where normal was precisely what he was. America was his *manifest destiny*. He had been afraid to take it all the way, trembled at the implications, worked to get straight A's in school and made good friends, helped the family out where he could, slowly showing everyone that he had earned the right to his own future.

Now, tossing his shirt aside, he sloshed knee deep into the water and watched surfers slash across it, and boats drift out and in. Maybe he'd be a filmmaker, an actor, or an artist or a writer. A screenwriter! Why not? Anything was possible in LA.

The water when he finally dove in was splintering cold, but still the wide-open ocean was his and wave over wave he swam, until fifty yards or so from shore he turned on his back and drifted, the warm sun on his belly and cold water undulating below, his body a kind of yin and yang.

For how long he floated he could not say, but it was long enough that when he looked up, he was fantastically far from shore—100 yards, maybe more. It was as though he'd traveled at warp speed from one reality to another in the blink of an eye.

He swam for several minutes, good, strong teenage strokes toward shore, and when he looked up to see how close he was, thinking he'd catch a wave the rest of the way in, he discovered that he might as well have been swimming in place, or backwards. Something diabolical was going on in the seas, and he started swimming with crazy resolve, looking up over the grey green humps to mark his progress. It was impossibly slow going, if he was going at all, and already his muscles were feeling scorched. To catch his breath he rolled over and floated on his back. A mix of self-pity and self-scorn for having swum so far out on his own filled him. Then suddenly, panic grabbed his heart. *People die in the ocean all the time*, he thought. Some people never reach the beach. He was on his stomach again—he couldn't wait, with his head down thrashing, god, oh god he was going to reach that beach or die trying, and then, as though the beach had mercifully leaped, there was sand beneath his feet.

He stood trembling, disoriented. Maybe an hour had passed; anyway, the sun was beginning to set, a golden coin dithering on the horizon line. Two women were weaving their way on skates up the bike path. Half a dozen others were perched on a short wall drinking and smoking, probably dope. Nobody had been watching out for him. Why should they? Everyone was doing *his own thing*. Adam reached for his towel and draped it over his head and shoulders and sat there for several minutes looking like a Muslim at the haj. The churning beauty wasn't so beautiful after all, was it? He hated them for their leisure—they were so relaxed, so oblivious. Overwhelmed with embarrassment, he wanted to leave, to flee, actually, but from what and where to?

My brother was in the deep of America, where there was everywhere to turn, and nowhere. Get used to it. "Either sink or swim," as the tough guys on TV say. The sun rapidly lowered into the phosphorescent seas, the clouds turning inky at the edges. He stayed until the horizon and ocean combined, blazing. He stayed until the light had all but drained away, and the sea looked like some hammered ore, cooled and grey.

It was getting on midnight when Adam made his way to Versailles. This was the fourth "high-end concept bar" that Sammy, a good acquaintance, had opened in so many years. Tired of managing "M," sick *and* tired of his partner Nick, and wanting to keep his options open, he had talked to Sammy about maybe starting a club somewhere *down the road*. Maybe something similar to "M," maybe somewhere like Silverlake. "*Let's keep the conversation going*," Sammy had told him, so when he called and asked Adam to come by and take a look at his newest venue—not just the physical establishment, but more importantly, the concept behind it—Adam took it as a sign he wanted to *further the conversation*. He obviously would have chosen another night to go, except Sammy had put Adam's name on that night's list. If Sammy called to ask his impression and Adam didn't have one, that would be the *end of the conversation*.

That's how it was with people like that, with people who had that kind of traction and money.

The girl with the pretty voice who had called to confirm he'd be coming had also said, "Look for the valet," and now he saw why: it was located in a residential neighborhood on a side street off Fountain, just below the Strip. He pulled up in his '86 Camry, and between a two-story-high stand of cypress trees the valet pointed to a flight of stairs. Halfway up, the façade came dramatically into view: a faux-French chateau right out of Disneyland, the kind of *voila* architecture that reminded him that LA had been a place of magic and dreams long before he arrived, and would remain so long after he was gone.

On a semicircular porch, two bouncers dressed in beautiful black suits stood in front of a suede cord with clipboards in hand. He gave them his name, and they kindly nodded and welcomed him in. Ferns in decorative urns were perched on tall pedestals on either side of a large beveled black door, its surface lustrous as river water. Next he was standing at the threshold of a stunning room, angelically lit, with marble floors, textured like melted wax, which flowed out to a balcony where men were drawing richly on cigars. Waitresses whose body suits conformed to their bodies like swords to their scabbards conveyed tall cocktails to couples lounging on divans and curled up on oversized velvet chairs. On low glass tables, champagne bottles were sweating in classic silver coolers.

So there he was on the first night of the riots, deciding on a sage green comfy-looking love seat close to the bar. He ordered his third martini of that evening; yes, he was buzzed, and maybe that was why the violent images jackknifing his brain were already beginning to fold up and fade away. Serving three-ounce martinis at $12 a pop (made from a $7 bottle of vodka), Sammy was well on his way to owning yet another home. Adam remembered he'd been talking up Costa Rica. It was an hour before "closing," and amazingly fresh flesh and credit was flooding through the door. Like the lithe, toned, and tanned blonde in the flashy short dress now sashaying up to the bar, her eyes studying the room for a place to sit.

Adam made some small talk. "Looking for anyone special?"

"Supposed to meet some friends. Guess they're late."

"Have a seat in the meantime," Adam said with a quiet smile on his face. Crazy handsome, he never needed to do much more than that. They introduced themselves. The girl's name was Alice.

"Alice," Adam repeated. "It's such a sweet, old-fashioned name. I like it."

"My parents were South Carolina hippies, supposedly. Alice's Restaurant. It was supposed to be some cool, spiritual, happy place that they all hung out in back then."

"Would you like a drink?"

She patted her tummy, which was barely even there.

"Maybe later."

"Lose any more you're going to vanish."

"Just a few."

She tilted her head and let her tanned, toned calf bump Adam's.

"I don't know," she said. "I just needed to get out."

"I hear you."

"People are animals. Know what I mean? What they did."

"Definitely. People are no damn good, a friend of mine always says. But since we're all we've got…"

"Maybe I'll take a sip from yours."

"It's more romantic anyway."

A waitress picked up the empty glass and cocktail napkin, and he ordered another.

"I would say you're very interesting looking," she said.

She took his hand and turned it palm up, studying it.

"Hmm."

"What do you see?"

"You definitely have an earth hand. Maybe in another life you were a cowboy, or a farmer. Close to the earth."

She slid a finger down the center of his palm, "That's sexy. You're kind of romantic, but emotionally you're unstable too. I don't see any signs of danger here." She let go of his hand, kind of pushing it away.

"Aren't dangerous men supposed to be a turn-on?"

"They used to be. Things are changing."

"Not from what I've seen."

A long, elegant martini glass appeared before them, its misty, shimmering opalescence a kind of mirage.

"Actually," she said, "I can tell by the way you pick up that martini glass that you're not dangerous. I was just double-checking. You like to drink, but you're not a drunk."

"For me, drinking is mostly celebration. Some people drink when they're sad. I drink when I'm happy, in order to be even happier."

"My father was a drunk. Same with my brothers, all the men in my family. All drunks. Are you always happy?"

"Wouldn't that be dull? "

"I just get that vibe from you."

"I've survived. Maybe what you're sensing is a survivor's contentment just to be alive."

"Me too. Boy did I survive."

"How'd you end up in LA?"

She told him her story, how at a resort town called Hilton Head Island she'd met a soap star. They'd hooked up, and in the course of what amounted to a week-long fuck he told her that he saw in her not just an actress, a dime a dozen, but a living, breathing artist in the vein of Brando, Bette Davis, or Meryl Streep. That affair altered the course of her aimless life. She was twenty years old, crashing in a shack on the beach, so she packed up, and in a beat-up Toyota she bought for five hundred bucks, made her way across the country, hoping to hang out with this actor. After putting in about a dozen calls with no call-back, one evening she drove to his house and waited for him until the wee hours. Around sunrise she realized that he would never be there for her like he had promised, and that probably he'd only said that he would hang out in order to shag her for the week. But she wasn't mad at him; no, she was grateful to him for getting her out of Hilton Head and putting her in touch with this haunting sense that there was something more.

"Know what I mean?" she said.

"It's the reason most of us are here," he said.

"Where did you say you're from?"

"Here. More or less."

"You don't meet natives all the time."

"We're hiding in the bush."

"What are you?" she asked him.

"Excuse me?"

"I mean Italian, Spanish? You're not Mexican, are you?"

"I'm American."

"I know th*aaa*t."

"Let's leave it there. I don't want to ruin the mood."

"The mood is good," she said.

"You're good."

"If you have love. If you don't have love, nothing is good."

"Isn't it the truth?"

"You see, I'm an adult child of an alcoholic." Instantly her face went slack, as though she were a wind-up doll that had run out of juice. Vaguely spooky.

"You okay?" Adam asked her.

"I'm great," she replied.

"Sorry to hear about that. Must've been tough. I bet it made you a target for bad characters."

"How did you know?"

"I've heard it a thousand times," he said. "I manage a bar."

"You don't even want to go there. You don't even want to know."

"Oh, I know."

"Like my first boyfriend when I came out here. I met him at a party up in the hills. I was sitting with one of my girlfriends when, from all the way across this crowded room, I saw him. He wasn't even that good looking, but I was drawn to him like a magnet."

"Turned out to be the worst character in the room."

"A criminal, a drug dealer. He fucked with me for one year. I don't even want to talk about it."

"Water under the bridge."

"He had this gorgeous house on the beach, just this side of Malibu on PCH. You should've seen the view. His bedroom, it had a fireplace, and looked out onto the ocean, and he had a rack of Armani suits, I swear, a whole rack that went the length of the closet, amazing. In a way he was kind of a nerd though; in a weird way. He drove a Jaguar, sure, one of those convertibles, but there was something about him that was kind of goofy, too. For one thing, he didn't do any drugs, he barely drank; he claimed to get these migraines if he did. Or, like he'd be dressed to kill, but would forget to tie his shoes; or he'd miss one of his belt loops, or his shirt would be sticking out, and on top of the fact that he wasn't all that great looking, I don't know, he kind of reminded me of someone who was *acting* like he was just rich, even though he was *really* rich. I mean, a guy has to have deep pockets to give you two thousand a week just for play money; that's what he called it, play money. In some ways he really was a sweet guy, and I liked that he was nerdy."

"What did he do for a living? Did you say he dealt drugs?"

"I wasn't just there for the money. I really liked this guy, and I was serious about me acting, my art, really serious. Anyway, he was in with this crowd, this porno crowd. They all worked out of the valley but they had places on the beach. There is a lot of money in porn; you wouldn't think so, but there is."

"No, I believe it. Porn is big business."

She jerked her head to the side, as though someone had called her name. Adam doubted she was really waiting for friends to show up—that was probably just a hatch she had secured in case she needed an escape—but maybe he was wrong. He turned to look. She was staring at an empty spot in the room.

"You've got radar out everywhere, don't you?"

"Think so."

"All this reading of people. All this vigilance."

"You make me want to relax. You make me not have to be vigilant." She lifted the martini glass and took another swig.

"This tastes good."

"Relax away. You deserve it."

She took yet another drink, almost like she was obeying an order.

"We'll just keep splitting them."

Adam waved the cocktail waitress over and ordered another.

"So he was in with these porno people. Ben, that was his

name. Ben. When you think of porno, you think of… I don't know what, but what I thought of was a bunch of wild, big-mouthed, dick-slinging braggarts."

"Dick-slinging. That's a good one."

"But these people, what amazed me the most was that they were so normal acting. We'd get together, order pizza and, you know, watch a movie and bullshit. I didn't think they were saints, but they were no worse than a lot of people. Some of them were even married. I met three couples, and they loved each other just like normal acting people. Sex, it was what they did for a living; a job. No big deal. In fact, when they couldn't do it good anymore, especially the guys, when they couldn't get wood fast or hard enough they got down—you know, because they fucked up at work. One of these guys, I swear, was so depressed he couldn't get it up anymore he actually killed himself. One of Ben's closest friends."

"Were there a lot of drugs? Lot a time there are drugs in these kind of things."

"That's the main reason they were Ben's friends. There's where most of Ben's money was made, from the drugs these people bought. But you know, they could also play monopoly and be happy."

"Hanging out with these people was Ben's way of establishing good business relationships?"

"No, it was more than that. He loved that crowd."

From the corner of his eye he thought he saw Sammy. He focused in: no, it wasn't Sammy. All Iranians, like all Armenians, kind of look alike.

"Sorry," he said. "I thought I saw a friend."

"That's okay."

"So you think these porn stars weren't sex-addicts or anything. It was like any other job. Say you go to work bagging groceries, and come home after eight hours of doing it—you don't become a grocery-bagging addict. Something like that?"

"Exactly like that."

"Wow."

"But, this was two years ago. I've totally changed. I wasn't even in touch with myself back then. I wouldn't be found dead around those people anymore, even if fucking on film was their job. I have more self respect. You see, I was never taught to have self respect. I never really loved myself. A lot of people do things because they don't love themselves."

"Maybe there is nothing to love. Maybe they have a good reason not to love themselves."

"That's a terrible thing to say."

"I don't love myself," he said. "In fact, there are times when I hate myself, and feel that the hatred is deserved."

"When people like you say that don't love themselves, that's because they don't take themselves so seriously. When people like me say that they don't love themselves, it's different. See, I bet you had a healthy family life."

"I think by definition a family is a neurotic structure that produces neurotic people. But there are degrees, true."

"That's the difference. There's normal—what you call 'neurotic'—and then there is dysfunctional. People come out of dysfunctional families emotionally crippled and neurotic. That's the reason I got involved with people like Ben."

Just thinking about him made her laugh in disgust. "Porno. It's totally exploiting women, you know. It's just another way of demeaning women, what men have been doing to women for thousands of years. Sexually abusing them, taking advantage of their sex. But guys are like that. It's like an animal thing."

"I'd like to think there are exceptions."

"Every guy does." She put a hand on his thigh, and said, "Don't worry."

"You don't worry either."

"So, Ben was in this crowd. We all hung out. *It's what they do*, I told myself. Until one day Ben asks me, 'have you ever thought of doing porn?'"

"No kidding. Your boyfriend."

"Living with him. Living together. Anyway, I passed it off as a joke at first. I mean, why would I want to do porno? But I was kind of hoping he'd think it was because I was so beautiful or something. I guess I was fishing for a complement, because he never said anything about how pretty I was."

"He was blind."

"You're sweet. You know that, you're really sweet. There's something sweet about you." She sighed, and continued: "So Ben tells me, 'I've been asked by John,' this was a producer-director friend of his, 'if you'd be interested in doing some acting.' That's what they called it, 'acting.'

"'And I wondered myself,' he tells me. 'You know, it's a way to break into the industry. A lot of girls start out that way, you'd be surprised.'"

"What a line."

"Yeah. Wasn't it, though? Wasn't it a line? So I ask him, 'Do you want me to do this, Ben?' and he goes, 'I think it would be a great idea. I thought that from the first day. I mean, you've got a great body.' I say, 'You know, Ben, you never complemented me before, why now?' 'Oh,' he goes. 'Well, we live together. That's my compliment. But now I'm talking about, you know, how other people would see you.'

"I ask him, 'So how about the issue of me fucking other guys? Is that an issue?' He says, 'Not if it helps your career.'"

"Career!"

"'Plus,' he says, get this, get this…"

"Career."

"Get this…." She grabbed his arm. Her grip was serious, almost threatening.

"Hey." Adam took his arm back and turned it to look at where she'd grabbed him. The flesh was vaguely dented.

"I'm not Ben."

"Sorry. I don't know why I'm telling you all this anyway."

"In any case, the guy is a pure jackass."

"I was sooooo hurt. I couldn't even say anything. I kept thinking, you know, that he'd let go of it. I was really hurt, but we'd been together for I don't know, six months? And like, that was the first time he'd pulled anything like *that.* Already, my self-esteem was really low. I'd been here for two years trying to make it happen, and you know, every month you feel more and more over the hill. I guess I was desperate, the reason I put up with him to begin with. I don't know, maybe a month passed before he brought it up again. I guess he was giving me time to think about it. It wasn't the sex with some guy I didn't know that bothered me the most, but I kept thinking, you know, what if someone back home picks this video up. It would shock them to death."

"I always wondered if the porn stars have parents, siblings, grandparents, know what I mean?"

"That's what stopped me dead." In a mock-hysterical voice, she said, "I mean, what if like my brother was like, jerking off to a video when all the sudden he sees that he's jerking off to me?"

"The reason I can't think of these porn actors as anything other than orphans, to be honest."

"And then I'd think, *that's a stupid reason not to do it.* I was their victim, not the other way around."

"Your family, you're talking about."

"Oh. I didn't tell you: I was sexually molested."

"So sorry."

"Oh, yeah. From five to twelve years old. All of them."

"Who is 'all of them'?"

"Dad, the two boys."

"Your brothers."

"Half. Half brothers."

"Wow."

"It was sick," she continued. "But I started to think—this is how bad my self-esteem was—I started to think, *maybe it isn't a bad idea.* You know, my perfect revenge on them for what they did all those years. Like I was bringing their dark secret out into the open. I kind of felt like a liberated woman from them when I thought like that."

"I can see that."

"You can?"

"You really *are* in touch with yourself, just like you said."

"I've always been able see through things; you'll be surprised. I lived it all out in my head, but I saw through everything and everybody. I was in touch with myself always, but I lived in fear."

"You left all that, and then you ended up with Ben."

"Oh. That. Well there I was trying to replay the past. I was trying to heal my past wounds that way. You see, if you can make it happen again, and avoid it, then you've somehow healed yourself."

"I never understood that. How you can make yourself better by repeating your mistakes?

"Not exactly that way. Anyway."

"I was always taught you had to learn from your mistakes in order to avoid repeating them next time around."

"I didn't say it right. Anyway, I told Ben, 'Okay, I'll do one, for you, if you really want.' I'll bet you can guess what he said to that. He said, 'Don't do it for me, sweetie, I want you to do it for yourself.' Can you believe that?"

"Yes."

"If you watch porno, maybe you saw it. It was called *Total Exposure*."

"Never saw that one that I remember."

"People don't remember the titles. Maybe you forgot."

"I don't think so."

"I did it with a pretty big star, Randy Hardaman."

"Okay."

"It was no big deal. I mean doing it. You'd be surprised; there is so much acting in sex to begin with. I mean in normal sex, it really isn't all that different. So we get a copy after it's made. They gave me like ten copies. Ten copies and two thousand dollars. Ben doesn't push right away, watching it, like, you know… well, anyway, one night we're getting nasty on the bed, and he says, 'Hey, what do you think? Let's put the video on.' 'The video,' he called it, THE video. I don't know why, but I'll never forget that. He didn't call it by its name, *Total Exposure*. He had a billion other videos but there was just one THE video. You know what I mean?"

"In a way."

"It's kinda funny how things stick in your mind."

"Isn't it?"

"Before I had a chance to think about it really, he hops out of bed, this big teenager's grin on his face, and pushes it into the machine. You can't blame me for thinking that his whole idea of getting me into a video was so that he could feed this weird sexual fantasy, some fantasy about doing me while watching a video where I'm doing another man, this Randy Hardaman."

"If that's the case," Adam said, "a helluva lot of planning went into it. Months of planning, from what you say."

"I know. But when comes to men's fantasy lives…" She chuckled, darkly. "Women are so simple. When it comes to sex, women are so simple compared to men."

"I can't argue with you there."

"So, you know, we're getting private, and then the part comes up where—I mean at least he didn't fast forward to my scene, that would be too obvious. He was sneaky—men are—the part comes up where I'm having sex with this Randy. And guess what happens."

"I can't, at this point, imagine."

"Couldn't stop giggling. Ben asks me, 'What's so funny?' and I couldn't really say. I just couldn't stop the giggling. I don't know if it was some kind of breakdown, or what? That was pretty much the bottom for me. I bottomed out there."

"More like you hit China."

"Wherever."

"You okay?"

"Of course." And just like that, she said, "Ready to go?"

They went to her place, a bungalow apartment set up just off Melrose near La Brea. They held hands like long-time lovers as she walked him through a garden courtyard filled with the smell of jasmine to her dinged-up front door. A vague fear, a kind of question trembled beneath his skin, and he couldn't tell whether she or the rioting was the root of that fear. In either case, sleeping with her was going to be the answer. There was already too much momentum to reverse. The ambient light coming through the windows caused her front room to glow a weird blue. She led him through it to her bedroom, a shabby little room with a low-slung futon, a few books piled on either side of where her head would rest.

At the first small press of her flesh to Adam's lips, everything she had told him about Ben, the skin flick, and her stolen tender youth faded into concepts. The mind might be in an epic battle with memory, but the body is forever exulting; like a mustang in a desert scene in a 70s movie she surged magnificently from a crucible of dust, swift, dazzling, her rising and falling almost mystical in the martini-buzzed light.

Afterward she fell asleep. So did Adam. But only an hour later he woke. An alleyway lamp deposited a jaundiced light into the room. His body felt hollow, crusty, and sour. A red LED hovering in the dark read 4:20 a.m., marking the start of a minor hangover. He was seriously hungry, actually picturing one of those combo breakfast plates at Norm's. But leaving in the middle of the night—how rude and demeaning that would be; the last thing *this* girl needed. So he fished out his skivvies from the deep of the sheets and walked in his bare feet to the kitchen, where the refrigerator was loudly humming, and opened the door. I imagine the sudden outpouring of light striking him as it might strike a character out of a Caravaggio painting.

No-fat milk, calorie-reduced margarine, three six-packs of diet-coke, carrots, celery, a half-loaf of brown bread, kosher dills, and weight-watchers mayonnaise; barely enough to sustain an apparition. On the other hand, this minimalist, virtually nihilistic approach to consumption must have made possible her stunning, toned thinness, her elongated mannerist casting-director-happy shape. Even so, as he stood there his hunger ballooned, and pickles wouldn't do. He grabbed the milk and reached for a box of puffed rice on the counter next to the fridge. The cupboards were empty except for drinking glasses, and oddly, cupcake-baking pans—kind of touching. A few hard-plastic dishes with faded floral patterns and dull utensils were strewn around the bottom of the sink; he found a lonely bowl in there and washed it out.

There was no dining table, nowhere to sit, so he took his cereal into her living room and turned on a tall halogen lamp next to the couch. It appeared she hasn't lived in her place for long; beneath the windows a small stereo-cd-tapeplayer-speaker combo unit sat on a naked board supported by cinder blocks. Against a wall opposite the couch was a cart, and on the cart a thirty-two-inch TV/VCR combo. In the cart's middle storage compartment were several videos: *Buns and Abs of Steel*, *Everyday Yoga*, and two Charlie Chaplin titles. The couch was upholstered with cheap, shiny, black cotton, on which he noticed a few nasty white splotches. He sat there with his cereal, grabbed the remote, and turned on the TV.

                        JOHN
     Tim, if I'm right, that is the *Times*
     Building.

                        TIM
          (live feed, through the noise of the
          helicopter, his voice somewhat choppy)
     I believe it is.

                        JOHN
     A venerable, can we say it, an iconic
     building in the heart of downtown.

[A wide shot. In the light of the street lamps,
people milling around, their heads like pin-
heads, in small groups, alone, moving across the
streets, after something, after nothing.]

                        JOHN
     Tim, do you, from your perspective up
     there, do you see any police, any sign
     of police activity there?

                        TIM
     We have seen police cars, yes, but their
     presence seems awfully light. It's hard
     to guess their strategy, right now,
     John. We are veering south now, you can
     see now, even from a distance, oh, we
     must be a couple of miles away, you can
     see several fires burning, this is near
     Florence and Normandie.

                        JOHN
     This, folks, was the scene of that
     terrible beating and violence we saw
     earlier today. I'll have to be honest
     Tim, there are days when all of us com-
     plain about how big and spread out Los
     Angeles is, not to discount the pain and
     suffering of a lot of people tonight,
     this is one of those times when it seems

a blessing.

                    TIM
We're showing you now, you should be
able to see on your monitor, we're showing you a good section of South Central.
We see many many fires now. People have
been setting structures on fire all
through the night. We can only wonder
what the morning will bring.

                    JOHN
            (a nervous chuckle)
It really appears to be spreading so
quickly I'm not sure…

                    TIM
Well we've been up here for several
hours now, and I can tell you that that
is what we're seeing. Now, here, we're
going to give you a close up of what's
going on down there.

[The camera panned in on a burning building
and held steady.]

                    JOHN
If you're wondering, folks, where the
fire department is, we're wondering as
well.

                    TIM
At this point, John, they are probably
overwhelmed.

[A two-story structure, a house, apartment,
or commercial building impossible to say,
so overwhelming were the flames. In the dancing
light of the fires, people were running here
and there, milling about, very occasionally a car
drowsily went by.]

                    JOHN
Those are people, Tim, probably from the
neighborhood.

                              TIM
          We imagine they are, John. And we can
          only imagine how they feel.

                             JOHN
          Folks, in case you missed the latest,
          and are still up at this hour, we need
          to let you know, especially if you use
          the freeway to get to work downtown,
          that the CHP has closed the exit ramps
          on the 101, downtown, and the 10 heading
          downtown.

                              TIM
          They are probably afraid of motorists
          turning innocently onto these streets.

                             JOHN
          That sounds right, Tim. Also, flight pat-
          terns, flight patterns have been altered
          for planes coming into LAX. We don't
          know for sure, but there is some indi-
          cation that some helicopters have been
          shot at. Tim, Tim...

                              TIM
          John? We heard you.

[The camera zoomed in even further, focusing on
two men sharing a bottle. One man slapped the
other on the back and handed over the bottle.
He took a swig and let the bottle swing before
sending it back. The camera turned away, as
though embarrassed, back to the building, which
was now burning so freely and extravagantly
that its burning seemed its fulfillment, not
something brought upon it from outside, but a
final cause within.]

                              TIM
          Stunning, John.

He muted the sound and slumped on the couch and nodded off
to sleep. Two, three hours passed before his mobile rang. It was
me, about ten o'clock my time. I'd finally gotten hold on him on

                              37

his new mobile phone, whose number I'd gotten from Sasha.

"What's going on with you people in LA?" I asked him.

"What time is it?"

"Ten East Coast."

"What do you mean, 'you people'?"

"I'd tell you 'wish you'd get the hell out of there,' but I know it wouldn't help."

"And where am I supposed to go?"

"Why are you whispering?"

"She's still asleep."

"You're at her place. Sound pretty hung over. I talked to Sasha…"

"I dropped her off and went to this new club."

He told me about his 'date,' in his typically unguarded and down-to-the-detail way.

"'*Total Exposure*'! Geezus. Well, now you can check 'porn actress' off the list."

"I don't keep a list," he said.

"You probably should—after that AIDS scare."

"Yeah."

"Are Mom and Dad okay?"

"Oh, shit."

They'd probably already left ten messages on his answering machine at home. They depended on him to brief them on anything out of the ordinary. He hadn't given them his mobile number yet.

"I need to call them," he said. "Talk to you later."

He was about to dial their number when he heard, "Hi."

He'd almost forgotten she lived there.

"Good morning."

He rose and walked over to her.

"Ummh." The hug was all in her voice. She turned around and stepped into the kitchen. "I'm so hungry."

"I found some cereal in the middle of the night and fell asleep."

"Take what you want."

"Wanna do breakfast? I mean, out."

"I've promised to practice some lines with a girlfriend

this morning."

"Okay."

"Sorry. We just have to get these lines rehearsed. It's this acting teacher of ours, she's like some Attila the Hun. She scares me sometimes, you know? She's so hard on us. But that's what it takes; that's our art, what it demands of us, you know."

"No problem," Adam replied. "Like you said, it's your art."

"It really is."

"You have my number don't you?"

"Yeah, I think so. Sorry, I really have to get ready."

"Oh, okay. Sorry."

"No. Don't be."

"Looks like you're in a rush."

She said, "I don't know what I'm in." She opened the 'fridge' and took out a pint of Ben and Jerry's. He hadn't bothered looking in the freezer, or he would've eaten it himself.

"Are you feeling all right?" he asked her.

"Oh, it's not that." In a kind of trance, she ambled over to the couch, picked up the remote, and switched channels. The Road Runner, zipping from hilltop to ravine. She poked the spoon into the container and into her mouth, and creamily slid it out.

A minute passed before she turned to him and asked, "Want some?"

The second he was in his car, he rang Mom up.

"We don't know what happened you."

"I was at the bar."

"You tell you no work last night."

"I went in for a drink."

"On day no work you go bar you work! *Akh!*"

"I was meeting a friend, that's all. You know, Sasha."

"Iranian girl."

"Yeah. Eric's good friend."

"I hope no the too-good friend." Mom didn't like Muslims, even if they hadn't set foot in a mosque since they were toddlers. "What they did that poor man, you see? *Vyrenee!*" The word meant "bestial" in Armenian.

39

"Is Dad at the store?"

"Where he be not store?"

"Maybe he should take the day off."

"They let everybody go *jooory*. Arsinee go. Not even go right bus, she."

"Okay mom."

"What okay."

"I gotta go."

"Where you go?"

"Work."

"I wish you get different work."

Holy Mud, the café where he daily ate a "continental breakfast," was bustling as usual. He fetched a paper from the kiosk and grabbed a spot on the patio. He was anxious to dive into the *Times*, but he needed to push some caffeine into his system. Nikki, one of the patio waitresses, was sitting at a table, chin in hand, with a couple of heavily pierced long-hair guys, probably rock musicians. He waved to get her attention, and she smiled in acknowledgment, as though she were a friend who would come over to say Hi after she'd wrapped up.

He opened the paper. The unrest had gained extravagant momentum during the night. One hundred buildings had been razed, the windows of the *LA Times* had been smashed, four people had been killed, and over a hundred injured. He also read that MACY's was having a "GIGANTIC STOREWIDE CLEARANCE," and MAY COMPANY's "YEARLY MAY-DAY SALE" was coming up, and ADRAYS was offering "SUPER REDUCTIONS OFF ALREADY LOW PRICES." Finally, Nikki came over, order book in hand.

"Sorry," she said.

"That's all right."

"Ugly scene last night, huh?"

"Four people were killed last night."

"All I heard is that that someone got beat up pretty bad at Denny's."

"Denny's?"

"On Gower," she clarified. "I slept through it; came home from work and nodded off. I must've gotten up around

Midnight. Then I went to a new club on Sunset. Anyway, I'm out of here if it gets worse. I hear the cops were nowhere. What do you want this morning? I mean, they're always there to fuck with your parties."

Adam ordered and turned back to the paper. That poor bastard in the truck, his name was Denny, Reginald Denny. He was hauling, as it turned out, some seventy tons of sand on an *eighteen-fucking-wheeler!* What was he doing in the middle of South Central with so much sand? And why didn't he use it to bury his would-be assassins alive? His face was broken, all fourteen bones. Who knew the face had that many bones? Now all fourteen were broken.

Adam looked up for a breather. He wasn't going to get one: briskly crossing the street was David, a painter, or rather a "Visual Artist" friend, stupendously handsome and who dressed like some well-heeled hobo: a long coat made of the finest leather over a ruggedly draped shirt with buttons that were unmistakably expensive, and as he drew closer, Adam saw he had three days' worth of beard going, as usual. He always had a three-day growth going, even if Adam should see him three days in a row. The shadow that beard cast, the whole rundown-for-show-look, the calculated skid-row theatrics, never failed to impress Adam, because Adam was never able to look haggard without actually being haggard.

As his friend's boot touched the sidewalk, Adam steeled himself for what he just knew would be a manic recitation of all the projects David was working on, from book projects to shows to teaching gigs abroad, lectures here and there, Munich, Barcelona.

"Hey, David," he said.

"Hey, Adam."

Adam shook his head, "Can you believe last night?"

"Fuck yeah," he said. "It was waiting to happen."

"My little cousin said the same thing. But he's a gangster."

"This fuck-hole of a city deserves what it gets. I don't give a shit. My world is everyplace but here. LA is my crash pad. I'm here to catch rays."

David showed his works in a big, beautiful gallery on

Wilshire, big enough for elephants to mix in, where his paintings, humongous and aggressive abstract-expressionist pieces, hung one to a wall. And yet he was still bitter; the Japanese and Koreans were all agog for his paintings, but Los Angelenos paid no attention to them. Everyone knew, he claimed, that the art scene for Visual Artists like himself had ended at the precise moment when Tom Solomon closed his garage doors.

Anyway, he'd just flown in from New York City, he told him, where he'd dined at *John's*.

"How was it?"

"Jasper was on a roll."

"Oh, that *Johns*."

"When I'm in the city we hang out. Anyway, he was in rare form. Just non-stop cutting jokes. What a sense of fucking humor, he had the whole table in stitches."

"Nice."

David reported that Bill—de Kooning that is—had just put together a new exhibition (an exhibition that turned out not to be so new, since we'd both seen it a few months before). David described Bill's new work as *dazzling* and *bold*, which wasn't Adam's impression at all; his impression was that Bill's newest work was good, but a little over-the-hill-and-over-the-top, nothing like the humanly tortured pieces he had produced when he and Arshile had hung out.

As David talked, he kept looking into the café, shifting his gaze from here to there.

"Meeting up this morning?"

So at Jaspers, he said, he was sitting next to another painter, he didn't say who, who'd recently gone to a lecture on contemporary art where David's paintings came up; the impression of the lecturer was that David's huge blobs and smears were nothing more than masculine phallic symbols, an attack on women, a recapitulation of the whole patriarchal thing.

Adam said, "That's some wild leap."

Actually, David told him, he liked the leap. He liked any interpretation of his paintings, because in the end the paintings didn't mean anything. Indeed, his paintings were what he called "parodical paintings."

Adam asked him what that was supposed to mean.

"Paintings that parody paintings with purpose and emotion." In essence, he explained, any attempt by anyone to assign them meaning was naïve, on the one hand, and precisely what he intended, on the other. "I mean," he said, "The point is that there is no point. Seducing people into giving it a meaning is its meaning."

Adam said, "Isn't the point that there isn't any point beside the point at this point?"

David didn't even flinch, but proceeded to finesse his comment, so that his pointlessness would seem novel and radical. But it didn't seem novel or radical; it seemed to have been crash-tested a thousand times in the same car, the same battered-beyond-belief dummy. Still, Adam nodded, politely.

Satisfied he'd salvaged his *point*, David strayed sideways to tell Adam what was really on his mind these days.

"Did you know Carrie left me?"

"No, man. We haven't talked in a while. Sorry."

She had been sleeping with Hugo something or other, a sculptor friend of his whom he'd known since high school, right under his nose. One day Hugo came over, and the two of them, the wife and Hugo, sat on the couch. They took each other's hands and proclaimed their love one for the other, and informed David of their intention to shack up, and said they hoped, really did, that it wouldn't *get in the way* of the friendship they all shared. For the first month, David explained, everybody was very mature and full of understanding and even goodwill, and they all saw each other from time to time and talked and carried on. But just recently, he confessed, the farce he'd for some reason put up with had begun to eat him alive. He spoke of how he'd wake in a rage, asking embarrassingly obvious questions like *how the fuck could she do that to me*, and *how could Hugo fuck my wife like that and then ask if I was still on for basketball Sunday morning*, and *doesn't five years of marriage mean anything?* It had gotten to the point he'd contemplated killing Hugo.

Adam said, "That never gets anyone anywhere, believe me."

They were situated near the front patio door, which meant that every minute or so they were each made to sustain a tiny concussion as another waitress, Michelle, a willowy beauty from Santa Barbara, brushed by to her tables outside.

"I'm headed in," David said, but before he did he asked Adam if he'd seen Sasha.

"Just last night."

He asked Adam to ask Sasha to call him.

"Stop by the bar tonight. She'll probably be there."

He just didn't understand why she was avoiding him and his work, because it was well known that he was one of the most important Visual Artists in the city. He gave Adam a "let's get together," and left.

Where the hell was Adam's cap and bagel? He looked around for Nikki; she was back at the musicians' table, deep in discussion, possibly probing for an opening on their next video; hard to know. In any case, there was no question that he might interrupt her, so he touched Michelle on the arm on her way back in and asked if she'd be kind enough to check on his order.

"I need that coffee bad this morning."

"Don't we all. Don't we all need a coffee bad? I'll see what's up with that."

Michelle possessed an angelic singing voice. When she'd first come to Los Angeles she'd invited Adam to a Christmas Eve choral concert at the Old Spanish Mission on the Santa Barbara Riviera. It had concluded with a hundred canters walking up the side aisles holding candles and singing *Silent Night*. He felt that evening the presence of the sacred in her voice. But three years later, after a seemingly endless rush of workshops and auditions, she'd lost the faith and had taken up pot smoking like Maui trailer trash.

Nikki finally returned with his order.

"Sorry for taking so long," she said.

The chasm between her sidereal ambitions and café waitress reality was so vast that a single wrong word or gesture was enough to upend her axis for days, so he simply said, "Thanks."

She said, "I guess everybody's a little out of it today. The mess out there and all."

"No sweat."

"You're such a nice person," she said.

"You are too, Nikki."

"That means a lot to me."

"And we can all afford to be a little nicer to each other right about now."

"But people aren't. I don't know why. I guess that's just how people are. Issues," she said, "everybody's got issues."

Issues spiraled into tragedies. They happened, of one sort of another, on a regular basis in LA, but because of the strict-prison-like reticulation of space, and over such an incalculable expanse, they seemed to happen in a different city altogether, at a snug remove. In some neighborhoods, like Adam's own, each block seemed its own cell, where just around the corner might live Nepalese throat singers, or a brood of witches. Now the boundaries were being breached, but because his section, the only part that really mattered, was still going about its business as usual, it was hard to fathom, the same way as a kid he couldn't fathom that he was part of the milky way, that he was gazing up there at the very thing of which he was a part. Adam paid the bill and headed out.

On the other hand, there were times when he was awed by how intimately and intelligently Los Angelenos were woven in; especially driving, when a semiotics all its own materialized, when a kind of primitive and reciprocating vibration moved you along in one piece like wild horses or wolves in great packs. The awe one felt at such moments was the awe of defying the self, or rather the more awesome feeling of being both on your own and in the flow.

This is what Adam was thinking when he turned up the narrow lane at whose far end his bar was located, and saw a ramshakle Chevy careering down the one-way in the *wrong fucking direction*. What the hell? The car guttered past him, the driver a young t-shirted black guy. Adam turned to watch him go, and then suddenly the car skidded to a tires-screeching stop. *Oh shit*, Adam thought, as the car backed up, weaving weirdly. Adam waited for the driver's eyes to line up with his frozen ones. "FUCK YOU WHITE BOY," he shouted, his face twisted with rage. Just as Adam thought, *Oh fuck, he's going to shoot me*, the driver punched the pedal and sped away. FUCK YOU WHITE BOY.

To Adam, a "white boy" was someone with pearly skin, freckles, and lanky limbs. White Boy was Nick—his partner at the bar—and that wasn't what Adam saw when he looked in the mirror. He finally reached the bar and sat down in front of his computer and tried to work on a spreadsheet. But "white boy" kept drumming at his head, the ugly injustice of it making him mad and sad at the same time. It brought back junior high school, all those feelings.

When Adam first came to America, he had enrolled in the local elementary school, where for two years he blended in fairly well; but by the time he reached junior high they had started "bussing," and so for a semester and a half he took that rolling purgatory across town to what they called a "minority school." When the bus door opened all forty students shuffled off the bus holding their breaths. Blackness was everywhere, alarming, that much of it all of a sudden, exotic, vaguely menacing, brothers and cousins of Crips and Bloods, all with searing wits, cocky rooster's walks, and the jazziest way with words. What exactly *he* was, with olive-brown skin and black hair and eyes as black as theirs, was a wide open question. Some figured he was a kind of *Messican*, some wondered whether *Arm-onion* was A-rab. *Say whah, Lebuhn-on where de fuck ih dat.* Syria, and Israel, in that general direction, he might've said, if he'd thought it would help.

In the meantime, he watched with horror—dozens of unambiguously white kids harassed and spit on and punched and tripped and made to squirm through the gauntlets of the hallways. He'd perfected his pace through it; not too slow not too fast, lest they prey on his fear, which he held in so tightly that by the time he hopped on the bus home he was close to shitting in the seat. Within a month two boys from *the bus* psychologically collapsed, and he never saw them again. Now and then, before he fell asleep, Martin Luther King would appear: his child-like face and river-big voice, telling Americans, "I HAVE A DREAM." Adam too had a dream, Dr. King, and a prayer: that as he slept God would transform him from whatever he was into a lustrous, swaggering, black kid. That he'd have a big fat Afro and *fuck you* attitude when he woke. Until that transubstantiation occurred, he'd use the grinding commute to mull over strategies to distance himself from his "whitey-ness."

He'd kept his heritage secret, out of shame, but eventually he began to wonder whether he'd be better off bringing it into play: bombs, guns, razor wire, militias, our uncle murdered in cold blood—he'd seen some shit in his day.

"Lebahn-on, huh?"

"That's where the war was, man, but I'm Armenian. Being Armenian in Lebanon is like being black in America."

"Armainyun."

"Exactly; Armain-yun. When you hear it, just think, OUR MAIN MAN. Get it: Our main man!" He spread his arms out. It was an all-in absurdist wager.

Their brains flickered as they sized up the pun. Suddenly laughter rose in their chests and sent their bodies into spasms. Were they mocking him? It took a minute for the matter to settle one way or the lethal other. Suddenly, they had smiles on their faces, and their heads began to bob like dashboard dogs. "Awright, den. Ah main man. U Coo."

Apparently, the issue was settled; as though once coo always coo; as though there were a directory in the black *Who-to-Hate* manual that he could turn to in case of just such a crisis.

He checked his messages, thinking Nick, who was in Paris or Milan or maybe Prague, would have called to leave him a contact number, but he hadn't. It was getting on ten o'clock when Ted, his bookkeeper, walked in and asked if he were "aware" of what was going on out there? They were starting to riot again. Adam told him about the black guy in the car. Ted said he'd heard something about the schools closing.

The phone rang. He answered on speaker. A bandleader wondering whether they were still on for tonight. Needed to know because they were all coming in from Encino. Adam had no idea and told him to check back in a couple of hours. The bandleader asked something about monies that were owed them from a previous gig, and Adam told him he'd given $200 in cash to the guitarist that very same night, and to talk to him about it.

He called it a day—although the day had just begun—and

headed home. Sirens, this way and that, were now slashing at the air, and as he turned the corner and started up the sidewalk he saw on the rooftops of the apartment buildings on his block people gawking at something transpiring to the south.

When he got up to the makeshift "viewing stand," he saw for himself: just how swiftly it was hard to say, but a cloud was migrating ever so slowly toward him like a humongous air-borne bruise. He heard "can't believe this," and "pisses me off" more than once. Some people were reporting to friends on their mobile phones, and others stood mum, snacking, as though they were at one of those IMAX flicks. Wilshire, half a block south of his building, was clogging up with traffic—people were rushing home.

Standing beside Adam were two upstairs tenants, Joanne and Derek, who he knew pretty well. Derek, mid-fifties and a recovering alcholic, had broken into The Industry doing commercials way back when, but after five years of casting-director neglect he'd turned wobbly, transluscent, a kind of human soap bubble ready at any second to burst. And he probably would have long ago had Joanne not been there for him. A therapist or counselor of some sort, blonde, petite and pretty, in conversation she had a way of super-gluing her eyes on you, and *hmmming* and nodding with a regularity that made it seem as though she were being tripped by a windup mechanism. He invited them to his apartment.

Derek made a quick detour to fetch something. He now strode into Adam's apartment to show just what: a gun, a gun that his father had owned. He carried it underneath his belt, the way you see Clint Eastwood do it in the movies, and now pulled it out and displayed it on the palm of his hand. Silver and shiny, it looked like a toy gun his dad had bequeathed him. In a kind of hysterical bony voice he had told Adam and Joanne that he'd already loaded it, adding, "I'll use it, by God." Even though it was clear he was acting out some vital part in his virtual repertoire, Adam cringed at the way he held the gun in his white-doddering-recovering-alcoholic hand, and he thought, by the time you find your mark you'll have several holes in your belly, so put it away before you accidentally shoot us both, chump.

Adam brought out tons of junk food; he emptied his cupboards of chips and dips, and some of those fried pork skins, and smoked oysters—this was no time to worry about cholesterol—and goldfish crackers, and he placed his cigarettes on the coffee table so that they would be within arm's reach, and he broke open bottles of Dos Equis, the small gathering shaping up like a Final Four party. Joanne, whose gaze was usually somewhere between surgical and seductive, now sat on the couch holding herself in her arms as though she could've used a shawl. Adam turned the TV on to see if what he saw out there was really happening—and it was fucking happening.

People were swarming a generic electronics store, tromping over broken glass and torn-down doors and fetching stuff and darting off, clearly experiencing the same heart-palpitating thrill that country kids feel raiding fruit orchards. The looters were carting out their wares and stacking them in the back of vans backed up into the parking stalls with such uncanny clockwork it might've been organized, if not verily prophesied in advance.

"Can you believe this shit?"

From out of the store next-door came boxes piled to the chin of one plunderer after another, NIKE, REEBOK, PUMA, ADDIDAS, WILSON, and SPAULDING—how many shoes can one person, one family, *even a Mexican family*, need? Maybe they were aiming to open their own store with the booty from this one. For shoes, he imagined the flea markets would be the venue of choice for the next year and a half. Then, amazingly, the camera poked into the store itself. Two men were stepping from one display table to the next because the catastro-clutter on the floor made the aisle virtually impassible. They looked up briefly, like cocksure coyotes, before returning to their business.

The news camera swung back outside to capture some hubbub. A couple of guys were trying to pry open a small appliance store door with a huge tire-iron, maybe three feet long. The crowd was egging them on with some apish chant—*HUH, HUH, HUH*. Tug-tug-tugging, the door finally popped open. The scrum roared and rushed forward, like kids scrambling for candy pouring from a piñata's belly.

Back at the sporting goods store, someone was now

pushing a canvas-sided cart the size of a small boat on rollers outside. When he got it to a clearing, he muscled it onto its side and stood back, cheerfully, an end-times Santa Claus. Folks nodded, thank you, and started going for footballs, ski jackets, and boots, grabbing in front and behind them, yet careful not to grab things from one another.

"Mind if I change channels?" Adam asked.

The therapist said, "Go ahead." Adam went ahead.

He'd lived in the city long enough to see dozens of movements take root, would-be converts crawling out of their holes and queuing up at makeshift shrines before which to lay their common sense for pulverization. Now, it seemed, they'd joined another "movement," the movement of "it's free for the taking." But why, why would these people, all stripes and colors, the perennial penniless, for sure, but also upholsterers and nannies and carpet layers and receptionists, folks with no criminal past, house painters and dental technicians—why, for a pair of sneakers, would these people throw years of more-or-less righteous living, no less righteous than his own, out the window? Because *everyone was doing it*? Was it that simple to explain? Because if they didn't, somebody else would? What will they tell their kids, or one another? Will they feel shame and hide their eyes, or will they compare notes, stolen stuff, who got what, don't mention where? As he watched the Latinos, who now seemed to outnumber the blacks ten to one looting-wise, he wondered, will they be able to face The Virgin? Will they be able to kneel at their homemade shrine tonight? And for what? A bag of diapers. A twelve-pack of Corona.

Adam had been consuming cigarettes at a demented pace, as were his neighbors, neither of whom he even knew smoked. His cigarettes were now nearly gone, and he needed to replenish his supply, so he excused himself to fetch a couple of packs from the market just around the corner.

Outside, white ashes twirled and drifted like snow in the shimmering chrome orange light. As he turned onto Wilshire, he saw that nearly all the shops were either shut or shutting down. Some had their front windows boarded up the way they do in hurricane country.

Luckily, his local mini-mart was open. It was owned by a short, stocky affable Afghani who spoke broken English. In line with the comically super-American names that foreigners often take, he went by the name *Mel*. Adam liked Mel because he had carried to the neighborhood some of the old-country shop-keeping customs that Adam knew as a kid. On any given day, Mel and a friend would sit on little fold-out chairs in front of his store, smoking, playing backgammon, and drinking Cokes. With a wave of the hand he extended credit if you were short a dime here or a quarter there, and occasionally he handed a stick of candy to kids who came for bread or milk. He'd pulled his chairs inside, and shuffled uneasily behind the register when Adam came in.

A little TV he had set on top a tall shelf was keeping him in the loop.

"Isn't this something, Mel?"

Mel pursed his lips and shook his head, a gesture of outrage more than disbelief. Then he swung a rifle out from beneath the counter.

"They come my store, I shoot."

"Calm down, Mel."

Mel smiled; he was missing a tooth, and fit the rifle back underneath the counter. The cigarette shelf, Adam noticed, was empty of his brand, and he told Mel that though he didn't patronize anybody else for smokes, it looked like he left him with little choice.

"I know you like the Camel." He lifted an open pack from his shirt pocket, and handed it over.

"I couldn't, Mel, not at a time like this."

Mel stabbed the pack at Adam's chest, Take.

"Appreciate it."

"You good customer."

"Well, what do I owe you?"

He crunched his shoulders, as though to say, "need you ask?"

He shook the pack; maybe half full—at full price? What the hell? Adam paid and paused at the threshold of the store to fire one up. He was a couple of nerve-steadying puffs into his cigarette when gunshots tore holes in the air. His mind seized; heat fled to his extremities. He turned to Mel, who was striding expertly toward the door, rifle in hand. There was a dry thickening in Adam's throat, a whack-whacking in his chest, as Mel stepped outside, looked left, then right. It was impossible to say where the shots had come from, how close, but he couldn't just stand there.

Mel brought the shotgun up to eye level, a sign that he'd give cover, and with his chin shooed Adam away.

His apartment was more or less half a block down, but that half a block felt like half a mile on a pasture pocked with landmines. When he opened the front security door to his complex, he stood, out of breath, and noticed that there was a towel bulging from beneath the door of the only black person in his building.

She was mid-twenties, thick as an oil drum, touchy, and private to the point of paranoia. Her apartment could've been a terrorist safehouse for how stealthily she slipped in and out, and for how securely it looked locked down: drapes were permanently drawn over every one of her many windows, even the huge picture window up front, even on the most exquisitely sunny day. Still, this was a new and absurd extreme: blocking light from the bottom of the door. Even the smallest inconvenience or request would cause her breathing to go hectic, so he was loathe to knock on the door: "I just wanted to see if you are all right," he imagined himself saying as an excuse, only to have her snarl back, "I didn't ask for your help. Why should I need help? Because I'm BLACK! Is that why?"

Or maybe, it occurred to him, she was committing suicide; maybe she was closing off any air-source to better gas herself with the stove. He bent over and sniffed.

The year before, nobody talked about it anymore, a girl down the hall had OD'd out of nowhere. They had carted her out in the middle of the afternoon when everyone was at work. A friend who came to fetch her belongings a few days later had floored everyone with the news. "She'd had psychological problems forever," her friend explained. "Nobody is to blame."

"It's sad," Adam had told her, "that's all. It's just terrible."

The girl had been from Michigan, pretty but not spectacularly so. She'd majored in drama, or stage, something of that sort, and she'd barely been in LA a year. She'd given up a hometown life to take her chances amid an endless bamboo field of novitiates bowing and straining toward the dazzling lights of the hippodrome. There were probably a dozen guys at her college who thought she was cute enough to marry, Harrys and Billys and Howies who would have just loved to take her down the aisle. But she'd chosen to come and take her chances, and IT had cut her down, and now when he walked down the long dark corridor to the back of the building, he could feel the stretch marks of the Hollywood death-star she'd gotten sucked into.

Back to the black girl. He got a flash of her blasting open the oven, and sticking her big head in there. He could see her blubbery body glued dead to the kitchen floor.

"What's-her-name next door has a towel shoved underneath her door," he told the therapist and her significant other the moment he walked back into his pad. "Looks suspicious."

"What do you think it means?" Joanne said. Her therapist clutch was obviously stuck.

"I don't know."

"Who cares," Derek said. "Who cares about her fat ass? Has she ever done anything for any of us?"

"Well no, but…"

"You might as just well say 'Black Ass,' Derek. Why do you talk like that? Please, not now. Not at a time like this. It's totally inappropriate to talk like that—especially now."

"It's the truth, that's why! Okay. Fat Black Ass. Is that better?"

She gasped, like some ingénue suffering a lout's advance.

They lived directly above Adam, which made him intimately familiar with their peculiar manner of redressing their relationship, and this was way out of the ordinary. Typically, Derek droned on, the sound coming through the floorboards like someone cranking a diesel engine, for fifteen, twenty minutes, before Joanne would suddenly start swinging her machete around, cutting him off and to pieces. So this brief exchange stunned Adam, and stunned her more. Maybe the gun in his drawers gave him the boost.

"I need a cigarette," she said, as if she hadn't already smoked two.

"Sure," Adam said. "Go ahead. Smoke your heart out."

"I gave up smoking three years ago, but I need one."

"They're there."

From the time the city was founded, Los Angelenos had lived obliviously with faults about to gape; wildfires aching to spring; gigantic mudslides happy to rake whole hills away. In all ways, it seemed, they lived like depraved despots live with the haunting specter of revolt; but this was something new even for the therapist, who right then could've used a session herself.

Thousands were draining into the streets, like ants, a colony of ants swarming from their anthills. It was even more astonishing to see a police corps that touted itself as the toughest and *most professional* in the nation, led by The Gatekeeper, a man who'd imposed on the city something that was just this side of martial law; whose use of military style tactics had turned the whole town into his quasi-fiefdom; who deployed battering rams to quite literally "bring down drug houses"; whose police force had conflated protection and aggression to such a degree that folks seized from fear when they were stopped for making so much as an illegal U-turn; who had inculcated the good cop/bad cop strategy into *every single cop* on the force, trained to go in an instant from Jeckyll to Hyde and back again on you (the precise psychological teeter-tottering that shrinks claim creates schizophrenics)—it was astonishing to see them all but disappeared.

A parking scooter had just stopped in front of his apartment and started ticketing. Adam said, "Look at this," to Derek, who erupted as though he'd been holding it in for a good many years.

"Fucks! Fucks!"

"What Derek? What?" The therapist stamped her cigarette out, as though it were the match to his fuse.

He bolted for the door. Adam followed. From the porch, Derek bellowed: "WHAT THE HELL ARE YOU DOING, YOU BITCH? THERE'S A RIOT IN THIS CITY!"

She looked up, her cursive frozen in the air.

With his neck outstretched for a little English, the commercial actor hollered: "HAVEN'T YOU HEARD, YOU BITCH? THERE'S A RIOT IN THIS CITY!"

"Just doing my job, sir. Is this your car?" She hooked a finger toward it.

"No, it's not my fucking car. But it's someone's car."

She looked at her watch. "It's twelve o'clock, sir. And it's street sweeping day."

"Maybe you didn't hear me? Do you want to get shot? It can happen on a day like this. Like that," he snapped his fingers.

She sprinted for her scooter-cab.

"Stay the fuck out of this neighborhood! Whore!"

"Take it easy on her," Adam said.

She grabbed her hand-held radio, and sprinted the scooter away.

"Poor thing is probably as disoriented as we are," said Adam.

"Yeah, call the cops! What's that?"

That was a black guy pulling across the street a clothing rack on wheels, with the clothes still racked. Adam assumed it was from the dry cleaning store around the corner.

"It's getting bad," Derek said, and then he wondered if he'd taken any clothes in that he hadn't picked up.

They went back inside. Passing the black woman's apartment, Adam pointed to the towel.

"I don't give a shit," Derek said. "I hope she's rotting in there."

The therapist was gone.

"I'll see you later," he said sheepishly, like all the sudden he remembered the deeper lessons of AA.

"Okay."

Adam called the Wizard who lived in the Hills, to see how he was holding up.

"Can you believe this?" Adam said.

"If you live long enough nothing surprises."

"I hope I never live that long."

"Don't talk like that; what nonsense!"

"I take that back. Sorry."

"In any case, don't worry about me."

Adam did worry about the Wizard. He loved the Wizard; the Wizard had been there when he'd hit bottom. He had been there when no one else was, when his body from its free-fall had arrived.

The Wizard asked, "But should I be worrying about you?"

"Just don't go outside, for any reason. It's getting really scary out there. What are you doing; what are you listening to?"

"Shostakovich." He invited Adam up to listen to Shostakovich with him.

"I don't think so. If you need anything, let me know."

"It is quite a mess on the freeways," the Wizard said. "Bumper to bumper."

"People are starting to get out of town. That's what that's about."

"What have I always told you: you have to find your way in between, you have to find a way to thrive in the cracks."

He loved it there, and he'd almost taught Adam to love it there as well, in the cracks, alongside the psychological misfits and addicts and strung-out vets and homeless and other social litter. Even as he sat in a highfalutin chair at UCLA, he'd abided, in his Wizardly way, by the pigsty ethic summed up in his favorite passage from his favorite book, Joyce's *Portrait of An Artist as a Young Man*: "The faint sour stink of rotted cabbages came toward him from the kitchen gardens on the rising ground above the river. He smiled to think that it was this disorder, the misrule and confusion of his father's house and the stagnation of vegetable life, which was to win the day in his soul."

"What's that noise?"

"A call is coming through. I love you. Keep safe, my old man."

Adam flashed over to the call.

"Are you okay down there?" It was his friend Brian, whom he'd met in Vegas at a bar owners' convention a few years earlier. "Looks like things are pretty heated."

"It's worse than you can imagine."

"Portland's fine. Come on up, we can party until it is

over."

"Right."

"Seriously. Is it happening anywhere near you?"

"What are you talking about? It's next door!"

"Really?"

"Shooting, looting, fires, the whole nine yards."

"I though it was just in Watts and Chinatown."

"You mean Koreatown."

"But you don't live anywhere near there. I though you said you lived near the Farmer's Market."

"Where the hell do you think that is? Out in the country?"

Brian had the idea—and if he did, so did millions—that the hysteria was drummed up by the media. He'd grown, as Adam had grown, as everyone in this country had grown, inured to catastrophe, so accustomed to seeing it framed at TV's scale, so used to stroking their peckers, munching on Fritos, shouting at the kids to shut the fuck up, while watching an entire world rock, that they could not fathom it, especially as the catastrophe was happening where the faux-catastrophe-fabricating-machine was located.

"Has it even hit places like Beverly Hills?"

"I'm sure it has."

"But you're not positive."

"What does it matter?"

"Seriously, why don't you just hop on a plane?"

"Oh yeah, and leave my parents. Anyway, I heard something about the airports closing."

"They're shooting at airplanes?"

When he hung up, he noted that Nick hadn't called. Was it possible that the news hadn't gotten overseas yet? The other possibility was that he'd taken the news in stride, thinking there was no way they were going to touch him. Nick was just the opposite of Adam: he assumed trouble would bypass him, while Adam assumed it would go out of its way to run him over.

[LIVE, the camera follows several dozen police-
men outfitted in riot gear, jogging down a street
somewhere in LA, to who knows where to do who

knows what. They look strikingly like extras on a
movie set.]

                    TED
          Trish, we now understand, we've just
          heard, that Governor Wilson has given
          orders for the National Guard to be
          deployed.

                    TRISH
          I'm sure this news about the National
          Guard will be welcomed by the LAPD.
          We've peeled away *Lieutenant Gerardo*
          for a second to get his sense of what is
          going on. Lieutenant?

                    LIEUTENANT
          They're just too many. The LAPD is not
          set up for something like this.

                    TRISH
          Who are these people?

                    LIEUTENANT
          At this point…?

                    TRISH
          Who is 'they' Lieutenant? Can you prom-
          ise the people of this city…

                    LIEUTENANT
          At this point we can't promise anything.

[We hear gunfire in the background.
Lieutenant turns his head, almost casually.]

                    LIEUTENANT
          Thanks. We have to get moving.

                    TRISH
          Lieutenant. To where?

                    LIEUTENANT
          We really do have to get moving.

                    TRISH
          Not really, I'm sure, what anyone wanted
          to hear, Ted. Maybe we will get some

In the meantime, there was a definite shift in the looters' tempo and mood, from swift, stealthy, angry, and energetic to good-natured and leisurely as families loading up for a spring fling. Some did the smashing—this seemed to be their *forte*—while others waited to rush forward, like groupies at a rock concert. Others self-consciously shuffled around outside, wanting in on the action but not willing to commit until a certain critical mass had developed in there in advance of them. Still others stood back from the mad rush, watching, wondering if it could be true that there would be no price to pay for paying no price. Capitalism will one day collapse from its own internal contradictions, Marx said. Adam Smith said that capitalism would grow and grow until it eventually led to the general good, a state of abundance for all. *At just this moment*, Adam thought, *both of them are on the money.*

"*Samy's Camera. Samy's Camera*," he heard. It was right down the street. The camera now joggled and then steadied and he saw smoke building over smoke over the building, a few humans darting out with bags full of whatever it was. *Samy's Camera! Samy's Camera* was on fire. Half the neighbors had bought something from Samy's Camera, but even for those who hadn't, Samy's had been there forever, a locally owned establishment, a little doe holding its own against the Godzillas, a place actually named after the guy who owned it!

Mom called, hysterical. Apparently they'd seen the same on their TV, and had rightly placed Samy's Camera just blocks from his apartment. Adam told her he sometimes shopped there. He told her, once again—as though it weren't already deadly obvious—that it was just down the street.

"*Vakh,*" Mom went. It was a muffled cry of terror. "Where are you?" she asked.

"Don't worry, home. I'm at home."

"I thought this was mobile..bobble..I don't know what."

"Do you and Dad want me to come?"

"No, no, honey. I just want call. You stay home."

"Are you sure?"

"Why come? Going get worse?"

Right away he called The Kurd, outside of The Wizard his dearest friend in LA. The Kurd had left the studio early, barely half an hour after he'd set up and started to work. "The place empty like everyone need go pee same time." Adam wanted to get over to our parents, but there was no way he was going to try it alone, so he asked The Kurd to ride shotgun; how on the mark the phrase suddenly was.

Outside the air was ugly as the air in a kitchen where pork chops had been left frying too long. He had just rounded the corner onto La Brea in his Toyota when he saw the smoke, rushing wildly up from behind two tall apartment buildings. It brought him to an idle, filled him with a kind of wonder, as though he were watching some stories-high genie unfurl from his lamp. Now he had rounded up on Samy's. The heat and sound were humongous. Fold upon fold of smoke, defying description, mounted skyward. At a distance, a few people were crying on each other's shoulders. Others stood stunned, in awe of its dark concentration of power, its ferocious and baroque complexity. He barreled up 3rd, saying goodbye forever to Samy's through the rearview mirror.

The Kurd was waiting on the sidewalk in front of his apartment, puffing on one of his hand-rolled cigarettes. He hopped in the car.

"What is happening? The whole city is going south psychedelic," The Kurd said, getting the idioms all mixed up as he so often and colorfully did. Adam told him that he'd just passed Samy's, and The Kurd said he'd seen it going up in smoke on TV, and that it was a vicious blow. In a city where it was often said you might as well get a Persian Carpet sewn for what it costs to order a set of prints, the guys who worked there were true professionals. They were fair, and they understood that "half the artists in the city live off the *cous cous.*"

Adam thanked him for coming along, and The Kurd said, "Of course, Buddy ("Buddy" was what he called Adam). That they should be driving together up Olympic toward Koreatown holding their breaths was not lost on either of them. Kurds were heinous to Armenian memory; a baser version of the Turks themselves, the genocidal advance guard on horseback, blindsiding the death caravans.

Adam had met The Kurd at the opening night of an exhibition of his work at a Santa Monica gallery that a friend of Sasha's, an Israeli named Ari, had recently opened. I was in town that weekend visiting our parents and catching up with my brother, and trying to smooth out a friendship with Sasha that had gotten into a complex emotional knot. On the drive there we learned from Sasha that the artist worked for the Disney studios and was "one the best scenic painters in the city," so Sasha and I expected paintings on the large side, like what you might find in the lobby of a fancy hotel or hanging in the foyer of a high-ceilinged, five-star restaurant, something to lend corporate environments a certain aesthetic exclusiveness. Or the opposite of that, possibly a series of paintings parodying Disney characters, Mickey doing Donald doggy style, etc. Parody or big and pointless beauty—that covered our thinking.

When we stepped into the gallery we discovered rugged, visceral pictures, built up with thickest layers of paint, impasto over impasto. Rust, mud, cobalt blue, sage green—nature's most hardscrabble colors put to use in the service of a ferocious theme, what can only be described as civilization at its brink. Forests quartered by real estate developers, a hilltop ravaged by fire, a modest wooden chair choked to death by branches and twisting vines.

After a few minutes together, Sasha and I peeled off, leaving Adam to study the paintings on his own. We agreed that even though his brushwork was confident and the surfaces technically daring, their tragically romantic themes amounted to commercial suicide in the current market. At the far end of the gallery, Adam was standing inches away from a 7 x 7 oil of a grand piano perched on the lip of a crumbling cliff. "Look at this," he nearly shouted at us. "This guy is driving dirt into the canvas with his fucking hands!" These paintings were troubling in exactly the same way that he was troubled. Sasha said, "He will never make it here," and then said why: "too painterly."

Adam said, "Too what? What the hell is that supposed to mean? You know I love you Sash, but sometimes you say the stupidest shit." Sasha sighed at her little naif and excused herself to find her Israeli friend. We'd arrived late, and the crowd had by this time thinned considerably, and so we had a chance to introduce ourselves to The Kurd. He stood about five-foot-eight, muscularly built, with a wide, handsome, rugged face, huge brown eyes, and eyelashes long as daddy-long-legs. A big mole perfectly centered on his forehead looked almost put there by pious design.

"You are Armenian?" He smiled warmly, and then said, "Paree yegar," *welcome*, in Armenian. He told us that he was Kurdish, but for the three years he studied art in Baghdad, his best friend was Armenian. He excused himself, and Sasha and the Israeli joined us in the center of the empty studio. They were discussing where to go and have a drink—Sasha was pushing for a new club on the promenade—when The Kurd returned with foldout chairs and a clear glass Mason jar filled with, he announced, homemade brew. Adam loved the idea of home-made brew and ached for a taste, but Sasha wanted to move along. I was kind of with her, but before we had a chance The Kurd poured us each a small tumbler full. "You are like a bird. Here, take this branch," he told Sasha, handing her a chair. Ari now told The Kurd who she was, in order to temper the scene. "Good," (he pronounced it "Gude"). "I love the downtown. Tell me what's going on down there downtown." Sasha, who'd done her graduate work in Contemporary Art History at NYU with a thesis on Korsuth, conveyed, still standing, the strategic impor-tance of a cultural complex downtown. After a study of the demographics, the politics, the history, and the geography of the city, downtown, she explained, was renaissance-bound. From the jumble of buildings and nowhere places where nowhere people congregated before moving onto another nowhere place; out of a city that grew like crabgrass, migrating horizontally, taking root everywhere but nowhere deep; out of a city set up like so many perishable movie sets, she was intent on cultivating a vir-tual avant-garden of Eden, where deeply rooted fruit-bearing art trees, apple and cherry and quince and persimmon, would flourish. But they needed, she said, public water, city water, state and national fertilizer.

She was happy to stay so long as the dais was hers, and Adam let her have it for ten or so minutes before he rather rudely jumped in. "Hey, he's the artist here. Tell me, how did you end up in America?"

The Kurd explained that he'd left Iraq some twenty years ago to visit some educated Kurdish friends in Chicago. He had brought a few working sketchbooks with him, and when they asked to see what he'd done, they were surprised at how good the work was. Next thing you know, he was applying to study at the Art Institute, there in Chicago. "What is they say, 'a dream it come true.' I danced for three days. But when I got to the Chicago nobody was doing art. Everybody was smoking weed and doing sex on the grass. Weeks passed, and this Hindu boy and me only one in studio. He would feed me a curry and I would feed him some dolma. Maybe now and then another student would come stoned in shaking like the tambourine, 'WHAT'S GOIN' ON, MAN!' They'd razor the canvas, or make big chalk circles and take shit in middle—cows eye, bull's-eye—I don't know what. Canvas is part of the system, they said. For me, stretching a canvas was like stretching out a lover on a bed. What did I know? I was nineteen year old. I was from a little straw and mud village from the Bible times. They were doing the bulls-eye and I was still doing goats."

Sasha, who'd *tired* of The Kurd, was smiling civilly and giving a head tick toward the entrance. I was getting into The Kurd's rhythm now myself, and Adam was sitting in that chair, chin in hand, like he was listening to a bedtime story, every now and then laughing hysterically and echoing The Kurd's expressions: "'CURSING THE CANVAS!' 'GOATS,' THAT KILLS ME!"

Then The Kurd dropped his hand on Adam's knee. "You know," he said, "I know, every Kurd, what happened your people. We know because we were there and we were partners in that terrible act. Not all, but many, primitive, vicious, greedy tribe people. I want to let you know I am sorry." He had a cheerful face that now surprised me at how earnestly and suddenly it saddened. Adam told him how happy he was to have met him. "Well then," Sasha said, hoping to move it along. What dumb luck, Adam continued, that we'd met Ari as well, and how very few places in the world still existed where "five people from four distinct tribes can gather under one roof, put down their swords, and get happily drunk. Isn't this living fucking proof that LA is one of the greatest cities in the world!"

Adam's enthusiasm was genuine, but the Ouzo, which our little group had now reduced by half, was damn near a hallucinogen. "What a journey, man" Adam told The Kurd.

"Not only miles," The Kurd said, and turned to study one of his paintings: the majestic tail of a whale dramatically rising from a churning sea. A beautiful painting that might've skirted the melodramatic if he'd not applied craqueleur, which had turned the water into what looked like a dried-up riverbed. "It's a great painting," Adam told him. "Thank you," The Kurd replied. "Thank you, my friend," Adam said. "The majesty is there, still recognizable, but broken into pieces."

It was probably that comment, so innocently yet eloquently put, that sealed his friendship with The Kurd, and that had the two of them now progressing unbelievably through the middle of Koreatown. "Can you look at this," The Kurd said, "Can you look at this!" Flames and smoke, spectacularly black, so thick he could barely see down to the next street light, gushed from one building and then another. Lebanese neighborhoods crushed by firebombs, Vietnamese villages blanketed with napalm, that's what it reminded Adam of. There was the Armenian Question resolved, The Kurdish Question open, and now The American Question. And nobody had seen the half of it.

A stereo-thundering Cadillac full of black-teens-whom-society-had-neglected shot past and skidded into the parking lot of a mini mall. The Kurd put a hand up to slow. The passengers, four in all, respectfully passed around a small ganja pipe, each took a solemn, almost sacramental hit, and then two got out of the car, one heading back to the trunk and the other toward one of the store's double doors. He gave it a quick tug. Locked, presumably empty, but who could say for sure. With a finger he lassoed the air, a "good to go," because now his friend took a canister from out of the trunk, lit it at arm's length and hurled the Molotov through a picture window. The glass shattered all at once, like a curtain collapsing. They got back into the car and motored up the road to their next job, as matter-of-factly as the DWP.

Adam followed them for half a mile before The Kurd said "Pull over." Adam did, into another Korean mini-mall. A dozen or so hair-netted *cholos* were sitting on car hoods chilling with cases of beer. The Kurd marched past them into a grocery store, Adam trailing. Noodles, packaged seaweed, bags of red and yellow spice, mud-colored beans, cans, and large jars of whatever weird things Koreans cooked up were in a shambles on the shelves or knocked clean off them. Several twenty-pound sacks of rice were here and there on the floor, like small dogs left for dead. *It was a Korean Kristallnacht.* A tattooed Latina gal, fat with baby, waddled a cart up an aisle of Korean cooking gadgets. She reached for a certain metal square-headed mallet, the meat-flattening kind, tested it on her palm, and then politely put it back.

Down in the produce section, four or five people were stuffing multi-ply garbage bags with whatever was in season; two boys, maybe nine or ten years old, had a fruit fight going. One flung an Asian pear at the other. The other volleyed back with a plum that almost struck their mother, who was emptying the onion bins. She turned in rage and cursed them in Spanish. The boys pointed fingers at each other; she stabbed her own finger at the empty bags; they needed to be helping! In the refrigerated section, gallon-size glass bottles of *kimchee* lay busted on the linoleum floor, still draining their crimson brine. The cabbages resembled large bloody organs layered in fat, the sum of the scene like a medical experiment gone berserk. The fumes were potent as pepper spray, so that Adam was forced to pull his shirt up over his nose. Oddly, no one else seemed bothered by the smell. Not even the kids. Maybe they'd been inoculated from all those jalapeños?

Then he saw an elderly Asian man with three boxes of rice cookers in his arms scurry up an aisle, and disappear into a storage room. It took a second to conclude the obvious: this man was the owner of the store, trying to stash away what he could, maybe hoping to plead for mercy when the pyromaniacs came. The shoppers paid him no mind, or maybe they were relieved he was there, in other words, it's not really stealing if you're here watching me take the stuff, in other words, if you own the store and you don't stop me, then what I am doing must be okay, in a way, right? Like you have insurance to cover it, like you wanted to thin down your inventory anyhow? The Kurd told you he'd seen enough. Adam was about to follow him out, when the owner shambled back up the aisle with his head lowered, as though in shame. When he looked up, and his eyes met Adam's, he froze, raising his hands in surrender. Adam said, "Don't worry," but it didn't help. His face was jumping with fear, like Adam had a gun leveled at his head. "No, no, no," Adam beseeched. The man turned clumsily to escape and slipped, his body slamming on the floor. Adam pitched forward to help, but the man cupped his hands in prayer for Adam to *please take mercy*. He made to his old feet trembling and lurched back down the aisle.

Trembling himself, Adam walked outside. The Kurd was sucking on a cigarette, with his eyes welded to a man with greasy matted hair and ripped jeans, homeless probably, readying to make his mark with a stainless steel trashcan that he was balancing on the back of his neck, a kind of alleyway Atlas. Half a dozen people, including a young boy and girl, looked on.

"Hurry," Atlas hollered to another guy, maybe a fellow traveler, who was down on one knee fussing with the zoom on a video camera, price tag still dangling. "Okay," he said. Everything for an instant froze, the cinematographer waved an arm, signaling *action*, and the man ran madly at a storefront howling like a samurai and then heaved the trashcan at a big window, but the trashcan bounced off. There was a collective sigh at the setback. He picked it up, loosely embarrassed, and with a kind of sick rage started swinging it at the window until the window had had enough. He stood there, wobbly with exhaustion, as the crowd whooped and cheered. That's when the camera guy turned to The Kurd and said, "It's history, ay," and chuckled, and The Kurd said, "And you are making it, man, you are making it."

A woman bolted out of a laundromat with a pile of clothes—whether they were hers or belonged to a customer who'd ditched them in a panic was anyone's guess. Gunshots creased the air, and everyone in harmony ducked. A block away, Koreans were firing wildly over the hoods of vehicles, causing the looters to scatter like vectors. Adam jumped back in the car and pulled out of the parking lot and aimed north up Western. A luxurious, drowsy, honey-colored light was slathered over everything as he rolled along in kind of creepy freedom through the stop signs and lights. He told The Kurd about the owner, how the old man had frozen, fell, and fled, and only then did it occur to Adam that he'd been holding his shirt over his nose: in that Korean's mind he probably fit the bill of the masked American outlaw or mobster, ready in cold blood to kill.

On the news they had said that the firemen couldn't catch up, but up close it looked like they hadn't made it down the ladder. Arsonists had even pitched their firebombs right through the slits of those accordion-like gates that some shops were rigged with. From every forth or fifth store, smoke and fire was getting sucked out like lava running in rapid reverse.

A pack of prostitutes were huddled near the bus stop at Santa Monica and Western, they and the parking monitors, apparently, the only ones still working the streets. "Are they men, boys, girls, or some combo meal?" The Kurd asked. Two high-heeled streetwalkers in tight-fitting outfits that showed super muscular bodies made the question entirely reasonable. The Kurd, whose Olympic-sized sexual appetite found obnoxious any law that might curb it, bet he could smorgasbord for pennies on the dollar on a day like this; "The police buy you motel just keep you off streets."

They were nearing Little Armenian. A major department store parking lot, one that the skycam had covered just an hour ago, showing a few people here and there, was now jammed front to back with vehicles.

It was one thing to see the mass looting on TV, where there is no space and there is no time, only a frictionless, cool interchangeability of wavelengths; only images switchable, reversible, pausible, fastforwardable, detailable, where it might've been anywhere, anytime. It was another thing altogether to see it LIVE, in person, where the atmosphere was, *I hate to tell you*, festive—a Grand Opening Celebration, a party with free hot dogs and sodas kind of thing. Some had brought their own sacks and duffle bags and dollies along, but most were sensibly putting the store's shopping carts to use: smiling; patting each other on the back, *Look what you got! Good for you!* News choppers, batteries of cameras on board, circled the sky like sharks zoning in on a meal. The looters seemed oblivious to the fact that they were practically self-documenting their crimes. Maybe these "opportunists," what the pundits were calling them, felt nameless, nameless to a *system* that had ignored them for so long that they no longer expected it ever to change. Perhaps in the flood of the moment each had turned blurry to himself as a salmon in a run of salmons, or perhaps their Warholian fifteen minutes had finally come around.

When Adam turned onto the Boulevard it was all but empty: no tourists, no mom and dad and the kids from Omaha and Detroit and DePaul and Bangor, cameras hanging from their necks, stooping to trace the stars with their fingers. They'd obviously retreated to their hotel rooms, from which they could probably see what Adam now saw: the palm trees lining either side of the freeway roaring like towering matchsticks. Over the phone, our parents had told him that it hadn't reached Little Armenia, but now as he crept—a kind of moving paralysis, really—up the Boulevard, he saw that word of mouth couldn't keep up with events on the ground. *Topalian's Auto Shop* had been broken into; small auto parts boxes were scattered on the cement drive leading in. The double doors were wide open at *Yerelian's Electronics.* And, oh shit, *Sako's Liquors* big picture windows were shattered. Inside, it looked like the epicenter of a tiny earthquake. Poor people were barely getting off the ground; they'd saved for years to start these businesses. The car was approaching Dad's tailor shop. Adam held his breath and quickly made the sign of the cross. That little shop was all Dad had—there was no telling what he'd do if the fire worshipers—what else might one call them at this juncture?—had gotten

68

to it: would Dad pack up and return to Beirut, kill himself, or kill our mom who had pushed us into the now appalling arms of America? No rioters; rolling further up, the reason why came into view: Armenian Power, a couple of dozen guys, maybe its entire heft, stood behind a barricade of cars in front of the Armenian Bakery, *ARARAT*. There was the baker's son, Asbed; there was Antranik, named after the leader of the failed Armenian revolt against the Turks; and there were Asbed, and Hovig and… well, all the other dropouts. On any given day you'd find them guarding the sidewalks, sucking on cigarettes as though it were their oxygen, the white smoke swirling into their mud-pie eyes, and asking in their own hard-to-follow dialect for money, work, or trouble. But that day, by God, they knew their station and purpose, they were primed for the fight, toting handguns and shotguns and a few death machines that might've been Uzis. The blacks and Latinos all looked mean, merciless, but they did not look like terrorists. For our own tribe of gangsters, Adam could feel something resembling pride bubbling up. Maybe we needed them after all; what a thought.

"The Armenian Militia," Adam told The Kurd,

The Kurd shook his head. "We come all the way America for this?"

PART 2

By the time he got to our parents' apartment, Adam's mind was gunked up with images black and viscous, like it had been pushed into one of those bubble-ups over at the tar pits. He wanted nothing more than a moment to come up from what he'd just witnessed when Mom shot out of the kitchen, her face stunned, LEBANON REDUX written across her forehead.

"What you do here? How you get here?"

"Hello," The Kurd said.

Adam said, "We drove."

He told Mom that he had asked The Kurd to come along because he wasn't sure what he'd run into. Our parents hated Kurds, but they liked *The Kurd*; his Armenian dazzled them.

"*Vakh*. You crazy!"

"The boy raised Lebanon," Dad roared from the family room. "Dohn worry him, Lucy."

"What raise Lebanon!"

Leaning into the TV, impeccably dressed, as usual, Dad stood to greet Adam with a kiss on each cheek and The Kurd with a solid handshake.

"What is this?" he asked in Armenian, his voice brimming with disgust. He really didn't want an answer. He formed the shape of a cup with the hand that was stabbing at the TV now, and spat into it, cursing in Arabic, a language he was especially well tooled-up in for just such situations.

Mom said, "Thank the God they no come here."

"Don't count on it, Mom."

"Why? What we do? Arto, what we do?"

"What these Korean they do? What you talking?"

"Hallo." Through the door came Auntie, smiling.

"Hi, Auntie."

"Hallo *hokees*, in English, 'my soul.'" She sashayed up to Adam and took his handsome face in her hands and shook her head in amazement at how well he'd turned out.

Dad barely looked up, "Ha, Arsinee."

"Hallo," she told The Kurd.

"You look ready for the disco," The Kurd told her.

The Kurd, whose heyday had been in Frisco, in the seventies, didn't really know disco was dead, but he was on to something: her white denim outfit, the rowdy gold jewelry dangling from her neck, wrists, and ears, and a gold foil belt wide enough to use for back support, all gave the impression she might be trying for some sort of comeback.

Mom asked, "No work today, Arsinee?"

"I dohn know."

"I don't think so Auntie," Adam said. "I don't think anyone is open today. You got dressed up for nothing."

The Kurd said, "Don't worry. I like woman dress pretty when the world it burn. Sexy." It was The Kurd's perverse flirtatious small talk. The mad visceral crush he had on her was well known to everyone in the family, and though she definitely felt something for The Kurd, he had no money, so she didn't long entertain it.

"Serop no return my call. I dohn know: Maybe he mad me."

Serop was the sleazy, barrel-chested Syrian jeweler who both employed and exploited her.

"I dohn know. Lucy, coffee, please," Dad announced.

"Maybe the something happen. I dohn know."

"Who knows anything anymore," The Kurd said in Armenian.

"I'll help, Mom."

In the kitchen she was rolling her eyes and wagging her head, starting in on Auntie's stupidity as though she'd just discovered it.

72

"Mom, give her a break. Jeezus. When people are that stupid you have to pity them."

"*Peety*," she sniggered, as if to say, *I should have been so lucky to be so pitiful.* "Why your brother no call?"

Adam showed her his mobile. "I've talked to him. He wanted to know how we're doing. Don't worry."

She shook her head in disappointment.

"Here Mom," he said, and took the coffee and some sugar cookies back to the living room. All three had lit up cigarettes and were sitting in a fog.

"When you smoke?" she scolded Dad, holding the demitasse for him to take.

"Dohn worry what I do dohn do *heemah* [now]."

Dad held the cigarette ambivalently off to the side and took the coffee in his free hand.

"*Merci.*"

"*I'm sorry*," Arsinee said to Mom, in an unctuous American accent. Her make-up was so thick it looked like it had been applied with a drywall trowel.

Dad slurped and made a face—too bitter. "Sweetheart, a little sugar more, please." He waited until she was out of earshot to say, "What, I get the cancer one cigarette?"

From the kitchen, "Explain me, how many the cancer need."

"Okayokay." He sheepishly stamped it out.

She returned and dumped a tablespoon of sugar into his cup. "*Merci.*"

"Blame the me," Arsinee said, her second *mea culpa* in so many minutes, in that same creepy faux-American voice. At this juncture, there was something definitely goading about it.

"Enough your fault!" Mom said. "He have the own brain!"

Auntie leaned back on the big brown couch, holding her cigarette at arms length, a kind of lazy *whatever* salute.

Adam had been waiting patiently for the confrontation to resolve to hand The Kurd his coffee, but The Kurd's attention was focused on Auntie's pillowy ass. At a time when jerky-thin was in, The Kurd had never lost his appetite for *the rumpus roast,* as he put it. Adam set the demitasse on a short table in front of The Kurd.

Dad reached over and patted his sister on the knee, "Dohn worry." He felt sorry for her because her husband had died a martyr's death in Lebanon and now she lived alone with her twenty-year-old gangster.

"I dohn know. They close bus." She took a luscious puff. "I have to be the Glendale twelve. Maybe tomorrow open. Arto, bus closed tomorrow too?"

"Okayokay I take you. Dohn worry bus."

"You take me tomorrow, Arto," Mom said. "Why your boss not take you, Arsinee?"

"Not job take me."

Mom said to herself, *No, my husband job!*

"Where?" Dad asked.

"Where what," Mom asked.

"Where I take you!"

"Kaiser! How many times I tell you? The God help me."

It was one thing for him to forget a Kaiser appointment pertaining to "sinus" or "skin" issues, but she was having what they called "female issues," and for him to forget about that—he could see it all over her face—hurt.

"Okayokay, we do the something."

"Dad," Adam said, just to break it up.

"Look this." Dad was referring to rioters using what looked to be an out-of-commission school bus to haul appliance store wares.

"Next, they bring the Amtrak," The Kurd said, chuckling darkly.

"I look enough," Lucy said. "Turn channel."

"I dohn know where your brother?" Dad asked. "Why he not telephone?"

Adam didn't answer.

"Anyway, Hovig protect us now."

"*Vakh!* You lose your husband Lebanon. You lose your boy too!" Mom laid into her,

"It's alright, Mom," Adam said.

"Why I lose?" She tapped out another cigarette.

"Please," The Kurd said. He thumbed at his lighter and brought it under her cigarette. "I don't know you have your

74

own," he said referring to her wildly long fingernails, which were painted fire-engine red.

She chuckled girlishly, nudging her big orange hairdo this way and that, slurped up the smoke and let it go, smiling.

"Let him be there," Dad said. "They come here they will see it."

Mom shouted, "What you talking? We no see already? The God help!"

"No, they come here, they will see it what we will do them."

There he went again, the blowfish; Big Brother getting bigger to show his little sister who was who, Big Brother who had taken charge ever since the day he walked through her door, on the third story of an apartment complex in Beirut, to deliver the bitter news of her husband's death.

. . .

IN THE SPRING OF 1975 there was an attack on a small group of Phlangists—for which everyone assumed Arafat and his PLO were responsible—and a swift and bloody counterattack on a busload of Palestinians that left thirty people dead. The effect was to light the fuse, tied to how much carnage we would soon discover. "We are Armenian-Christian. We have no trouble with anyone." That is what we said to ourselves and to each other— but no one else in Lebanon seemed to be listening. Passions were running wild again, new agendas and old vendettas were gaining ground. The Maronites; the Shia and their proxies; the Israelis and theirs. The pressure from every side was immense, and *Al-Mithaq al-watani*, the National Pact that gave all the players an "equal share" of power, was on ropes. Dad said at the time, "Who does this Arafat think he is? The Palestinians have upset the fruit cart."

Levon (Dad's best friend): "Don't blame the Palestinians. That is ridiculous. These Muslims have babies like mice. They want their fair share."

Uncle: "That cart was falling apart long before the Palestinians showed up. Blind we pushed it until it collapsed at our feet."

Levon: "I blame it on the Jews. They are the problem. Why should the Palestinians have to pay for the Germans' sins? Where did they think these people would go—into the sea? Are the Palestinians goats that can simply be shooed away? Why didn't the Germans give them half of Germany?"

Uncle: "It is too late to rewrite history."

Levon: "All we are doing in Lebanon is rewriting history."

Uncle: "They are using this as an excuse. The Arabs are using the Palestinians as a hammer to gain power. The bottom line, we have to protect ourselves. Nobody else will."

Dad: "Here and there we have some problem. What country doesn't?"

Uncle: "We are now house-guests—who have outstayed their welcome."

Dad: "There are a quarter million of us here. I don't think they can get rid of us so easily. Please, let's not exaggerate."

Grandma: "They are dusting their hands of us as we speak."

Uncle: "We won't let them. Not without a fight, they will not dust their hands of us like that."

Dad: "There need to be some adjustments. A few adjustments and we can save it from collapsing."

Grandma: "It is on your head already, I say. Our time here is over. In their eyes we are same as Jews. Stealing their wealth. The best way to get their jewels back is to get rid of us. Just the way they did in Turkey. It is an old story."

Now Adam finally understood what his friend, Mohamet, had meant when he said, "Armenians already have too much."

Five months before, Adam had met Mohamet on the Rouche. Our family didn't fish, but he'd been watching Andy and Opie as they ambled down a path with their fishing poles, whistling, and Adam wanted to try some of that, even if he were on his own, and even if he'd be fishing the Mediterranean and not a sweet, glassy American pond. He begged Dad for a rod and reel, but it was Uncle who listened, and for his birthday Uncle bought him more than he'd asked for: a tackle box with trays of sinkers and bobs and fancy feathery lures, a rod and a shiny red reel, made by *Abu Garcia*. (The strangest name you'd ever heard. An Arab who was Spanish?)

The following Saturday he headed out with his American fishing gear (which was actually Swedish) just after sunrise. He found a spot some distance away from the other fisherman so that he might take his time setting up without risking embarrassment. He followed the excellent instruction manual, and within no time he was ready to cast; but the line wouldn't go, and the lure whipped around like a wasp. What the....?

Across the way a boy about his age was casting his long bamboo pole with marvelous ease—the kind of ease that comes not only from fishing from a young age, but from watching a parent or grandparent fish from an even younger age. And look at the sweet silverblack mackerel he was bringing up on his measly line with its cork bob. Maybe American fishing poles only worked in America. Those long poles that real Arab fishermen used worked just fine. Finally he managed to get the line out there, but it had grown late, and so he left that day without even a sardine to fry. The boy he'd been watching had fish flopping out of his basket.

The next Saturday Adam saw the boy again and crept closer to see what he was using for bait: shrimp, he was cutting them into bite-size pieces. Adam chucked his feather lure and scrambled up to the Corniche to find a bag of shrimp.

When the boy saw Adam's line plop into the water, close enough to his own to cause him to look around to see who was cutting in, he turned around, his face frustrated, and then resigned, *Allah Inshallah*. Adam reeled in the line; its efficient whir causing the other boy now to freeze in wonder, then drop his pole and start over the rocks. He'd never seen one before, a reel. Adam showed him how it worked, and within a few minutes they were casting side by side.

That was the start of a friendship, Adam's first close Arab friend. Mohamet was a fisherman's son, and Adam's father was a structural engineer, but out there it was a wash. The city was to their backs, and the open sea was all that mattered; its glittering wonder; its salty satin smell, the wind brushing against the two of them gently as a cat, the outcroppings of rock and stands that nature had kindly furnished as plinths; what more than fishing could man be made for?

But then Adam noticed that if it were closing in on nine and the catch was bad, all the sudden worry would mount on Mohamet's face. It pained Adam to see it, and after a few weeks he began to slip him half his catch, even if it was two fish. Mohamet would make back toward his father with his long pole over his shoulder and the basket a little heavier than it had been just minutes before.

Then one morning, as Adam made for the sweet spot where he and Mohamet fished, Adam saw his friend huddled in discussion with four men, including his father. They were on their haunches, and a basket sat in the middle of their group, and now they stood and one man lifted something out of the basket. Mohamet's father grabbed him by the arm and led him up the rocks, while this other man fidgeted with this object in his hand and tossed it far off into the water. They all watched it splash and disappear.

Then there was a great rumble, and the seas erupted, a terrible geyser rising and crashing on itself like a building engineered for obliteration (we'd seen a handful of these by then). The waves thrashed at the rocks, and then, one by one, out of the pandemonium fish started surfacing. Mohamet was jumping for joy. They were all smiling, patting each other on the back. One of the men was now heaving a net out to catch the fish that bobbed by the dozens in sea foam that looked just like cotton candy.

Adam ran down the rocks, his heart racing. Mohamet took him by the hand and explained that it was a grenade. A grenade? "Look at all the fish," he said. "We will make what we need and more!"

While Adam was happy for him, any fish that hadn't been killed had likely fled; the day was over before it had even begun. Some fish had their heads lopped off; what was left of others was a little flesh hanging off the bone. Others were still alive, weirdly twitching. The fishermen were sorting through the nets, flinging the collateral damage back into the water. All of a sudden fishing was about killing fish.

Next week the poles were back. "They are hard to get as gold," Mohamet claimed about grenades.

"Where did they get it to begin with?" Adam asked.

"They are around now," Mohamet replied.

Why are they around now? Adam wondered.

One day, exactly a month after the grenade incident, Adam had pulled up his fifth dabous of the morning and was releasing the hook from its mouth when Mohamet took it from him and said, *"You already have too much."* His father had been fishing a hundred yards away, and now Mohamet looked over his shoulder as though to hide his words from him. Or maybe to show off?

"I decide what is too much for me," he told Mohamet. "Not you. Let go, it's not even off the hook yet."

"Armenians have too much," Mohamet said.

"Too much what?"

"Everything. Armenians own everything. "

"Who told you that?"

Mohamet said, "Everyone knows."

Adam said, "We have one car and an apartment."

He smiled a weird smile, as though to say, *Please know this is a game—but I am duty-bound to play it.*

Adam picked up the tackle box and told him if that was the way he felt he would never fish with him again. He needed to stick up for himself, but the sadness of loss pressed down on his shoulders as he made for home. "There are other Muslim boys to play with; don't pay attention to Mohamet," I told him.

But I was wrong. That very Saturday would be what we'd come to call Black Saturday. Four members of the Phalange were killed, and within hours they had set up roadblocks and checkpoints around the city. Up until then we kids had skirted the skirmishes; we'd continued meeting up with friends and arm-in-arm walking up the boardwalk. We'd scamper down to the pigeon rocks and take our shoes off and skip stones, or simply sift pebbles as the sun lowered behind us. Beirut was still our city, and we skipped up and down it with as much care as birds skipping from branch to branch.

But now we were reduced to two or so square blocks after school. Like turtles, we were reduced to staring out of our shells at one another. Now your life depended on what side of the line you lived on, whether you went to a church or a mosque.

Armenians had escaped the Turkish massacres not too many years ago and set up shop in Beirut proper, in a suburb called Bourj Hammoud, minding our own business, lighting our candles and breaking our bread.

We didn't have the luxury of fighting for an idea or even a nation; we were fighting for the right to be in this world, so some Armenians decided they needed to turn out a militia of their own. Auntie had no idea that her husband, a book-loving mid-level civil servant who had introduced us to Voltaire and Tolstoy before we were old enough to have any chance of fathoming a single one of their sentences, had joined, or that just two weeks before he had approached Dad to join as well.

It was mid-morning on a Saturday when Dad came through the door. He looked as though he'd left something important behind. "Sousan," he called and marched past Adam, who was on the floor reading a book on asteroids, his favorite subject. They met in the hallway. He spoke rapidly, and then she shrieked. They came out together.

Adam had heard the expression "white as a ghost" a dozen times, and there it was. Mom, "white as a ghost." Mom sat down and cried. Poor thing, she said, and said it again and again. Poor thing. Our uncle was dead, they told him.

"Where is Eric?" Dad asked.

"Football," Adam told him.

"Get your shoes on," Dad said. "I want you to come with me."

"Where?"

"Just come. We are going to Auntie's."

Adam didn't want to go; he wanted to wait until I got home to go in his place.

Adam rode shotgun while Dad barreled toward our aunt's apartment three miles away, around the roadblocks and past militias huddled in makeshift outposts. Here and there was a bombed-out building, a bridge that now looked like a high-diving board. Our beautiful Beirut, spooning the Mediterranean, was being broken into ugly pieces.

"They want this country to themselves," Adam remembered our uncle—our dead uncle!—saying about the Arabs. But

when a kid wanted something from another kid, the last thing
he wanted to do was destroy it, just the opposite, he wanted
to protect it from destruction. He wanted to get the kid who
owned it out of the way so that he could have that thing he
coveted. Adults destroyed the very things they claimed to want.
It screamed of hypocrisy. Hypocrisy was not something small;
hypocrisy drove all people, simple, sane people, to craziness.
Maybe adults didn't want the thing they claimed they wanted.
Maybe they just enjoyed destroying something that someone
else possessed. Hate didn't want anything but destruction.
Destruction for destruction's sake.

Soon enough, they were at Auntie's, Adam following Dad
up the three flights of stairs, three steps behind.

Dad plodded into the apartment and told her to sit. She
was already sitting, watching TV, our little cousin taking a nap.

"Arsinee, your husband… he is dead."

"What are you saying?" She shuddered, like glass under
immense pressure

"They were meeting in front of Levon's tobacco shop, on
Cypress Street in Bourj Hamoud," Dad explained.

She pulled at her long auburn hair and began turning in her
seat, as though to plead mercy from adjudicators gathered round.
"*Akh, Akh.*" The utterance was black, crow-like. "How? How!"

Adam looked to Dad to cough it up. What's wrong with
you? Tell her! Put her out of her pain!

The group of eight or nine men—Dad named a few of
them—heard tires squeal. They looked up from their coffees
and watched a car speeding away. Intuitively they dove to the
ground, and those who had weapons drew them. There was gunfire—*pop pop pop.* In the blink of an eye the car was gone and it
was over. Everyone rose and dusted himself off, except for our
uncle. He lay on the ground, a bullet through his neck.

Our bookish, revolutionary uncle; the one who rubbed
our heads; the one who carried us on his shoulders over the
rocky steps near the beach; the one who said "don't eat so fast,
the food isn't going to run away." That one. He was dead.

"Who will take care of me now? Who will take care of us?"

Dad answered her question before she had a chance to answer it for herself.

Maybe it was the size of Auntie's grief, or maybe Mom's burden, but up until Auntie and our cousin moved in, we'd never really thought of our family's three-bedroom apartment as cramped. Especially the hallway, down which Mom conveyed plate after plate of small cakes and mint tea to Auntie, who sat on the sofa crying into a handkerchief, taking mourners and listening to Om Kalsoum. No singer on earth sang with such otherworldly, even erotic sorrow; her voice was as big as a sanctuary, one where Auntie sat sobbing with her head in her hands for her forty days.

Our little cousin was too young to understand. Yes, he cried, but he cried because she cried. What he wanted was for the world to go back to being exactly as he'd known it. He believed it would. About his father he wondered, why had the man suddenly disappeared? How long would he be gone? About his father, the man in the box, lowered into the ground: How long will he be down there?

AT THE *hokee hahnkeest*, the "let the soul rest," I remember Mom seeming to be quietly at peace with herself, an *I have done my share with a good heart* aura surrounding her as she placed humongous platters brimming with food on the table. Dad, his voice cracking with emotion, toasted the memory of his brother-in-law, and the nobility of his cause, protecting them from a fate they were all too familiar with. The family and friends gathered round sadly clinked glasses.

Adam was seated with Hovig and me and half a dozen other kids at a small table when Auntie stood. Everything about her radiated vulnerability. Her breasts stood in stunning relief now against her slimmed-down body. With her white skin and black eyes, her lips red as blood, and her delicately concave neck that fanned out against the simple black collar of her black dress—she was beautiful, wildly beautiful. Neither Adam nor I could move our eyes from her.

The next day she was back on the couch—and on her own. Mom wasn't serving her—or anyone, for that matter—anymore.

Within a week, clothes were piling up in the closet and dust was gathering on the buffet; the world, just as the Bible said, was going from dust to dust. Dad had sent both of us a message in that car: "Boys, tighten your belts, the days of idling are over." But it wasn't until Mom collapsed that the message hit home.

Mom's retreat set in motion a kind of tectonic shift; our childhood, especially Adam's, was slipping away, and a new reality was furiously mounting. Naturally, we revolted against this unfair and sudden expulsion from our world, from everything that had meant so much to us; but who were we to complain, and who were we to complain to?

By the end of the school year order was collapsing around us, and we were ducking underneath our desks two days out of the week, and dashing into a bomb shelter beneath the gym the rest. Normal was gone, and another reality had commenced. Everyone would have to get used to it—but "it" came in unexpected shapes and forms. Everyone expected, for instance, that Auntie would wear a veil of widowhood for years to come, if not forever, but the opposite occurred: all the tears and sighs had apparently flushed her system clean. Auntie switched from mint tea to "calm the nerves" to demitasses of Turkish coffee to jack them up. Oma Kalsoum was out, and soap operas were in. She took up this newfangled cigarette, long and slender and white and better, they said, for your health. They smelled like filth and burned down so fast they were barely worth lighting up.

"Shouldn't she peel a few cucumbers?" Mom asked Dad. "Shouldn't she be caring for her own son?" Every time he'd muster a protest, the weight of her loss sat him back down. Every time he sat down, we'd stand up. "C'mon Hovig, let's go play outside."

Suitors started showing up, quietly, at first. "*Bonjour,*" for a cup of coffee, "*merci,*" conversing, "*rein,*" twittering laughter, relaxed, showing off, smiling as they picked up their jackets, "*Au revoir.*" Who were they to barge in and make themselves at home? Why was everyone forgetting? Not four months had passed, and Uncle's sudden martyr's death was old hat. Yes, Auntie was only twenty-six, ripe with beauty, but was that beauty in peril of rotting overnight? I was alarmed at the facility adults had for dusting the ashes away, for burying tragedy from sight. I had to agree with the widow Mrs. Bazazian, two doors down, that "The girl is out dating before her poor husband's body has had a chance to grow cold!" It was something new, to agree with an old spinster; a new feeling, wanting to protect memory, a kind of jealousy.

Though we didn't talk about it, Adam felt the same way. While I turned away in disgust, he began doing his homework smack in the middle of the living room where Auntie and her suitors took their tea and cake. Whenever it was feasible, he'd squeeze next to her on the couch to show them she had existing attachments they'd have come to terms with. He felt the victor when she brought him close and let his head rest on her breasts. But when she'd ask, "Love, would you get Mr. So-and-so some lemonade," and from the kitchen heard her giggle at their stupid jokes, Adam wondered if they all knew what he was up to. He'd rush back with the lemonade to see. No, they were giggling at something else, which was almost as bad—to really let loose, they needed him out of the room.

Mom was largely to blame for all this. She was the one inviting these men in; she was the one who had sent the word out that we needed to get Arsinee hooked up soon. It was part of her double-barreled strategy: pushing Arsinee into the arms of a suitor, and pushing Dad out of Lebanon. Dad didn't want to talk about either, really. He was protective of his sister, but it was the picture of America that made his eyes grow wide with worry.

He adored Lebanon. He knew his Beirut by heart—its fractured body had an itch here, a limp there, was all. What could that matter next to his favorite café, the street that tumbled onto the corniche, a closet of a store in Bourj Hamoud that slow cooked to-die-for chicken on a rotating spit, a little Sudanese man who rolled his cigars.

"I've lived here my whole life, and now I'm going to leave?" He laughed derisively. "This is my home, what are you talking?"

"Your home," Mom said, "your home! Look at it, your home! Your home is crumbling at your feet. Your home!"

Mom reminded him how he regularly dropped into conversation that he taught at the American University.

"You're proud to teach there, but you don't want to live there!"

Silly as the statement was at bottom, the paradox was hard to dismiss completely. Who could forget how he sauntered into the living room one afternoon, tipsy with pride, and announced that they'd asked him to teach structural engineering there, at the American University. "I guess they were looking for someone like me for some time." He'd whisper it to himself, "American University" (two of about fifty English words that he knew). The sound of it on his resumé. The sound of it on ours. Not the French school, our parents' alma mater, but the American school—not another word!

And so we did go, and we learned English from age five, and knew American history (as it would turn out) as well as, if not better than most Americans. We knew all the states, and the first ten presidents by heart; we'd memorized the openings of the Declaration and the Constitution. By the third grade, we'd already sailed halfway across the Atlantic. Its language was a con-fetti parade in our mouths.

"Dazzle," Adam said.

"Razzle," I said.

"What's that?"

"Like Dazzle; another word for it."

"Nice."

"Fine."

"Excellent."

"How about this word: 'Splendid.' You'll learn that later, maybe in the seventh grade."

"Splendid," Adam said.

Stringing English words together made both of us feel worldly, and this feeling would only grow as we absorbed the meaning for all of humanity of America's struggle for indepen-dence, a way of life then new to the human race.

None of this escaped Dad. His love-by-association was boundless, although as time went on, it became clear that he valued some distance from America too. When he brought the U.S. into focus as home, all he saw was a blur of humanity, a typhoon-size power, spewing napalm, roiling with riots, cutting down three good men in little more than five years, that "Tricky Dick" tripping over his own tongue on his way out.

The only possible civil society is one based on shared power, where you are left in peace to attend your schools and churches and make peace with your own God. *Democracy is fine idea, but people aren't.* No matter how hard you try, you will never be able to root out the identity of a people.

"Plus," Dad complained, "I will have to learn the American standards. Do you think that will happen overnight? I don't have the energy."

Mom said, "You have plenty of energy for other things. When you need to you become young like *that*!" She snapped her fingers.

It wasn't true. Adam and I had worried about Auntie, and Levon, and then we began to worry about mother—and we had both assumed until that point that Dad was taking care of himself. After all, he had mastered nature's fixed laws and strict harmonies and regularly applied them, at least in principle, to whatever problem, structural or human, he encountered.

So how awkward and pathetic he now looked, starting as briskly as ever toward the kitchen and then coming to a sudden stop at the threshold, waiting for whatever it was he'd come for to come back to mind. Food?

It wasn't just him. Under the threat of all-out war, most of the men we knew seemed bereft, vaguely depressed, like soccer balls left in the corner of the yard too long. "What's wrong with me," Dad started to say, "is there a hole in my head?" That hole gave him headaches, caused him to wake in the morning feeling drained. It was that hole that Mom believed she could push us through.

"Let us take our money and leave before we have nothing to leave with. You know people; you work with them every day, people who know people in the States. Let them help you find work there."

"I'm not a young man anymore."

Mom pointed to a friend in Los Angeles and a cousin in Fresno—also hardly "young men."

"Is this the world you want your children to know—guns and bombs? Do we need to lose you too before you learn?"

"When will you learn to leave me be? I have a thousand things on my mind—like feeding this family; now I have to think about moving to America too?"

If the lobbing back and forth of accusations, the crisscrossing of bullets, and the out-of-nowhere hate issuing from every corner of Beirut weren't enough, now we were made to suffer a mirror image of the conflict in the bitterly charged debate between our parents.

We tried to put our selfishness early to bed. We picked up after ourselves, and looked after our little cousin, Hovig; at church we prayed with special earnestness, vowing to God and each other to get along, to try to right every little wrong, as though tethered to our every misdeed and misjudgment were the massive misdeeds and misjudgments bulldozing the world around us. But the quieter and more devout we turned, the louder the hate and sacrilege grew, until Adam and I gradually turned on each other.

Dad had brought home a newfangled movie camera, maybe to buy our vote to stay.

"But we have to go," Adam said. "Mom is right."

I said, "You go then, with Mom, and I will stay."

"It doesn't work that way. What are you doing?" I was pointing the camera at him.

"Tell me why it doesn't work that way?"

"Why are you pointing that at me?"

"It's called shooting. I'm shooting you."

"That's what they call it? Like a gun!"

"Yeah. Tell me, why it doesn't work that way?"

"Because we're together; we're a family. We have to go together. I don't like you doing that. That's not why Dad bought it for us. Put that camera down."

"I don't even like you. Why would I put it down?"

"Why are you so mean to me?" He kicked me in the ribs.

"Why are you so violent?"

"I'm not violet."

87

"*Violent,* stupid, not *violet.* It means when you want to hurt somebody."

"Beirut is violent," he said. "Dad says it will change, but it won't. Nobody here wants to get along."

"Maybe you need to change."

"The Muslims need to change. They don't like anyone but themselves. Even Mohamet believes that. "

"Nothing that is happening has to do with Muslims, stupid."

"That's what Grandma says. I believe her."

I began shooting not only Adam, but everything. I shot even when I was out of film; just focusing and framing, zooming in and out. When I looked at the world with my own two eyes, everything seemed reduced to a single, asphyxiating point of view, but from behind the camera I found an infinite variety of perspectives, an alternative eye tailored for endless play. From behind the lens, you could fix a world that was not fixed; you could have your own say on how things would be arranged, and then rearrange them. From behind the lens, I found my need for my parents, my need for everyone, including Adam, dimmed alarmingly within a matter of weeks.

Adam, five years my junior, had no such tool; and so he did what so many kids his age did: he retreated into a cave, into Mher's cave. Now that I had found the camera, it was easier to watch him go.

As our grandmother told it, according to legend, Mher's mother and father die. With the world crumbling beneath his feet and nowhere else to turn, he turns to God: "The darkness is too much to bear," he says. "Give me a place to hide just until judgment day, when you return and settle the affairs of time. Then, I promise, I will come out." God takes pity on him. "Ride," he says, "with your horse far into the mountain, until you come upon a cave. You will know it is the right cave because when you ride past, its mouth will open. Take your horse in with you; when your horse's hind legs cross the threshold, the door will close."

Mher asks, "But where will my food come from?"

"One day a year, the door will open," God tells him, "so that you may go out and gather food."

Mher does as God tells him; he finds the cave and disappears. Year after year passes. In the shape of a celestial sphere, time spins like a pinwheel; its light leaks in from the bottom of the cave door. Mher grows big and strong and wise, and he writes his thoughts on the walls of the cave.

What does he write? Only one man knows, a *vartabed* (scholar) hiking in those mountains. He comes upon the cave and finds a way in, and what he sees on the wall he copies into a book; but because it is written in a unique alphabet, half Armenian, half not, it takes him twenty years to understand it. And look! When at last he translates it into the Armenian tongue, the vartabed goes mad from reading it! These mysteries make him lose his mind!

Grandma had enchanted us with that story, and now she put Adam squarely in the middle of it: "You will know when it time to come out, Mher," she told my brother. "But in the meantime, come and visit a little with your grandmother. Sit. *Egoor, Mher.*" *Come here, Mher.*" Adam didn't like being called Mehr.

"What Grandma?" he'd say, shuffling her way, sniffing up tears.

If anyone other than Grandma had called him that he would have taken it as a taunt. Though he didn't like the message, he trusted the messenger with his life.

"Don't worry about crying," she said. "Don't worry, my love, these are signs that you are full of life, that your *hahvahs* (your appetite, the flicker, the life force) is big.

"I wish my hahvahs wasn't so big, then, Grandma."

"Don't say that—*ahmot*—shame on you. Your hahvahs is all you have!"

Then why did it unsettle his bones, rear its nightmarish head when he slept. "Why am I not like other boys? Like Eric."

"Some have hot souls, some cooler. Some can see from a great distance, and others must roll around in it and put it their mouth before they decide."

Back to the turf war, Mom could not wait for Dad to make the exit call. Alas, he was mostly a victim of his gender. Grandma said, "At the end of the day, poor souls, their dam-sized egos can hardly handle a dribble. We must love them, but understand them for what they are. Their brains, listen to me girl, as they get older reduce to half a dozen parts, not particularly well connected. Look at a boy and imagine him a foot taller and with half the *hahvahs*, and there you have most middle-aged men. They puff their chests up like this, but you can barely use them to blow your nose in. Don't worry, it has always been that way, and it is in the sad clock ticking inside them. Women run against the clock; their strength gains as the hour proceeds, and they have put their duties of diapers and dishes and lipstick behind."

This was Grandma talking, a woman who knew what she talking about. The only member of her family to survive the death march, she was swept into a Lebanese orphanage run by a Turkish woman, a great friend of Ataturk, the founder of the Turkish republic. Like most men who only look to the future, he suffered no trace of the past, so he gave thousands of Armenian children Turkish names. Forget that you are Armenian; Turkish will now be your tongue; bite it and bow to Mecca.

From as far back as we could remember, Grandma felt our family's future was not in Lebanon, at least so long as it was populated by Muslims, whose religion was anti-hahvahs, explicitly created in order to push hahvahs down a hole and plug that hole by putting a million-man lid on it. She hated the Muslim faith, their endless prostrations and calls to prayer; "The jackasses are braying again," she would say. How can a people who must drop to their knees three times a day advance anywhere? How can a faith that does not allow women to attend the burial of their dead be anything other than half-cooked?

Dad would protest: How you can say that, Mother? Who took us in and fed us at the *mile-long table*?" It was the legendary length of the table where the orphans took their meals.

"Enough," Grandma said. "How long must we be grateful to them for handing us a crumb?"

Christians, those who dropped to their knees once a week, didn't fare much better. "The prayers they (the massacred) sent up," she'd wag a hand, "you could fill the sea with them." Still, out of respect for Dad, a committed deacon, the whole family would take to church, Grandmother trailing behind with her "two boys" in their Sunday best. As we sat and stood and kneeled and stood and sang the prayers, and watched the black-hooded priests, Dad now following piously behind them, chanting and jerking the censer, and as the ethereal voices of the choir and the incense rose with the smell of burning leaves, Grandma would remain seated, yawn, and yawn again, and then close her jade eyes and eventually nod off.

There was no wiser an idea in the world than the Americans' idea that the church should be put in a corner. "With one of those hats," she'd whisper, fitting an imaginary cone on either of our heads. We told her that Jefferson felt even the government should have limited power over the people, and that now and then a revolution from below was a recipe to ensure that it would stay that way. He's right! *Ahnshoosht!* Why should some egg-headed man in a sweaty shirt standing in front of a flag tell me how to live my life? Who are these people? I've lived ten lives to their half. Let them eat my spittle! Come here, sweetheart, let me see that picture. Yes, what a handsome man that Jefferson was. Nice nose? Look at that hair. How tall do they say he was? Elvis and Sinatra was one thing, but was it possible to be infatuated with a man dead for a hundred and fifty years? He was the man who let the *Sevs* (Black people) go? No, Grandma, that was Lincoln. Lincoln? Well, it's a good thing Lincoln let those people go. I'll tell you the truth, those people have hahvahs.

They weren't like our blacks, reed-thin, slump-shouldered men and women from the Sudan, limping up the street to toil away in homes; no, they thumbed their noses at the big shots, they had a smooth and rhythmic way of going in the middle of the street, in the middle of the storm! The way that Chuck Berry duck-walked across the floor... and that Queen Diana Ross Supreme, Look at that Sammy Davis swing and that Cassius Clay, he has a big mouth, sure, but what of it when a man is half cobra! Sad, sad what they did to that *Martinlu* King, such a sweet face, a baby, that's what his face reminded me of. But his

91

voice was a man's, one thousand percent man, and when he had that dream… they shut him up, that's what they do to people who dream, shoot them dead, shut them up. Anyway, look, there she is, built to take a thousand bullets, his daughter, that Billy Jean, god-be-with. I hope she puts that braggart Bobby Riggs Miggs in his place. He must've taken a white girl for a wife, that Martin, well, that's his business.

The point, precisely, of America.

It was a place where people traded what they made and bought what they needed, a great and vibrant bazaar, the only place people like Armenians had a chance. The Soviets wanted to turn us into Russians, and the Arabs wanted to make us Arabs—look how that Nasser drove us out of Egypt. For the time being they leave us alone in Iraq, but this boy Saddam doesn't look friendly. True, the Iranians are different—Persians, for centuries we traded princesses. But still, who knows what the future will hold? To tell you the truth, I don't like the look of that Shah, Ma, with that big nose and tight shoulders, he reminds me of a vulture.

Then the Syrians came, and Lebanon, for all its problems, was no longer Lebanon—not even the broken-boned Lebanon my father had held onto for his entire life. Now those who had left looked like prophets, and those of us who had stayed behind looked like fools. Now another reality was set in motion: the entire family had to go. Except for one hitch; Grandma, the impresario, wasn't budging.

"Get settled and then I will come."

"But Ma, nobody wanted to go more than you wanted to go. That's all you talk about." Mom, whose own parents were still in Iraq, needed her.

"Of course I want to go. But you first. What's wrong with that? The queen always sends her entourage in front of her."

"It's not that easy, Mom."

"Why are your thoughts always like that?"

"Like what? My thoughts."

"If you think it will be hard, it will be hard."

"I'm not going without you."

"Don't talk stupid, girl. You're not ten years old. Don't worry, I will come."

"It's dangerous, Mother. That's why everyone is leaving."

"My whole life I lived with daggers flashing around me. I should be afraid now?"

Then the visas came. There was much pleading and protest and back and forth in this tongue and that, until Dad put a stop to it.

"We will go, and in six months we will bring her."

Mom's plan was backfiring. She felt afraid and betrayed. Instead of rejoicing, she wept.

Those tears had dried up long ago, but as she sat on the armrest of the sofa with her hands on her knees, wearing the same flower-print apron she had worn in that kitchen in Beirut, Adam felt for her. With her parents in Iraq too frail to emigrate, and Grandmother dead and buried in Lebanon, she'd left a world behind, and for many years now we had doubted she'd ever be whole in America. The same with Dad; the very one who would take us out to a site to show us what he did, who likened a building project, big or small, to the human body: the skeleton, then the arteries, and lungs, and then the skin and finally we'd watch the blood of electricity turned on. Like the buildings he engineered, he had fashioned a life, it seemed, capable of withstanding multiple shocks, but in America the degree to which this tiny thing and that threw him off balance was a devastating discovery for all of us.

"What they do this?" Mom said. They watched as the entire rainbow coalition of colors now reached and clawed and climbed for things, the way refugees or victims of natural disasters scramble for rations.

"*Ahs martiquenera, ahs Koreanestzinera* ("these people, these Koreans"), the hard-working people, no?" Dad's voice was trembling; he was on the verge of tears.

"Sure enough, Dad."

"What happening, Arto?" asked Auntie. Weakness in others frightened her. There was only so much sympathy to go around and she wanted it all for herself.

Dad slung his arm around Adam and squeezed, trembling almost imperceptibly. Adam squeezed him back. The need for human contact among our people was acute. But at the same time that we embraced, we braced ourselves for the shock of loss; that explained the intensity, the trembling: "You will not take this from me!" Our love didn't idle, didn't cruise; when we started down its path, we saw a thousand landmines. We had never learned to mellow that love, to domesticate it, to channel it the way the Americans—who undoubtedly had just as deep a need for it—did, sitting across from each other, their legs stretched on ottomans, enjoying martinis and cutting jokes.

"Tell me, these Korean people, who they make trouble?" Dad pursed his trembling lips and wiped his nose with a handkerchief. For the fifteen years he'd lived in LA, the Koreans hardly existed.

"It's okay, Dad."

"What 'okay.' Don't tell American 'okay.'"

"Okay."

"What they do these people, these Korean, the Black people hate?" Auntie asked.

Mom said, "I dohn know. They say Korean treat the black people like the slave, the animal."

"The black people slave the Korean?"

"No, no, no. In store. The black people customer. Beer, the whiskey, cigarette, I dohn know, buy from the Korean."

"Charge too much? The welfare no pay?"

"I dohn know."

"Why Korean have store black people place."

"Money."

"Dangerous there, no?"

"I tell you, money, the cash money. Korean like the cash money. No the IRS."

Auntie said, "Why they no have own store, the black people. Black people buy black people. Better this way. Maybe take the welfare."

The Kurd wagged a finger, "They have no fear, the Korean people. Strong, like bamboo."

Dad said, "Before long go Jewish own liquor store; make too much money buy buildings, sell store Koreans. Now Jewish own too much buildings Los Angeles."

"Oh."

Dad said, "They come here with the nothing, no? No money, no the helping hand, nothing."

"Their country was torn apart, just like ours," Adam said.

Dad said, "Korea war, no?"

Auntie said, "Your dad no stupid."

"Nobody every thought he was, Auntie."

"I dohn know." The last word she sung an octave higher.

"Your brother make movie this. Why he go all the way Lebanon make movie?"

"Documentary, Dad. What he's doing is important. People need to be reminded not to forget."

"Hmph," Dad said. "I know nobody give these Korean the helping hand. Now they take from Korean hand. Take the hard-working people from their hand."

1. There was no greater crime. Hard working people—no greater honorific.

2. Taking from the hard-working hand violated the living and the dead.

3. What was stolen from the dead had to be returned; since the perpetrators hadn't so much as acknowledged that anything was stolen, that duty to "return" fell upon the backs of the living, the survivors.

4. One must return ounce by ounce what was lost.

5. Leaving no room for poetry. What right did one have to sit and think and spin, words or film, when the debt was still outstanding? Get off your ass and get to work!

6. But there is a rub: we had come from a world of craftsman and poets and artists; objects and artifacts of the highest quality were dreamed up and executed in the countless workshops of countless generations of Armenians. But it is equally true that those things had come to nothing in the end; those objects of transcendence had failed to deliver them from mortal death. In the end, they were mute. Pulverized. Ashes.

7. Those who made the money and built and rebuilt were honored. They were rebuilding from the ashes. They were helping pay down the debt the fastest.

8. Implicit hatred of artists; an implicit sense of their uselessness; they had shunned their responsibility:

a. They had failed or refused to suppress the poet in them;

b. "I could have been that, but I've taken my duty to the dead seriously," they were saying. "I've lived up to my obligations, but you? Who are you to indulge yourself with a pen or a brush? How dare you indulge yourself that way when our body is cut to pieces and scattered to the winds?"

c. Armenians had killed the artists inside themselves, a monumental sacrifice, to get on with the job of paying down the debt. The artists who had let the artists inside them live resented them in turn.

Adam was putting this together in his head (he later transcribed it into his journal) when Auntie shouted, "*ADAM, ADAM, LOOK, YOUR APARTMENT THERE, NO?*"

> TIM
> We are in mid-Wilshire now, folks, just
> around the corner from Sammy's Camera,
> which was set ablaze just hours ago.
> Trish?

"Yeah," said Adam. "And that's my gym."

["BLACK OWNED," a sign posted on its door
read. It was a local set-up that Adam doggedly
supported against the homogenization of the
city's gyms by a single corporate entity.]

> TRISH
> Yes, Jim. We are seeing, as you too can
> see, more and more of these types of
> signs popping up on windows. This gym is
> clearly owned by blacks.

[The camera now panned across two other stores,
hair weaving and nail-salons,
with similar signs.]

> TIM
> Disturbing, very disturbing.

> TRISH
> (contemplating the sign)
> It is.

                              TIM
      Very, but… in a way… in a way we can
      understand…

      "You 'M' bar there, no?" Mom pointed to the TV.
      "Why would they loot a bar?"
      "For drink," Mom said. "What, you think? Smoke dope,
mope, coke, no drink?"
      Dad asked, "Why we not go Fresno, I dohn know?"
      "It's happening everywhere, Dad. Not just here, not
anymore."
      "Riot on farm? What, you crazy, something?"

                              TIM
      We're going to switch now, folks, to Mel
      Martinez, who is in Beverly Hills. Mel?

                              MEL
      Yes, Jim. We're in Beverly Hills.

      [Some of the streets were cordoned off, and the
      camera showed a pretty good black-vested police
      presence.]

                              TIM
      What is the scene like there, Mel?

Compared to Koreatown, it was like a resort hamlet. Should
they hit Beverly Hills, no doubt the plunderers had sensed the
special price they'd pay. Maybe instinctively they knew the
Military Procession that would greet them should they try and
have their way, because it was one thing to tear apart the worlds
of immigrants who come from torn-up worlds to begin with, it
is one thing to see such people's hard work mocked and demolished, and another to see Calvin or Giorgio or Giafranco so
much as bitch-slapped. The absence of even a spent firecracker
in Beverly Hills, right there and then, vanquished any possible
explanation that might've been offered by any number of left-
ist economics classes at USC. If the uprising had anything to

                              97

do with wealth, the have-nots should've flooded to the multi-national slave-labor-intensive, prohibitively expensive, insured up the wazoo, MBA-run "designer" shops in Beverly Hills, the very archetype of fuck-you-poor-people, as naturally as water draining to the lowest point.

The Kurd and Adam had been thinking the same thing.

"Look this," The Kurd said, "they take their coffee and cake, like *pashas*."

                    MEL
    Ma'am, if you can give us a second…

Adam thought it looked like Alice, the very girl he'd slept with the night before. When the camera framed her face, his thought was confirmed.

"Shhh," he went.

"You know girl?"

"Yes."

"Who knows this girl that girl?" Mom said. "How many?"

In that slimy, super-American voice, Auntie said, "Let him have the fun."

To which Mom responded, "Fun. Mun."

                    MEL
    Are you a resident of Beverly Hills, or
    just shopping here today?

    [Alice stood with a few fancy shopping bags,
    her body beautiful beneath a crisp, off-white
    linen dress.]

                    ALICE
    Yes, I live here.

    [For as far as the eye could see there was
    nothing but boutiques, yet she looked over her
    shoulder as though to indicate a few doors down.]

                    MEL
    How are you feeling today?

"In fancy dress," Mom dropped in.

"Shh."

"What you get excited!?"

<pre>
                    MEL (cont.)
...this all affected you?

                    ALICE
Oh, it's, umh, very frightening. (With a
finger she pulled a few strands of hair
away from her face and smiled, weirdly).
Like everyone it just came out of
nowhere, so, you know... it took everyone
by surprise.

[A man with slicked back hair, looking
kind of like an Italian Mafioso, stepped up
and took her arm. She patted his hand.]
</pre>

Adam had had no idea she had a boyfriend. He wondered if Slick was the Malibu drug dealer. He was going to call her to see how she was making out.

<pre>
                    MEL
Do you feel safe here, in Beverly Hills?

                    ALICE
I do. I do feel safe. But that's just me.
</pre>

"Look her, she look me like the spah-ghetti." Mom stuck a pinky in the air.
Adam said, "Jesus."
"Watch mouth."
"He mean nothing," Auntie said.

<pre>
                    MEL
             Well thank you.

[She nodded, and the man guided her past Mel, who
dropped the mic to his side, clearly exhausted.]
</pre>

"I just wanted to hear her."
"Hear. Who she—Catholicos?"
"For Jesus' sake."
Mom covered her mouth, "What happen you?"
"Leave boy 'lone," Dad said.

"You like he talk that?"

"Forget it."

"Who girl… so 'portant?"

"Just a girl. I met her last night."

"Iranian girl you say last night with."

Now Adam was in a pickle.

Dad said, kind of saving him, "She have the problem maybe, huh?"

He'd picked up the catchall, "she has problems" from Adam, and he used it to get a discussion going or out of the way about any girl Adam had unsuccessfully dated.

Mom said, "They dohn know problem. Problem."

This was right up The Kurd's alley: "These American girls, they break the shopping bag and make it like the sky is falling."

"You hear what Kurd say?" Mom asked Adam.

"Yeah. I heard him."

The Kurd said, "Men like snail afraid. You say one word they drop the salt on your back."

"God be with her," Dad said.

Auntie said, "She be Beverly Hill; what she want more, 'god be with her'?"

"It's not always about money, Auntie."

"Of course, honey. Money not everything."

"DWP Company say this," Mom said.

"Okay, we go the Carousel," Auntie said. "You hungry, Kurd? You like the kebob?"

"I don't think so, Auntie," said Adam.

"Okay, you go the Abril and talk the Harout. We go Carousel Restaurant. Let's go." She rose with a flourish from the couch.

Abril, an Armenian bookstore, was one of Adam's favorite haunts. And Harout, the owner, one of his favorite people in LA. Auntie viewed bookishness as regressive, especially for a young man as debonair as Adam.

"You come?" she asked The Kurd.

As much as The Kurd would've liked to, he wasn't that stupid.

"Maybe next time," he said. "Adam is right, probably close."

She plopped back on the couch, disappointed that everyone was so negative.

There was a big back-and-forth about whether Adam and The Kurd should stay with them for the night, but The Kurd was eager to get home, and Adam wanted to get home, too. Through the picture window Mom watched Adam and The Kurd go, the rest of the family huddled around the TV.

"This TV," The Kurd said, "like it some camp fire. The caveman in the brain feel good, safety, so long it burn."

Adam knew a curfew was in place, but he couldn't fathom anyone taking it seriously. No sooner had he come up on Sunset, however, than he realized that nearly everyone had taken it seriously but him. The streets were empty, and even if it was plain as day he could go any way home (and at any speed, for that matter), he merely sat the car as though waiting for instructions until The Kurd told him, "Go, man, go." When he finally decided to cross the boulevard it was too late—two pairs of headlights on *both* fucking sides of the boulevard were coming wildly his way, and growing brighter. Stunned, he and The Kurd watched pathetic little low-riding Hondas shoot past, one then the other then oh god they slashed right through the red light.

He punched the pedal and zipped across the boulevard and started threading the side streets. If the boulevard possessed the egomaniacal expansiveness of a sociopath, then these side streets, as he jerked down them, felt like the suffocating ideations of a suicidal teen. At any instant, he imagined, someone might jump from behind a parked car and level a gun at his oncoming face. Just north of Willoughby a mom n' pop grocery was being gutted by dozens of men and women with their children in tow. Who else but neighbors would loot such a pathetic little neighborhood store?

He dropped The Kurd off. It was past 11:00 p.m., and the streets were eerily deserted—causing a new wave of anxiety to rise inside him. Back at home, three messages from Sasha were waiting for him: she was afraid to leave her apartment in one message, threatening to leave in the next, and in the last had ditched town on a flight out of LAX to she-didn't-say-where, obviously just before they'd closed the airport.

Two other messages were from employees, apologizing for not coming in (nobody else bothered), and the last was from the bandleader, asking whether their gig was still on. He turned the TV on only to discover that college kids in Atlanta were hurling rocks at cops. In Vegas, several people had been killed, including a young boy trapped in a building that had been set aflame. In San Francisco there was a mass protest. New York, Denver, Toledo, even fucking Peoria, Illinois, all had their share of pandemonium. Surely, Adam thought, Nick must've gotten news of the mayhem by now. That he hadn't called to see how he and "M" were doing told the whole story. The whole sad tale.

To convey what Nick and "M" had once meant to Adam, I am directed back to a dream Adam had when he was just fifteen. It is a few minutes before dawn, and Adam stands under a long portico in front of a wooden cart brimming with apricots and pomegranates and figs that he is there to sell. Others peddle chickens and ducks in cages, hand-carved ladles, rugs, and burlap bags brimming with spices, nuts, and seeds. Everybody is speaking in a different tongue but seems nonetheless at home, while Adam feels thrown there, lonely and confused.

The shadows are starting to thin, and he sees a young man walking swiftly and confidently down the boulevard, his blonde hair tousled, his chinos comfy if a bit rumpled. How cool and agile, how American he looks with his cardigan sweater tossed over his shoulders. How much future he carries in each of his steps. Suddenly he turns Adam's way and nods. Next, he waves for Adam to join him. Who are you? Where to? Adam slips past his cart and bolts toward him, and without a word they start running side by side, with all the fast faith of young men, past one vendor and another up the millennia-long colonnade.

Nick was that young man in Adam's dream, right down to the penny loafers. They'd gone a long way; for two years they worked the bar day and night, side by side, but then Nick lost interest and wanted instead to trot the globe with Alexandra, a fashion model.

"Hey," Nick said, "I need some time off."

Fine. "How long?"

"Don't know."

"Okay. A week, a month?" Trying to get at it another way, "Long enough that we're going to need some extra help?"

"Let me think about it." Up until that point, it had been let *us* think about it. Now it was let *me*.

Nick had come up with the idea of the bar. "M" they'd call it, Nick decided. They'd call it that without it calling itself that. No sign, no indication that it was there, much less of what went on or who was inside. If you advertise, it advertises that you need the advertisement. Give the impression of a place where people disappeared, or better, a place where people who needed to disappear appeared. Picture, he said, the opium dens of old, the early Christian churches, speakeasies.

It seemed suicidal, but the more Adam studied it, the clearer the concept grew, its illogical genius. They chose the location to fit: A 2000 square-foot box located across from a liquor store and next to an all-night laundry in a shabby mini-mall. A place where Central American day laborers dozed while their clothes tumbled dry, where drunks went for spare change, where hookers went for a fix.

Next, they worked up the design: a movie director's staging of Las Vegas, say, in the late-fifties. All burgundy and studded leather booths skirting the room, with small round tables in the middle, and at the far end a platform for bands and crooners who covered Billie Holiday, Frank Sinatra, and Pasty Cline.

Nick knew everyone, and he had a list. People on Nick's list start bringing in people on their own lists. Within a month, half a dozen B-list actors on any given night sat shoulder to shoulder with D-listers, fishing an olive out of a martini, nursing a neat glass of scotch. Then one of these B-listers brought an A-lister in. It was the start of something new, a kind of evolutionary leap. Adam had been helping the sound guy with some echo problem when all of the sudden the room abruptly, almost noisily, quieted down.

A group of women had come to the middle of the front room and were looking for a place to sit. Two A-Listers were among them. In a matter of seconds, Adam was parting the waters for her and her retinue. On the way to a "reserved" booth just off the stage, Adam could feel it on his neck, a thrumming borne of so many novitiates jerking at their wicks. The experience was nearly Catholic, and by the weekend people would wait in line, tongues hanging, for an hour merely to get a lick of the luminous silt their brilliant trains left on the floor.

To sift and sort and manage the flow, "M" needed a bouncer. Nick was right: it was the positive power of obscurity and shadows, from the smoky darkness of the booths to the one-letter name, that generated mood, depth, contour, and volume, that had set the place ablaze. He was a genius. "M" might as well have stood for *Money*. "Cash money," as Dad called it, every evening stacks of twenties thick as bricks.

Let "me" think about it.

For construction and equipment and all the rest, a little over $200,000, Nick had told Adam "Don't worry, I'll cover it." The partners had agreed to a salary of $37,000 a year until Nick's capital investment was paid back, at which point they'd both begin drawing profits from the business. He'd paid off that $200K in a little over two years, a crazy rate of return. From that point on it was all gravy, split, Adam assumed, 50-50.

Wrong. You see, Nick explained, that "up front money" assumed a high degree of "risk." That "initial funding" had actually bought him a big portion of the business—90 percent, to be precise. The math was straightforward. The logic was Business 101. More or less where they'd met.

At Hollywood High Adam had woven in and sometimes woven out of brown, black, yellow, and olive-skinned people. He felt UCLA, where half a dozen of his closest classmates were going, would mirror that experience on a larger scale, but Dad claimed that USC was where all well-to-do Los Angelenos sent their kids, and that that was where he would send Adam. He had never, in his entire life, been around so many people so white. In the middle of a lecture his compass would freeze on the fine, clean seams of the co-eds' jeans, the scent of their baby-blue polo shirts, the velvety sheen of their bass weejuns; in turn, this would lead him to imagine the size of their homes, where they vacationed, where their mothers shopped, even the size of their fathers' cocks—did money make your tool size superfluous?

Tommy's triumphant carriage pointed to a particular kind of reality, a particular dispensation. All fall long campus was rank with him and the other kind of Trojan, and everyone seemed ripe to take to the next level an already over-ripe privilege. With a kind of awe, he watched his classmates cheat on tests and gutter-talk about tit sucking and blowjobs and fart and cut out from studying as early as Thursday afternoon to tap the keg for a Saturday afternoon match.

Late in the spring term, Adam discovered the deep quiet of Doheny Library. Between classes he'd slip in there and pull up a chair and settle into his studies and daydream and take naps and wake and start again. Yes, he'd found sanctuary, but he found no fellowship there; the Asian varieties and super well-dressed Chicano kids, the blacks whose parents were invariably military or doctors, and of course, the pasty-faced whites, whose insane focus alarmed him. If the library had become a kind of cathedral for Adam, for them it was another suburban church; none of the liturgical mystery—the incense and lights and ethereal voices—but the filing in and filing out and mending their ways and checking-in their sex drives. Okay for a life in labs or pharmacies or dental clinics, but not for the life he dreamed of. So far, Art History and English Lit and Philosophy—these get-you-nowhere earth-movers—were what moved him. But he was there to get good grades in preparation for a professional degree, an MBA, or JD. And so he majored in business.

For his first elective, "business management," he was one of six in a group assigned to give recommendations to a jewelry store in dire financial straits located on Pico just north of Fairfax.

The partners had worked side by side at a big chain for ten years before taking their experience and best customers with them. They kept clean books, filed their taxes and paid their bills on time, and even helped sponsor a Little League team. Their expectations were perfectly reasonable.

After listening to their sad story for three two-hour briefings, Adam wanted to light a candle for them at church, but as the group assembled on the lawn for a brain storming session, he was forced to consider a more mundane solution: bigger signs, fliers handed out on street corners, gifts with every purchase.

Someone brought in graphs to show that the summer months were burying them; true, their revenues for the rest of the year were down, but only *slightly* down. Here their loans were on a variable interest rate; look how those rates had risen; look at what they'd been shelling out in payments! Business was complicated: getting to the bottom of why a business didn't work was like getting to the bottom of why life didn't work: each idea seemed as good *and* bad as the next.

Then Nick, who had been lying back on his elbows, his long legs crossed in front of him, a blade of grass between his almost comically big lips, pushed himself upright and said, "You know, with all due respect, guys, we're just talking to ourselves here. These people need help. These people need us to dig a little deeper for them." Dig a little deeper? Who was this guy? The same who'd stood chin in hand at the rear of the store during the briefings? He had huge facial features, and his skin was pockmarked by what must've been a serious case of acne when he was a teen. It was possible he'd been a somewhat homely, gangly kid, but over time his features had come together nicely, but not so nicely that he didn't have to make an effort.

"Bottom line," he said, "There's no 'big picture' here." He reached into his backpack and pulled the 'big picture' out: a map with red sticky stars showing the location of the other jewelry stores in the vicinity: one had been family run for thirty years; another was part of a chain that regularly offered huge discounts on "low-end material"; the third was where Orthodox Jews shopped. And that didn't include adjacent Beverly Hills, just a mile north, where the number of stars was enough to make you dizzy.

"What our clients need is a theme, a customer base—in short, a reason for being. We haven't asked, and neither have they, one simple question: What is my store's *identity?*" A good two thirds of the group hadn't supposed a store needed an identity beyond its name. In less than an hour, all were convinced that this was their one and only problem worth taking seriously. This Nick cut through the crap; he was a whiz kid; his very person summed up for Adam a particular kind of American brilliance.

Nick had a perfect Los Angeles pedigree—born and raised in Hancock Park, third generation USC, third generation Kappa Delta Gamma—and Adam fast became his best friend. He invited Adam to all the open-house frat parties, where he met girls and mixed it up and made connections with Reagan Republicans, barely veiled Ponzi schemers, budding natural gas speculators. These people weren't jacking off at school; between Jim Beam and Heineken chasers they were cooking up a thousand different "business models" to grow their fortunes.

What had kept him from getting his share for two years was fear: fear that he didn't deserve a share, that he was an interloper, a visitor who should be mindful of his place. The frat boys hadn't rejected him; he had rejected them, and in rejecting them, he had rejected himself. All that he'd put outside his reach was within reach. With his unassuming good looks and solicitous manner, Nick disarmed girls. They loved him, and low and behold, they loved Adam too. Adam loved them back. This one and that one, this way and that. What a life! What a fun fucking life. No need to get all strung out. When Nick ditched a girl or a girl ditched him, in fact, when anything got ditched, there was no need to obsessively rehash what *might have been if only...* "If only my aunt had balls, she'd be my uncle!" So true; right as it was tight.

Whenever a little fire started inside Adam, he reflexively picked up a bucket of water, sure that it would get out of hand if he didn't quickly put it out. Nick told him, "Put that thing down. You're not going to get burned." Maybe this was why Dad had wanted him to go to USC: he wanted Adam to get the big picture, the big American picture. He wanted him to have a picture besides the one he'd grown up with: sad-eyed saints; stiff, big-eyed sad people wearing halos on their bald heads.

From day one, he'd watched in awe as moneyed Los Angelenos swept leisurely up their long driveways or into Saks or day spas or five-star restaurants and all but disappeared. Right out of a Dickens novel, Adam pictured himself standing out in the cold as they clucked and quaffed scotch and made business deals and lighted up cigars.

But Nick's parents were nothing like that: they had a two-story June Street mansion, a Jaguar, and a Range Rover, and probably shopped and passed their afternoons precisely as he had always imagined rich people did—but all their material possessions seemed to serve a good-hearted cosmopolitanism that they were happy to extend.

Within a month after he met them they had adopted Adam as a brother to Nick, and he began spending more weekends at their home than he did at his own. He had assumed that people with money showed off to make the little guy feel bad, but in fact it was the other way around: people who didn't have money showed off to make other people who didn't have money feel worse.

In no time, everything he thought about rich people began to rearrange itself in his brain; his prejudices looked like prejudices. He'd never been so happy to be kicked in the ass, and soon enough our parents and nearly every Armenian he knew seemed steeped in and fated for pathos, as evidenced by everything about us, even down to our physical build. Armenians are bulky, cinched up like a choking crowd of roots, where these people possessed a certain grace that made their movements efficient and relaxed. The difference was between poetry (and not even free verse) and prose.

Sometimes we overthrow ourselves all at once, and at other times we do so by small, almost imperceptible revolutions. Suffice, by the end of his junior year, with Nick's help if not under his very tutelage, Adam's victory over his insecurities was complete, and the meaning, the nearly existential meaning of Tommy Trojan, was conspicuously clear. Now when he walked past him he felt a kind of quiet fraternity.

Nick had problems from the start, but Adam didn't allow them to register. In fact, he turned the most serious of these problems, alcoholism, into a near virtue. Nick downed liquor as casually as some Italians down espresso. His whole family were the same; scotch on the rocks or bloody Marys or gin and tonics—whatever it was, they imbibed all day long around a pool, flipping rib-eyes or doing the *Times* crossword. Armenians drank to celebrate or cast their worries aside or stoke their anguish. It always ended in parades, foolishness, dancing, wobbling about, and slurring nationalist slogans. But the more these people drank, the cooler and more relaxed they were, the more of themselves they exuded.

"Look, Adam, there's no need for either of us to get worked up."

"Hey man, the main thing is we're friends."

"For sure," Nick said.

"We started this together. We'll end it together."

"I don't know about that. I've got a lot of dough on the line."

"Nick, you've made it back how many times over?"

"Just doesn't feel that way."

"Anyway, when you said 'let *me* think about it,' that kind of upset me, Nick."

"For sure."

"Why all of a sudden *me* and not *us*? I felt like a frickin' bar-back."

"Sure. I understand, but look…" He pulled the CAPITALIZATION TABLE out of the filing cabinet. The two of them had drawn it up in case of just such an eventuality as this, in order to avoid confusion later on about who owned what share.

Of course Adam hadn't forgotten about it. He wasn't arguing its existence, only its relevance: "Look yourself; we had anticipated a more normal rate of return; in fact, we had anticipated a loss, for years one and two. Not until year five did we expect a complete payoff of the initial investment. Neither of us anticipated the bar doing as well as it has, and the table shows that too. Doesn't our ridiculous success count for something?"

Adam had hatched a plan to steer future profits from "M" to help Dad throw a shingle up over his own structural engineering firm. Unlike me, he refused to believe it when Dad said "The future is yours, not mine." Although it was painfully clear that Dad had been held together in Beirut by a vast, taken-for-granted social apparatus, which vanished the moment he stepped into America, Adam believed that with a little help Dad could jumpstart his career. Maybe it was too late for high-rises, but good engineers were still needed for small jobs, homes, retaining walls, add-ons, and whatnot. At some point, while Nick was abroad, Adam went to petition Nick's parents.

"Adam, come in. How have you been? Long time no see. Sit down; beer?"

He sat with a beer on their lovely outdoor wicker furniture, next to the splendid pool, and told them, with all the sadness he could bring to the surface without drowning in it, what had happened. He'd always admired their style, so different than the rancorous style we were accustomed to; they listened, nodded in agreement even if they disagreed, and dropped a conversation if it got too noisy, rather than doing things the way our people did, raising the tone of debate past reason, always to the next farcical pitch.

They understood, really they did: sometimes those new to business have a hard time taking a contract *seriously*. Sometimes they *rewrite* a contract in their own heads, as circumstances change. But all business, eventually, relies upon the soundness of a contract. Without a sound contract, commerce of any sort would grind to a halt: anybody could claim anything anywhere down the road. This is, essentially, what makes America different from other places—the Middle East, for instance. This is why people come to America from other places; because of the soundness of contracts, starting with the most important contract of all, the Constitution. They were so rational, so right, so white, it sent Adam's screaming heart to a corner for a slow bleed. Besides, the money that Nick had invested was his own money, drawn from a trust, not borrowed from them, as Adam had assumed (which was why he'd approached them in the first place). They were hardly in a position to step in. But look, Adam; if you need a loan, for any reason, don't hesitate to come to us. He didn't want a loan. Look----you're young, talented, educated: *just getting going.*

But Dad *wasn't* just getting going! The man felt done, and he needed some help. Adam had come to tell them all this, but with a hundred-percent certainty that it would lead to a lecture about immigrants, how one generation sacrifices for the next, how it had always been that way, he kept his feelings about Dad to himself, thanked them, and left.

A few days later, Nick called from Croatia to tell him, "looks like someone is shorting me." Not a month had passed that the bar hadn't made more money than it had the month before, but now the sales were evening out. If he'd been around, he would've also discovered that the leather booths, the carpets, and some of the fixtures were wearing out. That the A-listers, *who'd worn them out,* were taking a drink and moving on. It was going back to being a neighborhood bar, with a neighborhood bar's good but not dazzling profits. Instead, Nick was convinced the bartenders were pocketing cash payments; that the waitresses, in cahoots with the bartenders, were dishing out free drinks to their friends. The bar-backs, in cahoots with the waitresses, were sneaking home with bottles of high-end wine. What, did he have cameras embedded in the rooms? In any case, on the road, he had done some research. A Swiss touch-screen electronic payment system that tracked every pour was on its way. Within a few weeks, fifty thousand dollars worth of it was up and running. Now, strangely, the machine, Adam's enemy, was also his star witness; perversely he hoped profits would drop even further to confirm the downward trend and clear him of any residual suspicion. As it turned out, Nick accepted whatever it spit out with Basho-like equanimity. "What it is is what it is." Gravy enough to pay Adam's salary and net Nick $5,000 or so a month.

Adam was showing up to work, but he hadn't really been there for at least a year. He had left in one way, but in the other, with nowhere to go he'd stayed behind. That was why he'd talked to Sammy about opening a bar. But he was doing it behind Nick's back; that's why he felt guilty.

Koreatown was now lit up like an octogenarian's birthday cake—the skycam showed. According to news reports, "three new structures per minute" were going up in smoke, the kind of unbelievable figure that his inflamed brain couldn't work out the long-term math for, as elementary as it was. He closed his eyes, but light from the tube beat against his lids like a heart, his own heart, under terrible stress, and before he knew it he'd dropped off into a kind of willed coma. But no sooner had he found some blank-time there than he was whisked back to Alice's place, rap music from the apartment above rapping dully against his skull, and her wraith-like body undulating underneath his own. The memory of her—her bed, her apartment, her desperate

collection of books (*Franny and Zoey; The Bible; Misery*)—
these images, more than the images even of her body, clattered
through his brain until he bolted from the couch and made for
the shower. When he turned the water off he could hear a helicopter walloping the air seemingly inches above his head. He
grabbed a towel and threw open the curtains. A column of light
tottered in the street then came crashing through his window.
He fell back a step, closed the curtains, and watched it back and
forth swing.

He passed through every room in the house to make
sure all the windows were locked, as the light from the chopper thinned, then thickened, then thinned again. The bedroom
window, whose screen he had idiotically forgotten to replace,
was up. He closed it and quickly jumped into some pants, wondering whether he would have what it took to kill a man. The
one-time-commercial-actor's prissy little handgun looked pretty
good to him right then. He walked-ran to the kitchen. When
you don't have a gun, you go for a knife. Probably a bat or golf
club would do the job better, but in the movies a knife, the hill-
billy kin of a gun, is what everyone goes for, so that's what Adam
went for.

He stepped into the hallway with a steak knife and began
slinking down the length of the wall, and even though he knew
that this was all likely just his imagination, even though he knew
that the chances of anyone being there were near nil, just going
through the motions was jacking him up. By the time he reached
the office, where he was convinced the killer was "hiding," there
was no distance anymore between the character-role and himself,
a virtually Brandoesque performance.

Adam opened the door, and suddenly, like he was watching a movie trailer, he saw his body pathetically freeze as the
intruder just inside the room smoothly raised the gun to his
stunned head. He fought through the fear and flicked on the
light. Empty; only the closet was left. All shaking, all mocked up
with courage, he stepped up to the jamb, and holding the knife
in front of himself at arm's length, he parted the clothes and
jabbed into the bottom rack between the trousers. No shout, no
groans, no splatter of blood. The apartment was safe, but the

helicopter was tacking away. He listened until its sound thinned, and then he listened to the absence of sound. The chopper unit had given up, leaving the killer out there. It wasn't a question of whether he had a gun, but rather what type and what caliber.

He had always believed guns did more harm than good, because as he'd been told and told himself, most perceived threats were imaginary, and any real threat was best handled by police anyhow. He had always believed that gun owners were paranoid, tobacco-chewing wife beaters, the true "dangers from within." But of course, who would ever have envisioned a situation like this—not in America. "Paranoia is getting the facts straight," as William Burroughs in some delirium had put it. How right the junk-head was. He went for more knives and hid them in strategic easy-to-get-to spots around the apartment, and then, with a big honkin' butcher knife in hand, took a seat on the couch and kept his ears open.

On the TV, the sky cam had become strangely disembodied, a kind of extraterrestrial eye: Here you have a burning building, there you have a close-up, a few people scuttle about, a car cruises, a dog on his haunches stares. Maybe the cop-chopper had left because there was nobody to follow.

He heard rustling in the bushes outside and immediately his heart raced up into his head. Calm down. A cat or possum, or even the wisecracking coon that scavenged the garbage cans, that's what had made that noise. He thought, *All your reading has turned you into a kind of urchin. Instead of using your free time to hone your inner warrior, you'd used it to trim your brain with chintz. Nothing more than a sound, no, worse, the thought of a sound, brushes against you and all those knick-knacks come crashing.*

He needed to protect his vital organs. He pulled a few slender paperbacks from the shelves: Heidegger's, *A Question Concerning Technology*, a book he couldn't get through ten pages of, and the *Tractatus Philosphicus* that he read in one sitting, only to discover after he put it down that for all he understood, Wittgenstein might've been writing about arachnids. He shoved five or six books down his pants and up his shirt all the way to his chest.

The sound came again. This time, instead of numbing, it weirdly liberated his vocal chords: "GET THE FUCK OUT OF HERE!" He leaned over and got stuck in the ribs pretty good by those books, but because of his adrenaline-jazz he plowed right through the pain. "YOU FUCKING BASTARD, I'LL PLUG A BULLET IN YOUR FUCKING HEAD!"

When a sovereign dies, when the order is broken, anything goes, on all sides; the criminal must fear you as much as you fear him. Let him feel it. Let him! He opened the French window, insane, fucked up, he wanted to see him face to face, to be done with it one way or another.

That's when I called, on his home phone.

"Jesus, man," Adam said when he picked up. "I think someone is outside my place. I mean, I thought. I'm coming apart here."

"Take it easy. Are you sure?"

"All I know is next chance I get I'm buying a fucking pistol. It's getting 'everyone for himself' out there. Charlton Heston and his 'cold, dead hands' and all the other NRAers are laughing their asses off at the pathetic little KCRW *kum-ba-yah-ers* like me."

There was a knock at the door.

"Who is it?" he asked politely. He told me, "Someone's at the door. Hold on."

"You all right?" It was a woman's voice.

He opened the door. It was the fat black chick. He'd almost forgotten about her.

"Did you hear the helicopter?"

"Yeah. Come in." He tried to sweep her inside with a hand. He told me, "I'll call you back in a little bit. It's my neighbor."

She made her way into the room and looked around, then dropped her eyes to his shirt.

"What is that; what do you have on? Are those books?"

"Just a sec." He made for the bedroom, pulling the books out.

"Who were you yelling at? Do you have someone here? I don't want to bother."

"I thought there was someone out there who might be in here."

Her voice spiked. "He's in here!"

When he came up the hallway, she was pivoting back toward the door.

"No, no," he caught her by her arm. You could've tossed pizzas with it. "He's out there—I think."

"You think?"

"I didn't see him. Anyway, I checked the apartment. He's not in here. I scared them away or something."

"Them?"

"I don't know."

"But he was in here?"

"No, I thought he might be."

"Is he outside?"

"I heard something. Maybe I just heard it."

"Oh God." She put her hand on her heart and sat on the couch. "Mind if I sit? I'll just stay a minute."

"Absolutely."

There was no telling her tits from anything else. Even the beads of sweat on her brow were fat.

Adam said, "We were kind of worried about you."

"Who's we?"

"You know, people in the building."

"This is all so terrible," she said. She framed her head with her hands and stared at the dead TV screen.

"Where have you been?" he asked. "We haven't seen you."

"Inside. Watching."

"Alone."

"I was thinking about going home. My folks live in Bakersfield. Everybody at home is worried. Mom thinks I'm crazy for living here to start with. Now with these riots, I've got them worried sick."

"I think you need to be worried about yourself, not Mom, not at a time like this."

"I know," she replied. "I don't know why I keep worrying about her."

"This must be really hard for you… to watch."

"Why, because I'm black? Is that what you think?" She guffawed, her body jiggling.

"Well, I'd feel pretty bad if my people were out there ransacking the city."

"Your people. You mean white people. You mean the same people who ransacked us."

"You're the one who said it was terrible."

"I didn't say why it was terrible. See, you made an assumption. White people making assumptions about what black people think."

"Sorry."

"You have no idea what's really going on."

"I confess."

"For three hundred years you white people have treated us like animals, and now you're all surprised that we act just like you treat us. That's why it is terrible."

"'You white people.' You think I'm white? Do you consider me white?"

"Of course you're white."

The temperature in the room felt suddenly smothering. He went to open one of the front windows.

"What are you doing!"

He fanned the room with it.

"My family came here from Lebanon less than fifteen years ago. Is it fair to throw us in with Southern slave owners? I'm just asking."

"Would you please close that window?"

"What are you so afraid of? Your own people wouldn't attack you, would they?"

"They don't know any better," she said.

Because, Adam thought, you and your ilk keep excusing them. He went ahead and closed it, but now he wondered how he was going to get her off the couch. At the same time he wondered whether he should ask her if she wanted something to eat.

He began, "Well, I need to get to…"

"It doesn't matter when you came."

Instead of removing her body she shifted it around to get more comfortable.

He'd half lost track of the conversation.

"Sorry. Look. I feel like we're miles apart here, and it's really no time to hash it out."

"White people really need to open their eyes."

"And I really don't feel like I'm a party to this problem. If you only knew what we escaped."

"You can be from Canada or Spain or wherever you're from."

"Lebanon."

"Lebanon, Libya, wherever. When you land here, in America, no matter where you're from, you reap the rewards of slavery. And blacks don't have to be slaves to reap its curse. These are the 'facts as they are lived, not a theory as it is imagined,'" she said, obviously quoting someone. One of these African-American scholars at some state University? San Francisco State? Adam's curiosity was piqued. This conversation was no throw-away. This was one of those unvarnished moments well worth remembering, writing down.

"So I reap rewards I didn't ask for, just by being here? I have to pay a price, even as an exile from somewhere else?"

"Of course you do. If someone steals my car, and then sells it to you, do you get to keep it? Does the law let you keep it? You have to give it back. The victim has a right to ask for it back. That's the law." She looked away and chuckled, a strange chuckle, like there was someone inside her she was chuckling with.

She continued, "Do you get to park it next door to the person it was stolen from? Even though you didn't steal it, does that make it yours? This country was built up on the backs of slaves. It would be nothing without us. We own it, by our sweat and blood."

He said, "I mean, if you took that logic to heart, we'd have to unravel whole civilizations, back to the first humans even."

"Maybe whole civilizations should be unraveled."

"Maybe the trend is starting here."

"Who were these first humans, anyway? Blacks. Blacks are the original race. The closest to God. His chosen."

"I thought those were the Jews."

"So they tell the world. So they make the world believe."

"Boy, I just thought you had it against Koreans. What is your problem with them, by the way? Are Koreans white too? Aren't they considered yellow?"

"As bananas."

"Latasha Harland, is that what you have against them? That was one woman who shot one girl."

"Like a dog. One for the thousand others not caught on camera. Those bananas are whiter than white."

"So white isn't the color of your skin."

"What makes you think? There's plenty of black people that are white."

"Oreos. How about the opposite: can white people be black?"

"Some like to think. Makes them feel good."

"Is there a word for them?"

"You mean, Fig Newtons."

Society was looking more and more like a bake sale, how could he avoid the analogy. But that was hardly the issue; the issue he told her was: "Every day of the week blacks are shooting other blacks. Where's your outrage about that? Why don't you burn down each other's stores?"

"We have plenty of outrage about it. It's sickening. And we *are* burning down our own stores. Only the news doesn't cover that. When black people turn on blacks the cameras turn the other way. It's only news when black turn on whites."

"I suppose you're right, there. But isn't that black people's fault as well? That they turn their eyes away from their own sins and blame it on whites?"

"Our people are misled; blind, raging from they know not what. They need to find the way. And they will."

"I hope they do. I hope we all do. We can all use a little way right now."

"When they have their own land, their own home to go to, they will."

"You mean like Liberia?"

"Liberia!"

"Aren't they tearing each other apart there, Doe and what's-his-name, Taylor?" He'd maybe heard something about it on NPR.

"That's the white media talking." She snapped a hand open and shut a few times. "And no, not like that. Inside this country. A place carved out for us, right here."

"And where exactly 'inside this country' do you propose?"

"Not the useless dirt they gave the Indians, that's for sure. But good land, rich with minerals. Why not right here?"

"In LA?"

"This is what the Nation of Islam is asking for. That's what the Black Muslim Nation is about. Own our country, our own laws, run by our own people."

"Right here as in Los Angeles?"

"I don't see why not."

"Is this Farrakhan? Nation of Islam wackiness?"

"Minister Farrakhan just carries the message. I follow Allah, and Master W. Fard Muhammad."

He'd never heard of Fard and wasn't in a mood to get educated. He said, "Let me walk you back."

"You don't need do that."

She put up a hand, and moved it around, like she was polishing a mirror and then leveraged herself off the couch: "I'm fine. I'm fine, don't worry."

"I'm not worried. Just know that if you get scared you can knock on my door."

"Thanks. You too. You can knock on my door too."

"Good night."

"Thank you. You're a good person," she said.

"You are too."

"It's just that white people can't help it. They don't mean to be racist; it's in their blood."

He opened the door and watched her trudge back to her room, just up the empty hall.

. . .

When he rolled out of bed, after an all but sleepless night, it was almost ten. His bottom sheet was wrinkled with sweat. Congested, face swollen from all the ambient smoke, his brain foggy, he described it, "as Oxnard." A little like how he felt when sitting for fourteen hours in the cigarette-smoke-filled plane that brought us to America.

Two tenants in his building had decided to call it quits. Laura was cinching down a rope over a heap of furniture in the back of a pickup, Beverly Hillbillies style. Pam, the neighbor just behind him, was stuffing her studio apartment into a dented and rusted fourteen-foot moving van that barely looked up to the task of conveying her and her apartment across town, much less across the state to Santa Rosa, which, she now told him, was where her parents lived.

Though she'd moved in a year before, he barely knew her. Or rather, he knew her from her tired, stumbling walk home in the early mornings from the Westside club where she worked; he knew her from the music she listened to—Charlie Daniels and Willie Nelson; he knew her from her nervous rushing about readying for a date; her anger, the thud thud of her boots on the hardwood floor. He knew her from her silence, the contentedness of her silence on a Sunday afternoon.

"If you get back to town, look me up, please." It was a heartfelt gesture that fell flat, too much friendliness all at once; or worse, maybe she'd taken it as a last-second come-on. In any case, instead of an "of course I will look you up," she told him that she'd arrived at the moving company (an outfit that even under normal conditions was criminally mismanaged) at seven that morning, and a fight had already broken out because they'd booked more vans then they actually had on hand. It had gotten to the point, she claimed, that Los Angelenos were fetching vans from as far away as Bakersfield, a hundred miles up the freeway.

Up and down his street, dozens of people were scuttling back and forth between their apartments and their double-parked cars. In any given week, they occupied and vacated at astonishing rates, more or less like insects, but now watching them go they he felt sad, deeply sad, like he was watching persons whom he routinely had over for barbecue say forever "goodbye."

There was a two-blocks long line at the corner station, and with a big pole the owner was gouging up the price *fifty cents a gallon*. Where usually you couldn't find a single person to help, now to pump it out at breakneck speed a battalion of attendants was on hand, like some valet check-in at a Hollywood gala. As he turned up La Brea he kept his eyes from wandering into cars; in fact, he wanted nothing more than to become immaterial, a kind of mist that nothing, especially rage, might get purchase on.

His café had kept the faith. He took his regular table out on the patio, alongside a handful of regulars, each embroiled in the morning news. Each of them paused to say hi or nod, like all of a sudden they too sensed that they were a community, or rather, that they had been one all along. Two Humvees full of National Guard troops toting rifles barreled by. Dozens of deafening helicopters trolled the battered sky, like flying migraines. The chilling days of the cold war were over, and we were no longer living in some psychic subterranean fear of every man, woman, and child being turned in an instant to cinders by *the bomb*, but just when we thought that was over another kind of horror was taking root.

Then in the Humvees' wake, from who knows how far up the streets, in who knows what gang-banger's low-riding car: fook'emup, fook'emup, fook'emup, donttekdashit, donttekdashit, donttekdashit no-mo at some profane decibel level thumped the air. They all looked at each other, their faces liquefying with fear, and picked up their coffees and whatever else and darted like roaches inside.

Trying to come to terms with it, articles from every conceivable and inconceivable angle cascaded down the pages of the Los Angeles Times, a stupendous surfeit of reporting, from every angle, from every aspect, as though machines, located in a cool, frictionless, neutral zone, a virtual Switzerland of them, were doing the work. He imagined a time, maybe not far off, when all the people would disappear and the only things left would be these recording instruments and writing machines, a whole indefatigable viral army of them dictating to the last detail for some super historical aliens the last breath and whimper, the last drop of semen and blood. Michelle wove around the tables bending over to exchange ashtrays—some, he noticed, not even used—with all the nonchalance of a tanning commercial extra. He couldn't decide if none of this had bothered her, or if her focus was impaired because she was stoned, or if, scared stiff, she'd cut herself off. Her ass—the sheer platonic perfection of it—now seemed just that, an untouchable form there for disinterested contemplation. Here was a revelation: fear dries your dick up the same way it dries up your throat.

"Hey Michelle."

"Oh, I didn't even see you."

"Cap and bagel, please."

"They didn't come this morning. I guess everyone is afraid to drive."

"What do you have?"

"Coffee cake. The frozen kind."

"I'll take one of those. How are you doing through all of this?"

"Ryan has a gun and he really wants to use it."

"Scary."

"He slept with it by his side last night. I kept thinking it was going to go off by itself. That's why I look so miserable."

"You look fine, sweetie."

"You are such a nice person. I wish in my next life I could find someone like you."

It was a mind-bending comment, but his mind was already too bent to register it as anything other than perfectly plumb. He turned back to the paper. Deeper and deeper into the coverage, there was a distinct shift in reportorial tone: Indignation, fear, and disbelief had turned like acid on the reporter's usual objective perspective, and suddenly they were tooled up with all manner of flamboyancies, like "pandemonium." Bizarre phrases like "beaten nearly into oblivion," "a face emerges to transfix a moment in history," "spasms of destruction," "a bandage stripped off an open wound." More than that, for once the state of alert everyone was made to believe they constantly lived in was matched by an actual state of alert.

He really needed that coffee and cake, and he turned to see what was taking so long. The manager, a wiry Asian twenty-something who wore stylish sunglasses even in the dead of winter and claimed to have the best private porno collection in LA, had his arms wrapped around Michelle. Her face was buried in his chest, and he was looking at her beautiful bare shoulders like they were a winning hand that he was deciding exactly how to play.

"Did you order the coffee and cake?" he asked, pointing his chin at the counter where it sat getting cold.

"I'll get it, no problem. You all right, Michelle?"

She shook her head. "No."

"What's the matter sweetie?"

She shook her head again.

At any other hour he wanted to screw her blind, but just then he wanted to protect her, from the Asian porno addict, from the likes of men like himself. He wanted to wrap a shawl around her, put her in a car, and speed her away from LA; he wanted to take her body to a secret place where nobody could defile it; he wanted to save what innocence was left, maybe even restore what was lost.

On TV they announced that Rodney King was prepared to speak. Michelle pulled herself together for the big debut. No one had seen him since his face had been bashed in. He actually looked pretty slick. Dressed in a baggy black jacket, with his hair all glossily combed back, he shyly leaned into the microphones, and, and, and, and, said: "People, I just want to say, can we all get along?" Then something about justice will be done, something about the battle is lost but the war will still be won. Then again, "Can we all get along? Can we stop making it horrible for the older people and the kids?" He wasn't on long. And immediately, once he was done, Trish began to repeat those words, "'Can we all get along?' The voice of reason, the calm voice of reason."

                            TED
          You heard it, straight from the mouth of
          the man at the center of what is one of
          the worst civil uprisings we've seen in
          this country. Can anything be added to
          those words?

                           TRISH
          I don't think so.

                            TED
          Trish.

                           TRISH
          I don't think so, Ted. I think Rodney
          King has said what all of us feel right
          now. He has spoken for this community,
          for the world.

                            TED
          What's the mood there, Trish?

                           TRISH
          The mood here is respectful. Somber, but
          respectful. I think that everybody feels
          the truth in what he has said.

                            TED
          We've just heard Rodney King. His
          address was very short, and at the
          center of it were five very simple words:
          "Can we all get along." Here with us
          today are two people who we've asked to
          come into our studios to comment…

Adam took control of the remote like he owned the place and
switched channels. Everyone was now chanting it, "Can we all
get along?" It was as though, after mulling things over, God
had come up with an eleventh commandment, actually mel-
lowed into a kind of appeal; Can we all get along? Even so, those
five words, as much as they left unsaid, sounded Lincolnesque
compared to the politicians and sports stars and actors and civil
leaders knocking themselves out simply trying to find a word to

describe what was happening; a gang conspiracy, no, a riot, or maybe a civil disobedience, no, bigger, a revolution, or maybe a better word is revolt, how sounds uprising or insurrection? Too human. How about upheaval, a kind of now and again geological event? The sheer disposability of the words coming from every direction was almost as depressing as the absence of the right ones. Speaking of which: where the hell were the producers and directors, the bearers of the magic lantern, the avant-gardes of illumination, those whose every crumb of opinion people usually gobbled up? Nobody had heard from a single one of them yet. No, as the nightmare unfolded the spinners of dreams were fast asleep. Or perhaps, sequestered as they were in their heavenly estates, consumed as usual in their profligate affairs, they hardly took notice of the stupidity and baseness and self-destructiveness of the mortals down below.

Latasha Harland, he heard, Latasha Harland. By way of commentary, a black civil leader was now pounding her name into the city's skull. That murder was a lit fuse, the fuel packed, ready to explode, this black civil leader explained. Sure, maybe it started out as one thing, economic dead-endedness, or revenge against the admittedly sadistic LAPD. Maybe even a few Koreans had pushed a few black people too far. But none of that explained more than the first few hours and outbursts. No, it had quickly gathered its own abstruse logic, its own organic momentum; it had its own name. Marx envisioned a revolution, humans revolting against the capitalist social order that had fashioned their very souls. He believed that if people could see that they had actually made the Golden Calf that lorded over them, they would crush it and there would be no more Golden Calves. What he didn't realize is that people enjoy their Golden Calves, even those they've made, especially when they have no idea they've made them. They like to milk them, stacked up in the meat locker, floating in their swimming pools, like them as baubles dangling from their rearview mirrors. Far from crushing their Golden Calves, humans want to multiply them, feed and reproduce them, even if in the end there is nothing left to feed them but the last bit of human flesh itself. What do you call that?

Shaking free of these thoughts, he saw families of Hasidim crossing the street. It was Friday before Sabbath, and a few had kept the faith, trundling to temple on schedule in their big heavies; half of them looked like undertakers in spaghetti westerns, the rest like they were off to Dracula's birthday carrying the frosted cakes on their heads. In groups of three and four or more their kids trailed, the moms in stiff hairpieces, ugly skirts, and clunky shoes dutifully pulling up the ends.

The Wizard had introduced Adam to Martin Buber's collection *Tales of The Hasidim*, and those tales and parables reminded Adam of Christ's. "The world is full of enormous lights and mysteries, and man shuts them from himself with one small hand." Then he moved into their neighborhood, only to discover that all those mysteries had boiled down to black-garbed families shuffling back and forth to temple as though to a never-ending wake. Frankly, it was depressing to discover that this was how spiritual heavyweights acted. He had already allowed that the Hasidim were of this world and not of this world, okay, but now he felt they existed in a perversely clueless world.

Or maybe their ritual was different from his. He had headed to the temple-coffee-shop, while they were heading to the temple-temple. He read the Times, they read the Torah. He had always wondered how people bore news of approaching calamity and matter-of-factly went about their daily routine-ritual. Wouldn't their lives instantly change; wouldn't they immediately and tactically rebuff or retreat from the threat? As he looked at the Hasidim around him, looked at himself, he thought, no, the ritual is not the first thing that goes—it very well may be the last. The more imminent the threat, the more wild and thorny and poisonous the vegetation grows, the deeper the ritual roots sink.

He noticed that his coffee cup was shaking, the one in his hand. His nerves were teetering like a bridge, a bridge over which a dark cloud was also descending. He wanted to protect Michelle, yes, but from that failing bridge. Let's face it: He wanted to spirit her away from the dark cloud descending over himself. Just then, all the races and sects that called LA home, some so scarce as to be nearly extinct—Zoroastrians, Taoists, followers of Bubba Free John, and Swedenborgians, jazz artists, devotees of L. Ron, Save The Whalers, Mary Dalyians, Wheat Grass Drinkers and Star-Fuckers and All Night Nightclubbers, Channelers, and the Challenged of every possible human and non-human description, the millionaires in Ferraris, the threadbare thousands who roamed the streets at midnight, rain falling acid-like on their dreams—the whole impossible human lot of them amounted to a fantastical melting pot project gone apocalyptically wrong; or maybe it was wrong-headed from the start.

He felt as though his soul were eroding under their discharge, some spectacular deluge of it. Maybe the Hasidim were right; there seemed, just then, to be a sickening soundness to their thesis that ruination had been the state of the world since its inception. He was thinking of their creation myth, which went something like this: just before the world and all its things came into being, G-d withdrew into himself, bringing into existence a vacuum. From this vacuum emanated a ray of divine light, and this light was captured in vessels, but those vessels furthest from the source broke, and the light shattered and attached to broken fragments that tumbled to the Earth, and those broken fragments became the things of the world. Every rock, tree, book, and streetlamp, every word in the dictionary, carries a spark of divine light; human themselves are shards of light, bodies of light.

He wondered if the hell-broke-loose was inevitable—the pulverized air, the fire-crumbled buildings, the million smashed windows, the decimation of the very social order. One thousand structures, according to the best estimate of the Times, had been set ablaze or razed; twenty-five people had been killed, nearly three thousand injured, and the damage had been estimated at almost eight hundred million dollars—and only God at this point could see where the destruction would end.

Adam now desperately needed to see the Wizard; he needed to take to the hills.

PART 3

THERE WERE HARDLY ANY CARS on the road, so he reached
The Wizard's in less than ten minutes, half the usual time. He
hadn't bothered calling because showing up at The Wizard's was
almost like showing up at his own home.

The Wizard was sitting where he always sat, in his chair
that overlooked the city, listening to Bach and reading a book
on harmonics, or it could've been color theory. In any case,
whatever it was he was making a study of that day, his whole
detached professsorial vibe irritated Adam.

"What's the matter with you?" Adam asked.

"Nothing." The Wizard chuckled, kindly. "What have I
done, my boy? I'm just sitting here minding my own business."

Rusty, the weaker of The Wizard's two whippets, suddenly
appeared and jumped into The Wizard's lap for love.

He put his book down, and with two hands stroked the
whippet's long, sad, slender face.

"Take a seat. Put your feet up, as they say."

Adam was circling the room like a dog looking for a spot
to shit.

"It is quite a mess out there, isn't it?" said The Wizard.

"You make like it's a traffic jam." Adam told him that a
riot, a citywide riot was unfolding; the cops were nowhere to be
found. They'd given over entire sections of the city, and there
were gun-battles in Koreatown.

"Yes, yes. People are no damn good. I suppose I should

turn on the news. But really, what will I learn that isn't already obvious?" He paused a beat, then added, "From up here."

Actually, Adam could hardly see anything from up there anymore. There was so much smoke that the top layer of the Capitol Records building, less than a mile away, was but a vaguely defined flying saucer. The freeway and the charred heads of the tall Palm trees that lined it—he must've seen them flare up from where he sat.

"Oh yes, that was quite something," The Wizard said. He looked concerned, but not gravely so.

"Oh," he said, "did I talk to you about Karajan's *Gadfly?*"

The Wizard had created a castle in his brain, surrounded by a great moat. Whenever he needed to he retreated across the bridge and pulled it up behind him.

"The *Gadfly*, for God's sake!"

"Well, what they call the Romance piece, I think we both agree, is beautiful, but Karajan recreation of it is quite other-worldly. I've switched out of it, but if you'd like I can put it back on for you to listen to."

"I don't need to listen to that right now. Even your Bach is getting on my nerves."

"Bach?"

"You're in some kind of denial."

"Denial? My boy, at my age, there is no denying anything."

It was a stupid thing to say. After the life he'd lived, the strafing he'd endured.

"In any case," he said, "it's time for some lunch." He stood with a grunt, and tramped to the kitchen. The whippets, Landy and Rusty, followed behind in a line.

Adam didn't think of The Wizard as old, and he didn't like when he referred to his age. But The Wizard hit him over the head with it at regular intervals.

I've lived my life, we'll do whatever you'd like to do. It was The Wizard's refrain whenever they had had to choose between restaurants or movies or plays. When he said that, all Adam wanted to do was make The Wizard's day, do whatever it was The Wizard liked to do. Indeed, *just because* he wanted to do whatever it was Adam wanted to do, Adam wanted to do whatever it was The Wizard wanted to do. *No,* he'd tell The Wizard, *I've lived* my *life. We'll do what* you *want to do.* There was times when they ping-ponged back and forth for so long that they ended up doing something neither of them wanted to do.

The Wizard returned with lunch on a wooden tray: a fresh pear, canned baby peas, and meatloaf, *microwaved,* he announced, *to perfection.* He sat, lowering the tray onto his lap and tucking a napkin beneath his chin. "I suppose I should've offered you something," he said, and started in. The whippets stood to the side on their silly, spindly legs, waiting fretfully for leftovers. Between bites, The Wizard cast an eye their way and sighed.

"I dare say, these dogs will be my ruin."

"I dare say you were ruined well before the dogs showed up."

He smiled, *touché,* and as though his options had suddenly run out, he put the pear aside and set the tray on the floor with both hands. Right away, Landy bullied Rusty out of the picture.

"The underdog," he said. "But we mustn't interfere with their natural ordering." And so the three of them watched Landy gobble the lasagna up.

Trembling in defeat, Rusty jumped onto The Wizard's lap and began foraging for bits in The Wizard's goatee. The Wizard let him. When he was done, he lay lengthwise on The Wizard's lap.

"Small consolation," said The Wizard, stroking the dog's anemic little ribs tenderly. The Wizard had turned the dogs, especially Rusty, the runt, neurotic.

The Wizard turned to reach for a CD on the table just behind him. A bit awkwardly, since the dog was still on his lap, The Wizard tore the wrapper open with his teeth, lifted the CD out, and dropped it onto the carousel. He'd picked it up at Tower Records, he told Adam, a month ago; on one of those fabulous discount shelves. Touric doing Bach. Adam had no idea who Touric was.

"I do love this machine," The Wizard said. He had converted from LPs to CDs late in the game, but when he finally did convert he went straight for the carousel kind, which allowed him to efficiently study different takes on the same composition.

Side by side in the carousel he'd plop Feltsman and Gould and Richter, and now Touric, each doing in his or her own way the Well-Tempered Clavier. "The only way to get to the bottom of a piece of music," he mused, adding, "Naturally, there is no getting to the bottom of a really great piece of music, the very thing, I suppose, that makes it a really great piece of music to begin with."

The piano started up and he reached for a book.

He'd start into a subject—calligraphy, mysticism, black holes, or whatever—going through all the latest literature until it was piled up around him, until he could see through what he called "the whole nonsense, the whole tendentious, self-flattering avoidance of the really difficult problems," at which point he'd box them up and haul them to the local library for a tax-deductible donation that would go unused because throughout his entire life he'd never once managed to save a receipt.

"Why it is so difficult to a keep a box where I might put these receipts? Do you have any ideas how many thousands of dollars in tax deductions I've lost for the simple reason tht I can't hold onto a receipt! It's the madness. Yet another symptom of the madness."

Adam grabbed *Caravaggio* off the side table and began flipping through tipped-in reproductions of the old master's work; his stunning reds and blues, his seductive shadows and sensational strikes of light—all of it struck him just then as too dramatic, too staged. Adam let out a frustrated grunt, a kind of yelp.

"You *are* in bad shape." The Wizard had peaked over his book.

Adam reflected that it wasn't fair to bring his anxiety into The Wizard's home and expect him to share it. He began to think that maybe he should leave The Wizard in peace. But where would he go, short of home? Our parents' madhouse? The Kurd's? He loved The Kurd, but he'd also had enough of him. Adam couldn't get over the way The Kurd, despite the mayhem on TV, had locked his eyes on Auntie's ass like he meant to kill it with a single shot.

"Would you care for a game of chess?"

The Wizard put a hand out to the table just behind the large leather couch.

"Chess. Are you kidding me?"

"That ol' denialism sneaking in, I suppose."

The board showed that he was in the middle of a game. It wasn't uncommon for him to take two to three days to complete one.

"I feel like throwing up."

"Use the bathroom downstairs, please."

"Don't worry."

"In fact, why don't you go to your room and turn the TV on? At this point it's no use trying to pull your head out of it. Sometimes the trick is to stick your head farther in. Shrinks, I think, call it 'immersion therapy,' or some such nonsense. How has your sleep been?"

"Not good. I haven't slept in two days, really."

"You are welcome to stay as long as you like. I'll just be sitting here reading as usual. Go ahead."

Adam went ahead, downstairs to his small ten-foot-square room. Not an item had been moved, added, or subtracted, since he'd last stepped in there. Even the dust seemed no more or less. There was the full-size bed, and the small oak desk and floor-to-ceiling bookcase where The Wizard kept his philosophy and poetry; a twelve-inch TV (whose remote was broken) perched on a corner dresser.

He stepped out onto the bedroom balcony; the canyon was awash with a luxurious ochre-colored light that draped long, theatrical shadows on the slopes of the hills. After just a few minutes out there, he noticed his breath was getting wheezy, so he came back inside and eased onto the bed like an arthritic patient. The TV had become a feeding tube. He hungered for its food, though he knew its food was poison. The gnawing urge to turn it on was deep, down to the cellular level. He thought, *At this juncture what could possible enlighten you?* It was funny; when he was in The Wizard's house he talked and even thought like The Wizard. *Enlighten you? Relax. If The Wizard can do without it, so can you.* He went back and forth like this until the pressure was unbearable.

There she was, looking none the worse for the wear, lovely Trish, holding a mic in front of a black woman on a major boulevard, with two other black persons, a woman and a man, standing next to her.

> FIRST WOMAN
> It's like a hundred years ago—wild, wild west. There's no police. They're doing what they want.

> MAN
> This is our neighborhood. Our stores.

> SECOND WOMAN
> Sickness. What I feel is sickness.

> MAN
> How we supposed to get around? Mom, she's run out of medicine. How she supposed to get it now?

Then a gunshot. A car on the other side of the road blurily flew by. Everyone scrambled in panic and took cover behind a telephone booth. Adam wondered if this would be a first for him; seeing someone fucking killed on live TV.

> FIRST WOMAN
> Was that, what was that?

> SECOND WOMAN
> God. See. What I mean. Sickness. Help us.

He watched for hours, the feeling of defeat setting in him like cement, until around 8:00 p.m., when he trod upstairs to find some food; he hadn't eaten since morning.

The Wizard was dozing in his chair, the whippets curled up on the floor next to him. There wasn't much in the fridge—some Velveeta-style cheese, deli turkey, bread, eggs, and milk—and so he went for some canned spicy minestrone soup pushed deep into one of the cupboards. The Wizard rarely ate such food because it bothered "the valve."

He put the soup on the stove and stuck a slice of sourdough in the toaster. As he waited for the soup to come to a simmer he listened to The Wizard's serious-decibel-level snoring, snoring over Feltzman—or was it Richter or Touric playing?

When the soup was ready he took his dinner to the living

room and sat across from The Wizard in his armchair. While the soup had been heating the smell had struck him as strange, but now when he brought it to his mouth, he wanted to gag. Suddenly the minestrone smelled exactly like the vomit it resembled.

"I love it here," The Wizard would often say of his home. "I sit looking over the city while at the same time I am completely separated from it. I am in the middle of it in one way, and outside it in quite another." Now lights had been knocked out over huge sections of that very city. Here and there infernos glowed. Adam watched a car inch tentatively up the empty freeway. On the grid below, National Guard hummers stopped and then started and then stopped, retarded, ridiculously, like plastic glow-in-the dark worms. For the two years that Adam had lived with The Wizard, there were days on end they would rise only to find fog blanketing the city, and locked in in the fog they'd quietly turn to each other, The Wizard in his chair and Adam in his, and begin discussing whatever the matter was with an implicit sense that all was well, even divine out there. They would, like two ends of a taffy machine, begin pulling and folding and pulling and folding until the fog would lift and the city would take form below. And all along the freeway, the sound of traffic would rise up to them like the sound of the ocean.

Adam wondered if those days were over. He wondered if he'd ever feel toward the city the way he felt before this madness. We betrayed the sheer grace that had kept us aloft, he thought. We squandered it. We lived in ignorant bliss until that bliss consumed us.

He wanted to wake The Wizard to tell him what he thought, but he didn't dare. Dozing was sometimes the only way The Wizard—like Adam, a chronic insomniac—could catch sleep.

Adam's own exhaustion now hit him like a sledgehammer. It was the kind of exhaustion that in its perfection almost turns into its opposite, a kind of phantom wakefulness. It was no time to dick around; he hobbled downstairs to The Wizard's bathroom and started rummaging for whatever would do the trick: any number of benzos, Valium, Ativan, or Klonopin, whatever. All he found was oxycodone, a morphine-like concoction. The

Wizard kept a batch on hand for gallbladder attacks. (One night Adam had rushed him to the hospital for such an attack, and the doctor had prescribed them in case of another attack down the road. He was supposed to have the gallbladder removed, but he never did). He took two and lay back in bed.

On the TV was Ted. He looked exhausted, his necktie loose, his hair tousled., A spiffily dressed Hispanic Actor of repute sat to his left. They were in the middle of a conversation.

> HA
>
> …..of course we are all traumatized; of course we are all in shock, and there is no excuse for what we've seen and experienced, there is no way to excuse it, but that doesn't mean there aren't reasons.

> TED
>
> You are close to the Hispanic community. There are a lot of people out there who feel like you are a spokesman for that community.

> HA
>
> I consider myself a citizen of the world; if that makes a spokesman, then I accept that responsibility.

> TED
>
> What are your thoughts about, about the reasons we're seeing what we're seeing?

> HA
>
> It's no secret; this city is divided into two.

> TED
>
> Well, I think you would have a hard time finding anyone who disagrees with you about that; right now, I think you'd an awfully hard time finding a person…

> HA
>
> Those who have and those who have not.

It's not just people admitting it. It's people doing something about it. What we see on the surface is not what's happening beneath the surface. Look, we have to come to terms with the reality that the value system in this country is collapsing. We watch it every day on TV; our politicians and leaders…

                    TED
And right here, too. I just heard a story from a police officer: there were three kids, two nine-year-olds and a four-year-old, coming out of a store with some goods. When they asked them why are you doing this…

                    HA
I love those kids. You see, those kids, all those people out there today, they are part of us, and they are our family.

                    TED
… I was struck, for one, I was struck by what they said, they said they were looting because they didn't have anything else to do.

                    HA
Kids say things. Look, I embrace those kids. I embrace the looters; everybody out there is my brother.

                    TED
But if your brother tries to start your house on fire you have the right to stop him.

                    HA
You also have the duty to say, 'Brother, what are you doing? Let's sit and talk about this.' To understand where your brother is coming from. Look in the mirror. You know they say an eye for an eye, but everyone knows an eye for an eye turns the whole world blind.

How long before the fucking oxycodone kicks in? Adam wondered. Maybe he should've swallowed the pills with a large glass of water rather than a short gulp from the tap. Maybe, he thought, this city needed a good purging. Maybe the world has to purge now and then, irrespective of what and whom it purged. There were times when a world under the load of its own artifice was meant to collapse into ruin; the whole of its multitudinous lunacy. Yes, in spite of his love for this world, there was also a part of of Adam that couldn't wait for it to end, all this ridiculousness; all the billion layers of lies and deceit, yes, but also the hard-won layers of truth. He needed to feel that someday the complete sum would vanish.

This thought brought him a Zen-like clarity, a yogi's mindful calm. Maybe it was the oxycodone. The audio on the TV had become as soporific as a Buddhist chant. He could feel his limbs numbing, his body easing into a kind of warm, buzzing cloud. As a child, he'd one morning woken with a terrible fever. Grandma sat next to him the whole day as his body roiled with heat, and at some point in the middle of the tumult he suddenly found himself quieting. Outside the yellowing leaves trembled abstractly; the family chatter in the other room was white noise. He was swept up in the numinous beauty of leaving go, the exquisite throwawayness of everything. And then he felt something come to rest on the top of his hand. Grandma's hand, cool and smooth as a river stone. He moved it to his chest. Nothing might matter, but this does, he thought. In fact, all that matters is this Holy this.

. . .

Adam and The Wizard had first met three years before at a performance art event in one of those vast industrial lofts downtown. It was the third or fourth such performance Sasha had invited Adam to, and as with those others the crowd was dressed mostly in black, some in capes, and many in steel-toed boots. Waiting for the performance piece to commence, they sipped Perrier or seven-dollar bottles of wine, circling-studying three semi-permanent installations the way detectives might study a crime scene: ONE: a regimen of old fashioned telephones, all squat on the ground like plastic frogs; TWO: a great pile of children's shoes, very much like the kind of thing on display in Auschwitz, and from the middle of the pile the eerie sound of children, playing, crying, laughing; THREE: a dozen or so tiny shrines to the Virgin, like you find in the homes of little old Mexican ladies, facing oval mirrors, and between the mirrors and the virgin, votive candles that made for a warm spiritual halo. Someone announced the performance was about to begin, but the space was so large—the size of a football field—that it took another ten minutes to rustle the crowd around the circular stage.

Just in front of Adam stood Sasha; to his left a tall, elderly gentleman (The Wizard) in a frumpy wool suit, wearing thick glasses, and a Colonel Sandersesque goatee. It was streaked handsomely with grey, as was his youthfully wavy hair. To Adam's right stood a pretty brunette:

"His work," she told Adam, "is developed on the ideas of *duh-reed-uh*."

"You mean *Dairy-dah*," Sasha said.

"It's what he's doing to himself: deconstructing himself."

Sasha said, "He has AIDS."

The girl said, "But he's made it part of his Art. That's what art does. That's what makes it different."

Adam noticed now that her hands were too big, and that there was a rash-like bumpiness to her arms; her feet too, were big, too big and wide for a woman.

"I've been to probably a dozen of his performances," she said.

"I just heard of him."

"Oh, he's big."

"I don't doubt it," Adam replied.

She said, "Very controversial."

"Seems you have to be these days."

Could she be a man? From a kind of puzzle-solving perspective, Adam really wanted to know.

The girl said, "He usually shows with John Sissman."

"The fat guy." Adam had seen him a month earlier, lying on a bed in a bedroom that had been installed to full scale in the concrete basement of an abandoned industrial building off Spring Street. The room was full of memorabilia: books, trophies, banners, and posters; and in the middle of this room a huge circular bed, the kind on which centerfolds would lie in the early days of Playboy; except on this bed lay the fattest man Adam had ever seen, his tiny head propped up with an arm as big as a flour sack. The way the fat hung from his body reminded Adam precisely of a scoop of ice cream melting on a sidewalk.

"He was sure some fatty," he said, embarrassing Sasha. "I've never seen a man that fat before. He must've weighed a ton, literally."

The woman said, "You see, that's what everybody sees. At first. How fat he is. But you're supposed to see deeper than that. Deeper than the flesh. That's the point. That's his art."

Adam had a hunch that the guy was making a kind of sculpture out of his own body.

Wrong. "That kind of formalism has nothing to do with Sissman's work. Did you notice the pose he struck? Remember?"

"I agree," Sasha said.

Adam said, "Yeah, kind of creepy seductive."

Sasha told Adam, "It alludes to all those portraits of females reclining on couches. Ingres' *Odalisque*, etc." Now she gave it name. "Post-modern irony."

The woman said, "I think he's one of the deepest Artists there is. Like Cindy Sherman, but Live."

A spotlight jolted the stage awake. In the middle a man, maybe thirty, sat full-lotus wearing only a skin-tight pair of leather briefs. Tattooed from toe to bald head, he immediately brought to mind certain species of tropical snake. The stage began to turn slowly, lazy-Susan like, and for an hour or so he performed a series of meticulous operations on himself, one by one, pin by pin, inserting here, then there. With each lance Adam felt a ghostly echo of pain, as though the Performance Artist were a voodoo doll and Adam the cursee. Sasha and the rest of the audience were sophisticated; cool, there but not there, editors more than witnesses, clearly able to see the *concepts* behind the pins and needles. Adam looked for an escape route, but he was boxed in, trapped in a shoulder-to-shoulder crowd.

He dropped his eyes to his sneakers: after all he'd seen his family go through, he couldn't figure out why this guy wasn't raising his voice in thanks rather than vexing his flesh. Weirdly, anger flared up in him. *Fuck this, I'm out of here*, he decided, when he heard someone loudly groan. It was the elderly man standing to his left; he was bobbing and ducking his head, as if bullets were whizzing above it. The Performance Artist, who on any given day might've freelanced as a contortionist, was now pushing a long skewer through two fleshy points behind his back. It was too much for Colonel Sanders: he stuck his big hands over his eyes, as kids do during a scary movie.

After it was done, there was a general sigh of relief; the bar opened and everyone got back to cavorting. Adam followed The Wizard, curious to know who he was, maybe the PA's father or uncle. But no sooner was The Wizard deep into the performance piece than he was deep out of it and into the building itself, surveying the physical space, bumping into people, *oh, I'm sorry*, as he took in the thirty-foot high ceilings, *Pardon me*, the exposed vents and pipes, and a great square cement column that he circled a couple of times, scrutinizing its volume and apparently its texture, because now he paused to pet it, like a dog he hoped to befriend.

"What're you looking at?" Adam asked him.

"Oh," he said. "I'm admiring this building. By exposing its innards it has become a kind of living thing, no?"

"Yeah, I suppose you're right."

"A perfect setting for art, much better than these scrubbed up spaces they call museums. I'm sure they did not choose it for this reason, probably they chose it because it was cheap, but sometimes genius is simply tripped-upon. Yes, *tripped-upon* genius always makes me happy."

Tripped-upon genius. Adam loved that. He was right, there was nothing more magical than tripped-upon genius. But only a genius would know when he'd tripped on it. Adam needed to know what The Wizard thought of the show.

"Not my cup of tea, I'm afraid. Too religious. It all reminds me of those sad, deluded South Americans who climb up a cross and pound a few nails through their hands and feet to show their piety on Good Friday."

The Wizard was right; there was something weirdly spiritual about it, but here was the rub—nobody believed in God anymore, which made it even weirder.

It was a mouthful to express, so he just said, "Interesting."

"A word your generation uses when it is at a loss to explain it any other way. One wonders what makes you all so timid."

"We're afraid of embarrassment?"

"The way, perhaps, my generation was afraid of shame."

"But speaking of timid; I saw you cover your eyes. Sorry to eavesdrop."

"Oh," he said. "That. I suppose that is all just reflex."

"From what?"

"I was a prisoner of war in Burma," he said, and turned back to the cement column. Adam thought he'd lost him, but apparently The Wizard was just rebooting, because he now returned from wherever to tell about that "mad Joseph Bueys and his Coyote," one of the first ever performance art pieces. He'd been in New York at the time of the exhibit, visiting friends. Everyone was talking about it, and so he decided to go. The way Bueys befriended that animal, "his reaching out in hopes of sinking into its brain, was among the beautiful things I've ever witnessed." It convinced The Wizard that at the bottom of all art was a need to connect; "nearly every gesture of art, even the most cynical," he said, "has something to do with humans' need for love."

Adam said, "Even a tattooed guy sewing his butt shut? Hard to see where the love is there?"

The Wizard guffawed, his big body lurching forward, back and forward. It was good to see The Wizard laugh so hard. Adam was inspired to see a man his age laugh with such abandon. He laughed the way Grandma laughed.

Would he like a glass of wine? If he'd like, they could sit down and take that glass of wine together.

For an hour or so, through one, two, three glasses of wine, they talked about art; picking each other's brains, is the way The

Wizard put it, although Adam felt that for him, the pickings were slim. His own art education was limited to a single art history class in college, a number of monographs he'd purchased for study, and gallery gallivanting with Sasha. Adam had squirreled away few ideas, and it didn't seem to bother The Wizard in the least that they were naïve and jumbled, maybe because The Wizard's brain was just as much a jumble, though obviously a jumble spread across a sprawling estate. From one wing to the other he'd march, not particularly concerned whether anything he returned with ("Sad, those line drawings of Picasso, the God of Art felled by plain old age.") was at all connected to whatever he'd returned with before ("quite mysterious this Englishman Tobey") or after.

The Wizard was brilliant, but less like a diamond then a shoreline with jagged outcroppings when the sun hits it just so. Adam wanted to continue the conversation, however much it was over his head, but the crowd was thinning, and the lights one by one had been turned on, and so he asked The Wizard if he wanted to grab some dinner. The Wizard looked at his watch, a clunky one with a turquoise band, not at all in keeping with his gabardine suit, and said, "It's yet early. Let's go have a bite."

Sasha wasn't happy that she was getting cut loose because there was a party she wanted to go to and she didn't want to go to it alone. Adam promised he'd catch up with her tomorrow, and in no time they were cruising across downtown in the Wizard's beat-up Pontiac, into the heart of an installation that made the one they'd just seen seem amateurish: a virtual freight train of refrigerator boxes and stove boxes, and an occasional wooden packing crate with people sleeping inside, milling about, chatting, pitching pennies, a few huddled around a fire burning in a trash can. Downtown was not *abandoned* the way all the cultural connoisseurs and downtown-worry-warts-who-wanted-to-clean-it-up claimed, not abandoned in the least. In fact, just the opposite, it was hopping, and virtually Dadaist in design. Once the blue suits had evacuated, these alcoholics, transients, schizophrenics, had had in a matter of two, three hours thrown up another structure, "entirely alien from and at the same time entirely symbiotic with the one *above.*" Such was The Wizard's analysis.

"You must admit," The Wizard said, "it makes what we saw tonight in the warehouse seem quite superfluous."

"Indeed," Adam said, a word he believed The Wizard would approve of.

It was nearly 10:00 p.m. when they got to Gorky's, a Russian-themed Brewery in the flower district. The Wizard just loved the red, white, and black Soviet industrial feel of the place, he told Adam. Sidling side by side, cafeteria-style toward the steaming troughs of food, The Wizard kept bumping into Adam, the usual spacers having obviously disintegrated with his advanced age. They carried their trays to a table near the window, where The Wizard got down to business, tucking his napkin beneath his chin, slathering sour cream over his latkes, and then aggressively shaking out the applesauce from a little bowl. Hands and elbows, he started in.

After devouring a couple of latkes, he came up for air, a chunk stuck in the shrubbery. "Not bad," he said, "not bad," and then with a finger cleaned the little bowl and poked that finger into his mouth.

What an odd fellow. "You're quite the cultural junky to tramp downtown on a Wednesday night to see a performance art piece," Adam told him.

The Wizard said he enjoyed getting his fingers dirty in the streets as well as in the library, and that he'd learned the value of cruising such scenes in France, where he took a semester at the Sorbonne, shortly after the War.

"Foucault got me into it," he said, and then he told Adam how he'd met Foucault one cold Paris morning while waiting in line to get into the *Bibliothèque nationale.* The Wizard noticed directly in front of him a bald head that turned out to be Foucault's bald head. The great French historian was working up a paper on madness at the time, and since the *Bibliothèque* got only a few hours of artificial light a day, he'd arrived, like The Wizard, as early as possible to take advantage of the natural light that poured through the windows. Foucault was a generous person—indeed, a gentle person, not the bitter, cynical sort of French scholar he'd seen hundreds of over his lifetime.

Adam told The Wizard he had majored in business. He told him he'd heard of Foucault (although he really hadn't) but that was about it.

"I admire business," The Wizard said. "It is straight to the point: profit."

"True."

"In academic rackets, it's also about profit, but camouflaged by endless jargon and justifications."

Adam watched The Wizard's super-long, bony fingers scrabble like crab legs over the table for a napkin and begin to fold it this way and that.

"My brother is a documentary filmmaker living in New York," Adam told him. "He's read all that philosophy stuff from top to bottom. He graduated from NYU."

In no time, The Wizard had produced a remarkably fine origami with that napkin, and now he tossed it on the table, as though having entertained himself with the making of it was satisfaction enough.

"As I said, most of it isn't worth the bother," The Wizard said.

"Then what kept you in it for so long?"

"I used the academy for my own selfish pursuits. I have always loved learning for learning's sake, as they say, and there was no better place to do it. I did what they expected me to do, but only in order to make time to do what I wanted to do."

Adam told The Wizard, "I feel like I'm in training for something, but just what that 'something' is is beyond my reach."

The Wizard waved the suggestion away with a hand. "It always feels beyond one's reach until one reaches it, at which point it goes out of reach again."

A philologist by training, he had started his career working on Chaucer and Gawain. Then he got involved with mythology before discovering that, "The demotic (which Adam heard as "demonic") mode of expression, say, the way your Lizzie Bordens told their stories," was what really caught his ear. For the past

145

twenty years, he said, he'd worked on folk ballads and what he called "Negro songs," and then smack in the middle of Gorky's he began to sing one.

"Crazy!" Adam was dazzled. And then The Wizard sang another, at which point people began to stare. Adam was dazzled, not only because the song and the way he sang it was so wonderful, but because his feelings for those old Negro songs gave him a window into what made this man tick. The Wizard had an ear, an appetite for those voices that were left out in the cold. Adam might just then have been the old Negro singer The Wizard was emulating.

He finished the song and said, "Gorky wasn't actually Gorky, but rather Alexy Peshkov."

"Gorky," Adam told him, "was also not in fact Gorky, but Vostanik Adoian."

"Indeed. The bitter ones," he said.

"Indeed."

Adam picked up the origami. "Mind it I take this?"

"What for?"

He put in his coat pocket: "I don't know. Maybe a memento of our first date."

IT WASN'T LONG BEFORE they had their second. Only a few days later, Adam was zipping down Wilshire toward Westwood in the middle of the day to lunch with a seventy-year-old professor of English. Adam might've been headed to a date with an Elle fashion model, such was his nervous exhilaration.

The secretary at the front desk asked, "Your name? You're not a student here, are you?"

In her role as gatekeeper she could probably smell from half a mile away that he had majored in business, and at USC to boot.

"If you'll take a seat," she said, "I will let him know you are here."

The Wizard just then walked into the office area with his notes in hand. As he asked the secretary if she would *be so kind* as to type them up and have them distributed to the rest of the faculty, Adam watched as though he were standing behind a one-way mirror. The Wizard was a very tall man, and he stooped over just barely, the way a person does when trying to catch words from the mouth of a child. He wore a blue suit, and a tie that was tied in the old fashioned style. His shirt was too tight in the collar, and the sleeves were possibly three inches short of his wrists.

The secretary said she would be happy to type those notes up, and that, "This young man is here to see you."

"Oh," he said, and turned to face Adam. "Come in, come in." Adam stood there for a second, unsure if the man knew who he was. Then The Wizard did a double take and said, "Oh, indeed. Adam!" Come in, come in." Adam followed him down a corridor, The Wizard explaining, as though Adam strode by his side and not two steps behind him, that he was reading a book. The book was something he'd read years ago, and while reading it he realized he had missed the entire point of the book the first time he had read it, which made him wonder if upon re-reading it he hadn't missed the point again, which in turn made him wonder if one can ever know anything or if it's all, as they say, "a process," not a very satisfying conclusion if one doesn't know what one is "processing toward," in which case the *whole fancy notion* of process is just a sad excuse.

For what? Adam wanted to ask, but now he was in The Wizard's office: two large picture windows with the shades drawn halfway; dim but not gloomy. A mess of files and piles of books and papers and binders and more files. "Sit down," he told Adam. "Put your feet up, as they say."

Luckily, he sat up high enough so that the piles of books and papers on his desk didn't make much of a difference.

"Now, what I can I do for you?"

"Well, we were going to have lunch..."

"Oh yes. Well then, should we go?"

Adam had the impression that The Wizard would have made the same offer if a vagrant had been sitting across from him.

They started across campus toward the village, The Wizard's body veering slightly from side to side, so that every few steps Adam would get nudged. Adam liked the nudging, as though it didn't matter because they'd known each other for years. The Wizard crossed Le Conte carelessly as one might cross an empty alleyway and pointed up the street to a family-owned

Greek restaurant because, "What is the point in paying twenty dollars for lunch at some fancy eatery when people who carry old-country recipes with them for generations make the best food in the village." Into the tiny café they stepped.

No sooner had they entered than they were seated by the owner. Super-courteously, with one big hand flopped on top of the other on the table, The Wizard ordered for the two of them, "the positively fabulous lamb burger."

"The bread must be crusty on the outside and holey on the inside; the only way to soak the juices up without getting soggy." He now recalled the best burger he'd ever had, made by an old Armenian refugee in a Cambridge deli. "He'd chop parsley and onion and toss in a handful of lamb, I believe, a pinch of two or three spices, a drop or two of sweat, and work it all together with his hands and then slap it flat on a grease-glazed grill and drop an old red brick on top." The Wizard didn't understand at the time, oh, this must've been fifty-two, three, his first years as a grad student at Harvard, the brilliance of the brick: it ricocheted the spitting juices back into the burger. The food came. Adam went at it.

"Isn't this magnificent," he said.

Adam agreed that it was, and identified cumin as one of the ingredients.

"Suhmer is cumin," The Wizard sung. "Yes, you may be right. You're a very bright boy. How about the sweet tartness? Can you taste it. What is it? Vinegar? Balsamic Vinegar?"

"I think you're right there. I think they squirt a little balsamic into the mix. Americans use Worcestershire the same way."

"Americans. You're right, they do. You're a bright boy, indeed."

"I was raised on this kind of food."

He dabbed at his face with the napkin and then kind of tossed it back on the table. Adam has been distracted by hamburger juice beaded in The Wizard's goatee, so he was relieved The Wizard had finally gotten to it.

"When making a burger, one can't fret about spit on the griddle, or you meddle with the spirit of the operation," he said.

It occurred to Adam that at one time The Wizard must have been just like him, someone who gussied his most precious thoughts up. He seemed to be thinking aloud when he spoke, as though he couldn't help himself or didn't care to.

"Anyway," he said, "would you like desert? Go ahead, have some. You're young, after all."

"No thank you."

"Go ahead," he said.

Adam picked up the menu.

"Thanks, but..."

"You must. I insist."

"Okay. The tiramisu looks pretty good."

The Wizard flagged the waiter down.

"It's an old country custom," he said. "The first 'no thanks' means that you are acknowledging the gift, the second recognizes the sacrifice being made on your behalf. In cultures where food is short, a family member, probably, will be left hungry when a guest is served."

The Wizard had been educating the owner, who, with a hand on the table, had been waiting.

"The third no, of course, means no."

"Can I get you anything, sir?"

"Oh yes. The young man would like a tiramisu."

OVER THE NEXT COUPLE OF MONTHS, The Wizard filled Adam in on the details of his life. He was born in Missouri, on a farm inherited by his mother, whom The Wizard described as a "Bavarian peasant girl." His father, "congenitally unfit" for farm work, was professionally "I do not know quite what, an autodidact of sorts, I suppose," who whiled away his days in the attic of the house studying philosophy and theology. So the mother ended up running the farm, along with a full-time hand, a big black man named Albert. The Wizard was the baby of the family, the third of three boys, and they were all obliged to pitch in, picking peaches, milking cows, pruning, whatever was needed, both before and after school.

"The turning point in this bucolic life of ours," The Wizard told Adam, "came for me at the age of nine when I rather stupidly leaped from a barn loft onto a bed of hay and gravely wrenched my back." The injury left him a "good-for-nothing" so far as farm work went. Enslaved by a back-brace, which he was forced to wear until he was twenty years old, The Wizard became "almost by default, an inward-turning person," an avid reader of books and a patient student of how things were done and why. For instance, how the black cook, Mrs. De Grape, kept a large pan in the back of the oven into which she'd put a whole rabbit, stale vegetables, potatoes, and a handful of herbs, and at low heat allow it to cook for a day or two, making a wonderful, fragrant stew. "Some of life's tastiest concoctions come of things left to cook at low heat for days."

Near the end of the harvest season, a strong wind would come and shake the few remaining peaches from their branches, and these were used for pies. "What is left for waste makes the sweetest of fillings."

He told Adam about the honey bread Mrs. De Grape made from stale pieces of bread. She'd throw them into a blue lard barrel, and when the barrel was full she'd add milk, eggs, sugar, preserved fruit—raisins, persimmons, and dates—add cinnamon and nutmeg, scrape it all out, and shape it into loaves. The Wizard said he could still smell it baking, could still see how, in the morning, the farmhands would slice off hefty pieces of honey bread and with a cup of coffee sit down to eat at the small kitchen table with morning light blanketing the room. A certain amount of honey bread would always go stale, and one day The Wizard saw Mrs. De Grape take that leftover bread and drop it into the blue lard barrel to start another batch; it was then that The Wizard learned that each batch starts from the last; he was struck by the "almost metaphysical implications," that is, "That each cake would be present in the next cake; and that one could follow back the cake one was eating to the cake before it, and the cake before that, until one reached the very first cake ever baked by Mrs. De Grape."

He was drafted during the war, serving as a message decoder on the Pacific front. His cohorts were the best minds

America had to offer. "Intellectual Aces," he called them. They worked side by side, poring over letters and scraps of paper they'd been handed or retrieved themselves off the bodies of the dead, sometimes picking through blood and urine and shit ("the bowels, I discovered, discharge at the point of death") to get to them. During one such operation, The Wizard and a few of his fellow decoders were captured by irregulars in the Burmese Army, who extorted money from the US in exchange for their release.

Just before he'd gone to war, The Wizard had married a longtime family friend. His cellmate, who was from a prominent New England family, was also married, with two children. To get through the days, they showed each other pictures and shared stories—and whatever slop was passed to them through the cage. For warmth, emotional as well as physical, The Wizard and this American slept close. "It was in a prison in Burma, believing each day would be my last, that I discovered that I was gay," he told Adam.

No sooner was he released from the Burmese prison than his jeep was hit by mortar fire while careering toward the fallout from a firefight. The shrapnel ripped into his upper stomach.

They sewed him up and explained that he would never be the same; his lower esophagus was hanging on by a thread.

The Wizard soon discovered what this meant: food would refuse to go down, and sometimes when it did go down it would bubble up and charge right up through his throat. Back home, Purple Heart in hand, he quietly divorced his wife and watched himself turn to skin and bones, his digestive system no more serviceable than a backed-up sewer line. He reached out to the Veterans' Administration Hospital, where a surgeon told him about an experimental implant that was designed to do more or less what the esophagus was designed to do. The procedure was risky, but without any other option, he agreed. Of the little more than 100 persons who'd had "the valve" installed, only a handful survived longer than a year.

The Wizard was one of them, but it was hardly smooth sailing once it was "cobbled" in. If he wasn't careful what he ate, the valve would "act up," and he'd have to excuse himself to throw up in the nearest toilet. He took it easy at home, but when dining out, he usually said to hell with it and went for the kind of spicy, rich foods that drove the valve mad: any number of Mexican dishes at El Cholos', fried chicken and waffles at Roscoe's, *osso bucco* at Columbia Bar and Grill, or a brick-thick pastrami at Canter's, whatever, he would go for them even if he knew his chances of keeping them down were 50-50 even on a good night. "Excuse me," The Wizard would tell Adam in the middle of a heavenly meal, "the valve refuses to cooperate." For The Wizard it amounted to nothing less than a double blow, a *defaite complete,* if it spoiled Adam's meal too, so Adam had learned to eat right through the valve's "moods."

Adam would call him out of nowhere for a mid-day movie, museum exhibition, play, or poetry reading, and follow up with an early dinner and discuss what they'd seen or heard, taking it apart and reassembling it like two boys tinkering in an alleyway with a contraption they'd discovered. Adam kept his friendship with The Wizard a secret from our parents, but it soon became impossible to keep them out of the loop, so he played to their old-world sentiments: he'd met an elderly man who was becoming the grandfather he never had. Perhaps they pictured them sitting on a park bench together quietly chatting or feeding squirrels, but it was nothing like that, except maybe that Adam was the squirrel The Wizard was feeding.

When Adam left The Wizard, driving back down the hill toward mid-Wilshire, he felt that in a matter of just two or three hours something had transpired inside him, like his brain had gone from seeing in one dimension to two, then three, and four. The feeling was intoxicating, almost addictive; He refused to ask, "What the hell does The Wizard see in me?" because answering that question, even wrongly, might break the spell. He kept the friendship a secret, but he also wanted to keep the secret of it secret from himself. Still, weeks would pass before he'd call his friend again, his awkward genius pal. He'd abandon him for the fast-talking, wisecracking characters around the block who promised him the moon and delivered him nothing.

And then, a year into his friendship, a year weaving into his life and out, he put the strength of their friendship to a test.

Out of nowhere he'd gotten a call from a girl named Heidi, a Jamaican sound editor he'd slept with two or three times a year and half before. He'd almost forgotten about her, but now she was on the line explaining that she'd recently gotten tested for AIDS, and that she had tested positive.

"Why are you even calling me. We slept together, I don't know, a year and half ago."

"Oh," she said, "I could swear it was last March."

"No, it wasn't."

"They said I should call everyone I slept with over the last year."

Adam quickly sifted through his memory to nail it down. To the best of his recollection it had been a little under *two* years.

She said, "I feel so bad now. I'm really sorry about that. I'm just so worried that I infected other people."

"No problem. I'm sorry for you."

"Yeah," she said. "I don't even know how I got it. Please don't tell anyone."

"I'm worried about you. Hey, if you need anything, let me know."

The Armenian paranoid gene kicked right in. Not half an hour after he'd hung up with her he made an appointment to get tested and stripped in front of the mirror, looking for any lesion, any fucking blemish that might signal that weird skin disease that AIDS patients got. He wondered if a certain mole, which he'd had since birth, had changed shape and hue. His breathing was more hectic than usual, a slight wheezing that was detectable if he listened obsessively and closely enough. Why were his sheets so wrinkled? Was he sweating in his sleep? Profusely sweating? Within the month, the cool playboy on the prowl was now quivering like a field mouse in a Duarte "Testing Clinic." They drew three vials and told him they'd call with the results in two weeks, and for two weeks his mouth felt packed with clay.

The death he'd certainly contracted was his just deserts for thinking the poisonous sin out there could be absorbed into his system as harmlessly as a mosquito bite. He saw himself sitting down to explain to our parents that he had AIDS, AIDS,

AIDS—whenever he closed his eyes, it pulsed-blinked in his head like some seedy red-light district.

"When do you find out?" I asked him.

"Two weeks, they said. Why does it take so long?"

"I have no idea. I wouldn't worry about it. Like you said, it was a year and a half ago."

"I'm not so sure anymore. It might've been like a year."

"Next week it'll be last month."

"I can't remember."

"You know how you let your brain get the better of you."

"I don't know why I've always been like this. I don't like being this way. I want to change."

"Maybe you just need a change of *scene*. How about getting away a few days in the desert, Joshua Tree?"

"Take a notebook with you and write it out of your system," I told him. "Sometimes, it's the only thing that helps me, writing it out."

"Why would I write when I can just think it? What's the big difference?"

"You sound like a Neanderthal. Why would you think it when you can drink it away!"

"Tried that."

Adam decided to take some time on the desert to clear his head. He barreled beyond San Bernardino and the gently weaving hills and then swept down into the glittering repose of the desert floor, where the sublimely disorienting power of that space and light almost instantly began its steadying work on him.

For two days he hiked up the trails and climbed those outlandish stone monuments, like stacked pavers milled by the gods, the wind and sun, healing-dazzling on his skin. He felt small, perfectly so, a fleck of quartz, a millisecond in geology's colossally long timeline, under whose magnifying power man, blind to himself as an ant, came into focus. At night, in his little pup tent, he wrote down his thoughts, just as I had prescribed. The vast pulsing field of stars coaxed his mind back from the dark place his anxiety had sent it, where serious questions, beyond the far-fetched possibility of AIDS, drifted into sight. His life, he concluded, had become an orgiastic clutter. He'd thought it would organize itself, or that like some fractal there was a hidden symmetry in all the chaos. That if he just ran fast enough that order and worldly success would catch up with him. He had been trading needles (metaphorically), and trading sex (literally), for the sake of finding a home because at the root of his being he felt an outcast. He had made himself believe that "M" and Nick would provide him a kind of home base, and that from that home base he'd feed and supply not only himself but also our marooned parents. But there was no home base outside of one's self. He needed to find his "own center;" sleep with fewer women; meditate. Drink *way* less. See The Wizard more often. Maybe do Tai Chi.

After three days in Joshua Tree, he felt "a new man," scrubbed clean, buffed almost to a burnish. That explained his near ebullience as he left the desert, and an hour and half later climbed to the Forest Lawn crest, just beyond Pomona. There it was, spread out in front of him. The Angelic Land—its mishmash of hills (e.g. Holmby and Mission and Grenada) and villages (Baldwin) and squares (Chesterfield and Windsor) and heights (Angeleno and mounts (Washington) and lakes (Balboa) and parks (Expo and Echo) and woods (Holly and West and Oak) and the countless micro-cities that ramified from the "center" like the kill radius from a nuclear blast, all of it resolved into a vast and glittering physical abstraction.

Humans had constructed a reality down below that was spectacular, perhaps even spectral; home to millions but mysteriously more than home to them, because even when they left the city, its ethereal reach would abide. Becky, whom he'd dated for three months, one day packed her bags for Ojai to "recover" and never came back. Joe, who played a mean trumpet but couldn't get enough work, returned to central Washington where his family farmed apples; and of course there was the suicidal girl from Michigan, the one who'd had "psychological problems for a long time," the one whose friend had claimed, "Nobody is to blame." The city could do without any of them, and sometimes, it seemed, without anyone at all. Maybe our parents were right; in a city like Los Angeles, maybe one needed a real home, in his case, alongside a *clean* (the word no longer just figurative)

Armenian girl. Maybe just going to Bodhi Tree couldn't solve it.

Two day after he returned home, he discovered that he didn't have AIDS. Though he'd come within an inch of concluding as much himself, he also felt God had given him the scare. Mom had been collecting the names of a potential wife for years. Within no time he found himself ushered by one or the other parent into their tidy cigarette-smoke-clouded living rooms, where his "date" and the balance of the family—grandparents included—was waiting for him on big, floral design, claw foot couches.

Coffee? Please, take; any number of nuts, dried fruit, and sugar cookies on cheap crystal serving dishes. While the girl he'd come whistling for sat to the side mute as an urn, Adam was forced to confess that he did not belong to their political parties or fraternal organizations, and he hadn't bothered to pick up the Daily Azbarez in years, so how could he possibly know that Russian nationalist gangs were terrorizing Armenian day laborers in Moscow? He had been listening to Nirvana and Violent Femmes and Nine Inch Nails and getting acquainted with early Dylan, and he hadn't heard of the Armenian singers traveling through town or the newest Glendale clubs, and the winners of the Armenian Olympics were as remote to his consciousness as the winners of the Special Olympics.

After four or five dates, he had second thoughts about "this clean Armenian girl thing," and the guilt he'd felt for disconnecting from his tribe. Why should he feel guilt? Every Armenian he knew, even the ones born in America, were doing it, becoming-American, in a different but no less head-over-heels way. What else explained their flaming orange hairdos and transmission-challenged Mercedes and Byzantine purses and rings big as pork-knuckles, if not a desire to become red-blooded Americans by surrounding themselves with European symbols of style and sophistication?

He might've said he was drowning in their shallows, if he weren't daily mixing with a crowd globally famous for its shallowness in the place where the shallow-making industry was found.

In any case, just because Mom had a dozen or so girls waiting in the wings did not mean they were waiting for the likes of him. The manager of an *odar* (non-Armenian) bar who wore tennis shoes, beat-up jeans, a backward-turned cap, and an array of t-shirts printed at a Melrose studio wasn't even on their radar.

He would give it one more try. Sophia was a natural beauty, somewhat shy, and surely a virgin. Her family were dissidents from Iran, and her father, a one-time concert pianist now working as a taxi-driver, seemed to have put all his unusable talent to use securing his daughter's future. At a coffee shop on Beverly she told him about her dreams of traveling to Paris and London, and how she was on her way to visit relatives in Buenos Aires when her father panicked at the last minute and virtually pulled her off the plane. This she conveyed matter-of-factly, without a trace of anger or sadness, as if fate had intervened. Adam was used to young women bucking authority—not only their distant fathers, but also any stand-ins—and now he was faced with the opposite. He could almost feel her father's eyes perched on his shoulders as they walked together out the door. He began to feel self conscious about even holding this girl's hand.

One evening he took her to the movies, after which they sat in front of her parents' house for half an hour talking. Quietly he twined her fingers between his own, and in a flash he saw a life together: a tidy Glendale home, families in the backyard making shish kebob and drinking Armenian cognac, the song of our native tongue in the air. He went for a kiss, her lips, far from pulling back (what he definitely expected) gripped his with ravishing intensity. Under his hands her body was red hot as glass and ready to blow into shape. In Armenian weddings the bride and groom are made to touch foreheads for minutes on end to signify "oneness," and at just that second he felt as though they were already soldered together.

It scared "the living shit out of him." He didn't want to be soldered to anyone, and definitely not after the first kiss. He stopped calling her, and shamefully stopped returning her calls. Even though Adam had shied away from Armenian girls in the past, he had also assumed they'd be there for the winning when he was ready. What he did not see coming was this: his Odyssey, true to the original, had permanently changed him. The Him that was supposed to be there for them was gone.

Within two months of his desert experience Adam had fallen from his high place of illumination and was staring down to the bottom of a well. It made him queasy. When Nick shambled in bleary-eyed one morning and start bragging of an after-hours private party that included three girls, three bottles of rare agaves tequila in a penthouse big as a gym off Sunset, Adam felt nausea creep up his throat. When one of his lovely regulars walked into the bar with the finest, most delicately drawn lips now swollen to the bursting point by some Beverly Hills surgeon, he couldn't help but want to puncture those lips like a boil. At certain points in the evening the chatter and clinking and crooning in the bar collected like living misery in his chest, and he'd run into the office to hide.

He'd rushed headlong into the dancing light of the Magic Lantern and had burned his ridiculous self to a cinder, betraying himself, his past, and our parents; but more than anyone, Grandma. Rather than safeguarding the love and sweetness she had given him, a kind of body armor that she'd spent years forging, he felt that he had thrashed it beyond recognition.

Grandma's sweetness had all but leached away; he could no longer taste it. In fact he could no longer taste anything anymore, and the only person he felt who was left to turn to was The Wizard, whom he'd known for less than a year.

That was why he found himself knocking timidly at The Wizard's front door one afternoon, actually one knock short of turning back, when The Wizard opened it and said, "Come in, Come in," his suddenly worried look confirming the mess Adam had made of himself.

The Wizard offered him something to eat or drink, and Adam told him he didn't have the appetite, that he'd come over because he wasn't "feeling well."

"I see," The Wizard said, and asked if he'd like to lie down in one of the spare bedrooms downstairs. He wanted to desperately, but another part of him was afraid of being alone. The Wizard seemed to have read his mind, because he said, "I'll be right here reading, as usual. You go on downstairs, I'll come and see how you're doing in a bit."

He made his way down the stairs and into the small room

and collapsed on the bed with a thousand pounds of sand on his chest, sinking deeper and deeper into whatever it was he'd sunk into.

When finally The Wizard came and sat on the edge of that spare bed—which would soon become Adam's bed—and asked what was wrong, he hated himself too much to say. But what choice did he have? He had to say something, so he did say, "I've failed at everything. Everything I touch turns to shit. I feel like an orphan, a fraction, a lost part. It would have been better if I had never been born."

"Hmm," The Wizard said. "Well then, know that you can stay here until the rest of you shows up. Don't worry about a thing. You're safe here."

Adam stayed in that room for nearly a week, an excruciating week, before finally stumbling out The Wizard's front door and into a psychiatrist's office. He found himself in a small white room with two chairs, and a man with a white lab coat, Dr. Hartstein. He was a smallish man with doll-like hands who wore spectacles, a tie, and black shoes. In a jumbled, mumbled way Adam conveyed to him that as far back as he could remember life had felt like a roller coaster, alternately exhilarating and terrorizing. He told him now how there were days on end when he didn't even need sleep, that's how shot-full of energy Adam was, and there were other times when he could barely drag himself from bed. Since he was ten years old, he told Hartstein, he'd been obsessed with death, sometimes picturing dozens of times a day ways he might die. Oddly, there was something else he could no longer avoid: he had failed to calculate the consequences of his actions, not because he was stupid, but because something in him was determined to fly directly in the face of these consequences, as though to contest them, which in many cases was no less suicidal than contesting the law of gravity. To escape, he wanted either to die, or to change so drastically that when he finally arrived at the end of the journey he knew he had to make, he would no longer recognize himself.

Hartstein took very efficient notes, "working up" Adam's case. When he'd finished working it up, he finally piped up: Adam was not a depressive, but a manic-depressive; *bi-polar affective disorder* was the name he gave it (The Wizard preferred manic-depressive, so the two of them stayed with that).

On one hand, Adam had known for years that he would someday be sitting in front of this man, telling him exactly what he was telling him, and that in an even deeper way he'd known all along that what he'd experienced for over fifteen years was not normal, only normal for him, and that Hartstein's diagnosis was perfectly sound. On the other hand, he thought, *You must be mad to tell me I am mad.*

And then Hartstein told Adam he was going to prescribe lithium.

"Lithium is an element; I learned about it in the ninth grade. I don't want to take it."

"It's the right drug for you."

"It's a metal. I don't want that stuff."

Where and when he'd arrived to such a hard-nosed opinion about lithium he could not say, but there it was, coming out of him as though he'd spent years deploring it.

"I think it will help."

"How long do you want me to take it?"

"Let's see how it works for you."

"But how long?"

"Probably the rest of your life."

"I don't want to be taking some metal for the next sixty years!"

They went back and forth this way until finally Hartstein prescribed something else, a distant cousin of lithium but not lithium itself. Numb, Adam drove back to The Wizard's house and told him what the shrink had prescribed. That was when The Wizard told Adam that he too believed him to be mad.

"I always knew it," The Wizard said. "I always sensed you were one of the boys."

"The Boys," he called them, an impressive yet mortally damaged fraternity. There was Van Gogh, of course, and his cohort Gauguin, and Fitzgerald, Hemingway, Eliot, Pound; there was Thomas Wolfe and Virginia Woolf, nearly all the romantic poets, with the exception, perhaps, of Wordsworth. Rothko, Gorky, Pollock, and countless unnamed others. The

Wizard was an expert at sniffing out a fraternity member from biographical data—extravagant and dangerous behavior, drinking to the point of no return, gambling to the point of bankruptcy, or mindless womanizing.

They had tried, he told Adam, to put him on lithium as well, but he too had refused it. "But look for yourself," he said, and took from a bookcase a *Physician's Desk Reference*, a thick manual that told Adam everything he could ever want to know (and much more) about every drug currently prescribe-able in the vast American arsenal of prescribe-able drugs. That manual and its description, to the most minute and harrowing detail, of the drug to which he was about to commit his physiology, confirmed the terrible reality of his illness like no doctor's diagnosis ever could. He put the prescription in a drawer and went back to bed.

Eventually he took the drug, but he didn't take it for long because the very week he began to feel better he showed it the door. The minute he began to *feel* better he assumed that he *was* better, and that the madness had passed like a cold. The maddening effect of suddenly, *and without medical supervision*, uncoupling his physiology from the drugs, was far worse than the madness itself. In trying to describe what it felt like he was reduced to wild metaphors: a jar of worms churning, or a rat gnawing from the inside of your chest out.

Hartstein told him to keep a JOURNAL, which he did keep with rare discipline, pouring into it not only how he felt when under the influence of each of the drugs, but also what he felt and maybe why he felt it, from the past hour to as far back as he could remember. Over the course of a year and a half, he stupidly started and stopped his medication four times. He would quit, only to find himself begging for an appointment again. Naturally, he was the bane of his psychiatrist, who wasn't trained merely to help Adam "over the hump," especially when he'd determined that Adam's hump was as large as Ararat.

On Adam's last visit, "Hartstein, Holstein, Hatestein, or whatever the fuck his name is" (this was how Adam had come to concatenate it) entered the room and said, "Well, well," like a pipe-smoking Oxford don, and opposite Adam took an orange chair so unrelentingly ugly that Adam had found himself beating back the urge to kick it over for the half-hour he'd been waiting.

"That is a very ugly chair. Thank you for covering it," were Adam's first words.

The shrink jotted something down and proceeded to ask him all the properly obvious questions: why had he stopped taking the medicine? (Because I felt better); had he been drinking? (Yes, extravagantly); for how long did he take them before quitting (I forget); had he, Hartstein, not advised against dropping the medicine (Again, what was the point if I felt better?). After each answer Hartstein scribbled away on his note pad, barely bothering to make eye contact.

Adam told me a little later that he had no excuse, "But fuck if I was going to give the bastard the satisfaction of my feeling ashamed." After completing his "evaluation," half an hour or so of it, he told Adam that he needed to be on lithium. Of course Adam wouldn't take it. Lithium was *"out of the question,"* just like the last three times Hartstein had prescribed it. End of discussion. The psychiatrist stood up abruptly from his ugly chair and marched out of the room. Days later Adam got a letter from him on his official letterhead: he summarized in calm detail Adam's psychological history, his own diagnosis, the lengths to which he'd gone to treat "it," and his regret for Adam's insolence. He suggested LITHIUM once again, and signed his name.

After over a year battling his demons, including *Hearststein*, the arch demon, a virtual Lucifer, finally his chances for a medical cure were finished. Adam had backed himself into a corner with nowhere to turn. He'd kept me abreast of his troubles, but because he didn't want to worry me he also kept the details to a minimum. Or maybe he didn't want to hear me out, once again. Not a month went by when I wasn't pressing him to make changes to his life. It wasn't only the bar, and Nick's betrayal, it was the whole lot of LA posers, glad-handing and slapping together deals and making promises that never panned out—he had to get away from all of them. I bought into the fact that he was a victim, of mania *and* depression, but I also couldn't help feeling that he was loading bullets into the pistol that his neural chemistry held to his head.

In the car with Dad, on the way to Auntie's home to deliver the news that her husband had been killed, Adam had felt more alone than he'd ever before felt in his life; crushed, but also strangely opened up to an entirely new (if terrible) reality that had sent a mountain of doubt and cynicism cascading through his system. Still, Dad's behavior, Uncle's death, and the scorched world he passed were nothing new to the world. Eventually that reality would have gotten titrated into his system. But this was different, a symptom, it seemed, of a new and terrible dispensation: lying in bed one late evening after closing up the bar, he remembered staring into the darkness and feeling it precisely, like a speck, an inconsequentiality, a mote of dust drifting in an indifferent and endless stream of incandescence.

Two days later he called in "sick." The Wizard was out with what he called "My Gay Group." He didn't like the gay scene—too cliquish and swishy for his taste—but once a week he'd meet up with gay friends in Hollywood just to keep his finger on the pulse. It was getting on 10:00 p.m. when Adam took a bottle of tequila to the patio, not even bothering with a glass. He'd gone from hitting a series of dead ends to feeling very nearly constructed of them. He'd gone from gnawing and scratching to gnawing and scratching at himself until there was nothing to scratch and gnaw at. He wanted to pull his life out of himself the way one might pull a slide from a slide projector's carousel. One minute he would be in full color on a screen, and the next minute the screen would go white. It was that whiteness he dearly, almost romantically wanted.

He finished the pint of tequila in less than an hour and went to the kitchen and grabbed a knife and sat with his back to the dishwasher. The cool, smooth slope of the knife-edge felt good against his flesh. Really good; damn near like a healing wand. He slid it across his arms and throat and chest, toying with himself, as if he were some Easter Ham that he was ready to score. Finally, he made a quick slash against his left wrist and watched the blood come. The pain was breathtaking, but just as breathtaking was the blood, the way it bloomed, like a stand of hibiscus flowers blooming out of him at some time-lapsed speed, over and over again. It didn't feel anything like he thought it would feel. How long did it take? The flower kept blooming and bursting, and now he saw it make way and spread and cut a remarkably exquisite pattern on the white linoleum floor. He almost forgot why he was there, or even whose blood it was. In any case, he delayed long enough that The Wizard had finally come home. The kitchen was right off the front foyer.

"What in the world are you doing!" His panicked voice was very nearly a remonstrance.

"I was trying to kill myself," Adam whispered.

"Lord! Are you crazy? What madness!" He pulled a per-colator coffee machine cord from out of a drawer and cinched it around Adam's arm. Adam watched him go through the motions. "What a mess you've made!" Adam's nose seconded the claim: the sudden smell of blood, rich, rusty, repulsively sweet. The Wizard needed to get Adam to a hospital, but a kind of belligerent downward driving exhaustion kept "the boy" glued to the floor. Somehow he packed Adam into the car and drove him down to Kaiser on Sunset. They stitched him up, and after a seventy-two-hour "suicide watch," they released Adam into The Wizard's care.

At the hospital, Adam couldn't stop ruminating on the shockingly detached way he'd watched the life flow out of him. Now, at home, he made The Wizard vow to keep things secret. The Wizard made Adam vow in return that he'd never try that again, or else he would tell Mom and Dad.

The Wizard told Adam that he'd held off advising him on how to treat his madness because he felt that what he'd dis-covered was good for *him*, but not necessarily good for Adam. "But you've left me no choice," he said. Adam thought his solu-tion would be some mixed cocktail of philosophy and meds, and maybe music and art. But The Wizard told him that after trying this and that—but like Adam, never lithium—he'd finally decided that the only answer, let's call it medicine, that worked for him was to *endure*.

He had come to this conclusion, he told Adam, after the death of his lover and friend. They lived hundreds of miles apart, The Wizard down South, his lover, who was also a professor, up North. But they would spend weekends and holidays and summers together. He was a remarkable man. "The finest and most refined character, but also, like you and me," he explained, "*one of the boys.*" The relationship lasted for ten years, the truest and deepest love he'd ever known. "He called me one evening very late—jarring me from sleep—and told me I had to come see him immediately. He'd been in bad shape for a month, so his desperate call was not a complete surprise, and it was three days before my deadline for submitting grades. I told him I would hop on the first plane out of Los Angeles right after I'd submitted grades, but that it was simply impossible for me to leave just then. Why impossible, you ask? You see, there is often a hyper-responsible cant to those afflicted with the disease, a supercharged, nearly moral imperative to do one's duty in the face of whatever it is—the mania speaking. This determination to stay the course rather than open my eyes to what he'd clearly put in front of me is why I say 'impossible.' What I mean is, 'impossible for someone like me.' I told him to call me every five minutes, if necessary. The very next day he killed himself. Of course I ask myself, 'What if you had dropped everything right then and there,' a question I will never be able to answer because it assumes me to have been someone other than who I was at the time. Nonetheless, I did ask the question—indeed, tormenting myself to the point of paralysis with it. The most difficult thing is to accept that the course of one's life is the only possible course life could have taken; if we were other than who we were, it would have turned out differently, but we are who we are, so everything turns out exactly as it should, even if it shouldn't. This is the most difficult thing to accept; fate is fair, too fair. It coolly steps aside, allowing life to run its own terribly inevitable course. I couldn't accept this at the time. I couldn't even see it in these terms for many years."

During his twenties and thirties, The Wizard had bouts of depression that required psychiatric intervention. He'd undergone analysis and taken this medicine and that medicine, which kept the depression within a certain manageable range of expression. But at the age thirty-seven, he told Adam, it struck him like a 9.0 magnitude quake. It was during this deepest, most terrible bout of depression, in the wake of his lover's death, that he decided that quietly enduring was the only answer.

Endure. It sounded harsh and teeth-gritting, if not, frankly, Cro-Magnon. But the more Adam queried him on what he meant, the more he came to understand that in practice, *Endure* was more like accepting with lowered head one's fate, the entire organic complex of the way your brain was set up. The question is not "'Who am I?,' a rather ridiculous, impossible to answer, and ultimately vain question, but 'What am I?' or better, 'Of what am I composed?'"

The composition, he told Adam, is incontrovertible. "Scriabin can be played a hundred different ways, but the notes themselves do not change; the Moonlight Sonata can be played angrily, scornfully, contemplatively, or romantically, but in the end you are still left playing the Moonlight Sonata—even if, in the end, it is played in such a way that nobody recognizes it for the Moonlight Sonata." He told Adam, "The only thing under my control was the way I played these notes, the dynamics I brought to them."

And then he said, "I dare not lie at this point, my boy: If you are anything like me, it will take a lifetime of practice to bring the score under any truly satisfying degree of control." He advised, "You might try quieting down. Start there. Simply quieting down the composition a bit."

There was no composition; there was only a riot of notes, an excruciating sound-torrent, a noise bomb that kept detonating in Adam's head. In practice, quieting down the composition meant nothing to Adam. But The Wizard meant something to him that not even Mom or Dad or I meant to him. The feeling was wrapped up in the improbable, even preposterous nature of their blessed friendship: the fact that he was a gay Jewish English professor and Adam was a straight Christian bar owner, that Adam was young and he was old. The fact that from the heart of this preposterousness the two of them had found each other in a city where such friendships were supposed to be impossible to find, much less nurture. Look at how The Wizard peeked over his book, or into Adam's room: "How are you doing, my boy?" See the rich, spicy catastrophic-for-the-valve foods he toted in from Trader Joe's, asking "Can I make you something to eat?" Adam had never even taken into account the exertion required for The Wizard to play the flotilla to his roiling seas. An invisible hand had brought Adam and The Wizard together. And look how he'd slapped it away. Even if he felt he didn't owe it to himself, even if he felt he hadn't a self to owe anything to, he owed it to The Wizard to try to Endure, for The Wizard's sake, for all our sakes.

He'd gone to work, hardly missing a day, but even while he was throwing together schedules and handing out checks and calming down bartenders, he'd learned to foster another way of playing his composition. It had happened very slowly, only after months of terrible struggle. He'd quietly learned to take the waves and elongate them a bit, to let them swell and roll up to the beach rather than smash against it. Slowly but surely, as they say, he'd found that the ocean no longer frightened him; in fact, it felt friendly, even familiar. He couldn't have gotten there if he'd not moved into The Wizard's. The Wizard had saved his life. That's why he called him The Wizard.

. . .

He could hear The Wizard respectfully tip-toeing up the stairs right behind his headboard. The clock read 10:00 a.m. He'd been sleeping for a good eleven hours. He was alert, but not quite ready to get up, so he lay there quietly. The TV's appeal, its magnetic draw on his nervous system, reduced to filings, was magically gone. He could just hear Gould playing upstairs, Gould humming and The Wizard humming along with him. He got out of bed and headed for the shower. Likely, nobody had showered in there since he'd last showered in there: in the shower were a yellowing bottle of Neutrogena shampoo, a rusty razor blade, and a stale bar of soap.

The Wizard took short showers; ever since his days in the Army, he couldn't stand in a shower in good conscience for more than five minutes, thinking a buddy needed to get in there after him, and a buddy after that. There was therefore always an abundance, a superabundance of hot water, so Adam showered forever, letting the water slowly burn the fogginess away. To his "I feel like an outcast," The Wizard has simply answered, "I'll just be sitting here, reading as usual." He'd said it then, and he'd said it again. His dear friend could sense that he was not well. He'd chosen his words carefully.

"Good morning, Lad. Slept well, I hope."

"Very well. With a little help from some of your friends."

"Took some medicine did you?"

"That stuff for your gall-bladder attacks."

"I really do need to get it removed."

Adam poured a cup of coffee. The air outside seemed to have cleared some.

"Grab some breakfast. I can see you didn't eat much last night. You left your bowl full of soup on the table, by the way."

"I couldn't get it down. Sorry about that."

"I suppose I should be used to your slobbishness."

"Like you're Mister Clean."

"Please." He ran his fingers through his thick, wavy air, and said, "That chap is bald."

Adam took the minestrone to the kitchen and made two slices of buttered toast, which he topped with The Wizard's favorite marmalade, King Kelley. It was unthinkable that he'd come out and say "I Love You" to The Wizard; a declaration like that would get a "Please, leave the schmaltz at the door" in return.

The Wizard looked up from the book he was reading and his eyes caught Adam's.

"What are you staring at, for goodness' sake? Are you still angry with me?"

"No," Adam replied.

"Good."

"I am little confused."

"Would it make any difference if I told you I was boiling with anxiety the way you were last night?"

"You weren't even on simmer."

He chuckled. "My boy, what's happening is nothing new to the world."

"It's about registering reality as it is. It's about what's happening now."

"You're beginning to sound like Ram Dass."

"Ram who?"

"Maybe I've already registered it. A hundred times over. The fact is, what's happening down below is run-of-the-mill stuff, rather humdrum."

"Then register it again, for all those people whose lives are being turned upside down. I bet you'd feel differently if the fire had made its way up here. Wouldn't be so run-of-the-mill then."

"It didn't this time, but it may the next. I'll save those tears for then. You wouldn't want me to squander the few I have.'

"Do you know how many buildings have gone up in smoke, already?"

"No idea."

"They're estimating nearly 6,000. Hundreds of millions of dollars' worth of destruction."

"Imagine all the plumbing and roofing and cement people who will be put to work by all this rebuilding."

"When it's all said and done, they're saying it could be the most destructive riot in US history."

"It's a stigma we will soon cast aside, I assure you. They will work their way out of the rubble. They always do. Even birds manage to rebuild their nests after a fire. Sometimes the new nest is grander than the one they lost."

"And sometimes people say is 'enough is enough,' and simply give up."

"Yes they do. Still, I make you a wager; in twenty years, this city will bustle more than either of us can imagine."

He now told The Wizard that he'd been out there, in the middle of it. He told him about what he'd seen, the old Korean shop owner scuttling up the aisle and pleading for mercy when he saw Adam all masked-up like a bandit.

He said, "I wanted to help him, but for the rest of his life he'll remember me for wanting to kill him."

"The longer view shows us that he'll forget. It's the human way, it's the *Amuhricun* way."

"I thought your people coined the slogan, 'Never Forget.'"

"We also coined 'let the dead bury the dead,' thanks to a certain Rabbi. But Jews *are* living proof that people move on. So are your people. The truth of it should be as evident to you as it is to me."

"Last night I had this feeling, this thought, that maybe now and then we need a flood to wash the crap away. But we were the Turks' crap and you were the Germans'; and then we were the Lebanese's crap; now America's—so where does that leave my mom and dad, and I suppose, me?"

"Yes, one person's deluge is another person's push-broom."

"I wouldn't go that far with it."

"You're young, why should you? On the other hand, it may have nothing to do with age. Even when I was young I didn't long entertain a romantic image of the world the way you do. I felt from early on that I needed to stay nimble, to be different things to different people, in different situations. I was Jewish, and I was gay, and then I was an invalid, and then a manic-depressive. My entire life I had to live with all this, and then learn to hide it from view. I had to break myself into bits, so that the whole was indecipherable. It's a more common practice than you think. We divide ourselves in order to conquer what we can. "

"But all that gave you an inside view. You've told me that as well."

"I was conscious that I was deceiving people. And then I was conscious that others deceive themselves without being conscious of it."

"Do you feel there is a part of us that does not deceive?"

"Something authentic at the heart of us…"

"Something like that."

"You know how I feel about that kind of thing. No, I'm sorry to say I don't think there is."

"I think there is. I think there is a kind of caretaker of the fragments. A charitable spirit that holds the whole in a kind of trust for us."

"And in heaven we will cash that trust in," The Wizard said, chuckling warmly.

"And in the meantime," Adam said, "we get to live in LA, as close to heaven as an earthly place ever was."

"A starry-eyed statement if I've ever heard one. What makes you so endearing, my boy, and at the same time, I'm sorry to say, so callow."

Callow. If anybody else had said it, Adam would've slung an arrow back, but The Wizard had said it, and so Adam nodded, and asked what The Wizard was reading.

"Nothing special," The Wizard replied. But he did have a question: he'd meant to ask Adam about it how many times before, but these days thoughts that seemed so urgent one moment passed through his brain like trifles the next. In any case, he had been reading the Russian Mandelstam's "long, largely forgettable essay, *Journey to Armenia*," and in the reading of it something had struck him, and since he had "*a real, live Armenian*" sitting in front of him, he wondered what Adam would make of it:

"Mandelstam was clearly enchanted with the Armenian people—as was Coleridge, by the way, who studied the Armenian language at an Armenian monastery on an island off of Venice."

"San Lazzaro, I think," Adam said.

"Very well might be. In any case, during the course of Mandelstam's peregrinations through Armenia—oh, it must've been in the 30s—he wrote that the Armenians were not a metaphysical people. I was quite struck by this observation. The Armenians surely were a religious people. What do you imagine Mandelstam meant when he went out of his way to make this point, that they aren't metaphysical?"

"I don't know," Adam said. "Maybe it's because we're stuck in the world at our feet. No maneouvering room for metaphysics. I mean, just look at our words. The word for *blood* in Armenian is *ayroon;* you can hear it running. The English word *water* evaporates in your mouth, but the Armenian word, *joor*—it's like burbling from a tap."

The Wizard smiled; he just loved this line of thinking, this way of speaking. It spurred Adam on. "The word *hatz,* like teeth grabbing it," Adam said, "is bread. And *gaht,* 'milk'; you can almost hear a child gulping it down.

He offered up half a dozen other words, for *onion and apple and heart and plow,* reveling in how each sounded, how sound they sounded next to their English equivalents, until he was laughing, from a kind of breakthrough, as though words themselves were the key to safeguaring the world, as though with them in hand the very things to which they pointed were beyond the reach of destruction.

The Wizard said, "You've hit upon quite a tonic, my boy. You always surprise me. I just knew you'd give me something to think about." With that, The Wizard went back to his book.

He had become a substitute for Grandma; he had taken up her role in Adam's life.

She would have come herself, except she knew that her time was running out, and that she wouldn't survive the trip. She loved to busy herself in the kitchen, and like all good cooks had the knack of juggling three or four things at once. But during the last few months in Lebanon she would sometimes lie down, leaving a bunch of celery half chopped on the counter. We were all too harried and turned in upon our own worries to pay attention, and because Grandma's *hahvahs* was so strong, we assumed her body, however old, was just as strong. One time she was lying on the couch, her hands politely folded on her chest, and Adam sensed, the way certain animals sense the earth quivering before it quakes, that something was wrong, and he tiptoed over to see.

"Grandma," he asked, his heart pausing for an answer. She opened an eye and smiled. "What, did you think your grandmother was dead?" She made him laugh, and his image of her, forever there, was fortified. After that, whenever he sensed that weakness he explained it away; he ignored it. We all did.

It was just as she wanted it, if not just as she had planned it. Her heart was failing, and she must've felt small tremors in there and known that if she let us know we would never pack up and leave; we would never get to America. Adam missed her *hahvahs*. Maybe because, more than anything else, just then, *hahvahs* seemed to be draining from the world. Or perhaps the spark had turned into a flame, and that flame had turned into an inferno, an inferno that answered to nothing but its own monstrous appetite. *Tertevadz*, torn to shreds. It is what we had done down there. And Adam had fled to The Wizard like a bird—*turchoon. Tur*—the "r" beating the way wings beat—*choon*—quick as a sneeze the bird shoots away. Onomatopoeia, they called it, and dusted their hands. *Hos Avazan muh gah* (here is the little

172

bird-bath), Grandma sang. *Mechuh turchoon yegav* (and into
it a little bird flew). One toe for each bird, and for each bird
that flew into the bath she raised a toe. Five birds on each foot.
Each a surprise when it arrived. She must've learned it from her
mother; she must have. Probably her mother sang it to her to
bring calm to her heart on their long walk through the desert;
maybe a thousand mothers sang it to their children on their five-
hundred-miles march.

"Are you up to a game of chess?" The Wizard asked him.

Adam didn't answer.

"Perhaps a little later," he said.

Finally, Adam came to: "Sorry."

"Chess?"

The board showed that he was in the middle of a game
against himself: "Don't you want to finish your game first?"

"Those two can play anytime they want."

"Let's give it a try."

"Well, then."

They came to the table and took their seats and put the
pieces in place, The Wizard white and Adam black.

The Wizard could beat him with his eyes closed. He could
see three to four moves ahead, while Adam began to stumble
after two; Adam would throw himself out there, trying for an
early kill, while The Wizard patiently worked to tear the earth
from beneath Adam's feet. He would always play like that, but
Adam wasn't playing like that that day. After the game had been
going on an hour, The Wizard was only ahead by three pawns
and a knight.

"Something has gotten into you," he said.

Adam said nothing, enjoying leaving him to guess what.

"Whatever it is, it won't ultimately work here, my boy."

"Just watch."

"The watching will have to wait. I need to use the john."

"Not the valve I hope."

"Oh no. Just a regular visit."

"Then be my guest."

"Be my guest."

Adam got up for a stretch and a can of Coke. When The Wizard returned, he asked who had taught him to play chess. When did he learn?

"My father taught me," The Wizard replied, "when I was just a kid, barely six years old or so."

Adam knew The Wizard's father had been what The Wizard called an "autodidact," and that in their farmhouse attic he'd put together an impressive floor-to-ceiling collection of books written in French and German and English, and also a few in Hebrew. He once told Adam how exotic the authors' names had been to his ears as a child: Aristophanes and Paracelsus (this sounded like the name of an instrument for measuring the temperature in Paris), Albertus Magnus (a gigantic magnet), Leibniz and Spinoza (a type of exotic weaving machine), and Maimonides (a disease that only mothers contracted).

Now, The Wizard explained, in the middle of this quiet attic room, just above yet worlds away from the hustle and bustle of farm life, The Wizard's father had also set up two chairs and table for chess. On Saturday afternoons they would play for several hours up there, his father trapping him from this direction and that direction. The sliding shadows the million dazzling particles of dust, the must of books, the smooth, finger-oiled wood. "These," The Wizard said, "were magical things and moments for me. The only time really, I had my father to myself."

His father taught chess to The Wizard patiently and well—not well enough that The Wizard could beat his father, but well enough that he twice brought him to a stalemate. He was an interesting man: he never allowed The Wizard to beat him, and he never gloated over winning. Indeed, there were times when The Wizard noticed a definite reluctance when he announced "checkmate."

"One of the only ways my father ever let me know he cared for me," The Wizard said, "was when I sensed this reluctance to checkmate. How I loved him for the quiet way in which he checkmated me. 'In the end, however, I will not let you beat me, because if I do, how will you know when you have actually beaten me?' It was a maxim he never crossed."

The Wizard explained that circumstance had failed his father. "A man whose energy and intellect dwarfed the primitive tools he had at hand, he was left alone to pound and grind away at becoming a philosopher, and when a person is left alone with such primitive tools, he inevitably leaves behind a terrible mess, hardly the work of genius that in his solitude he imagines. The most hapless works of philosophy are produced in just such solitary circumstances, with just such primitive tools."

When The Wizard's father died, his mother quite literally pitched his books out the attic window and set a great pile of them ablaze. She needed the room for sewing. The only papers she saved from oblivion were those penned by her husband, including a philosophical magnum opus he'd spent god-only-knows how many years writing. "I was afraid for the longest time to open that book to discover what I knew I would discover. That he had produced little more than rubbish, and once again spent god-only-knows how many years at it. *What a waste, a sad waste*, I thought at the time; Mother was right, he squandered his life up there in that attic."

When his mother died and the family farm was sold, The Wizard found his father's manuscript in a small leather suitcase beneath the very same table upon which they played chess. His brothers and sisters had no use for it, it goes without saying, so the suitcase and all it contained were orphaned to him.

It struck Adam that The Wizard had described the contents as "orphaned," and he now asked The Wizard if he still had the "orphans." The Wizard said they were somewhere downstairs, in the basement with all the other junk, and that if he had the patience to dig it up, Adam was more than welcome to read the book himself. He then said he'd only once barely glanced at it. It just pained him too much. That book stood for his father's stubbornness and vanity. "In the end," The Wizard said, "he was a rather ridiculous little man, my father."

The harsh opinion pointed to the cruel side of The Wizard. This cruelty had occasionally reared its head at Adam as well, and though he had learned to sidestep it, there were times when it came at him like a rocket and left him dazed. More than once, exhausted by Adam's imbecility, he'd wave away with a hand whatever mishmash Adam had floated into the conversation, or nail a "rubbish" sign on it, or warn Adam that, "you're not as clever as you think." It took all the ego strength at Adam's disposal to stand tall during these episodes.

Though The Wizard was cruel, he was also conscious of his cruelty and quick to nip it in the bud, at least with Adam. "Pay no mind to what I say; it is the mean streak in me." Adam accepted his "mean streak," not only because he apologized but also because there was no way to disconnect that meanness from his generosity. As with all great and generous minds, he'd reach a point where he could brook no more folly, and in one high-pressured gesture he'd flush it into the gutter. Over the years he'd flushed into the gutter dozens of friends, professors, and acquaintances at dinner parties and colloquiums, and though he'd learned to bite his tongue, there were moments when he simply lost himself in the moment and flushed. In a way Adam admired his cruelty; he admired the brutal tightness of his brain.

But The Wizard had balked at the cruelty of this statement, and wanted Adam to know it wasn't merely cruel: his harsh attitude toward his father, whom he barely knew beyond the square of that chess board, who puzzled him, but to whom he was nonetheless deeply devoted, had to do with the circumstances surrounding his death. His father did not like farm work and was not good at it, but one day he'd decided to fix the tire on a tractor. While he was jacking it up, the jack gave and the hub dropped on his lower leg. "It was a crushing injury and within two days gangrene had set in. The doctor came and immediately determined there was no way to stop it spreading short of amputation." His father wanted no part of it. "'I won't live that way! I won't live that way!' he told us."

Thinking he was too stunned to see straight, the family waited. But one day passed, then two, until his fever grew and the children began to panic. Still he wouldn't budge. The Wizard was anguished, and puzzled. He was only eight years old at the time, and at night he'd pore over the meaning of those words, "I won't live that way." One morning he woke with a revelation: when his father had said, "I won't live that way," he had meant,

"If I get the wooden leg, I will die!" Fever had clouded his understanding, and he'd gotten the doctor's advice backwards! He believed the wooden leg would kill him, literally. Everyone had misunderstood what his father was trying to say. Certain that he would save the day, he ran to his father's bedside to explain. The stench, he said, was dizzying; thick and foul; "The precise corpse-like smell that I'd grow to know well years later polluted the room."

The Wizard told himself he must endure, and without even a tissue to cover his mouth and nose came to his father's bedside and explained. His father, who had grown horribly weak, listened, and then suddenly rose from his fevered fatigue and bellowed, "Why is no one respecting my wishes?" The man was trembling, his eyes bulging: "Not even you, my youngest son! Not even you!"

"His ego wouldn't let the leg go," The Wizard said, "and in no time he was dead. I'm afraid my mother was happy to be rid of him. He and his books served no purpose. Indeed, they were a chain around the family's neck, and now she was free to use his small remittance, as they called it, to get things fixed that he might've fixed himself if he hadn't been so fruitlessly bound to his so-called intellectual pursuits. Within a year, she was seeing one of our farm hands, with whom, undoubtedly, she'd had a longstanding love affair. We knew him as Albert, a black man who lived in a small shack on the corner of the farm. Two or three nights a week we'd hear the door creak open and the sound of Albert's huge feet take the stairs. It was all terribly Victorian.

"All that being said, it was all dreadfully mundane, the entire fiasco boiling down to little more than the sad consequences of my father's mundane stubbornness and vanity—dare I say, a *Jewish* stubbornness and vanity." He reached for a tissue and dabbed a tear from beneath his glasses. "If I could live with the brace, he could live with a wooden leg. That was how I saw it. But he would rather have died than walk with a prosthetic.

"So here is the crux: the same stubbornness and vanity that led to his death was preceded by his mule-like work on that book. Why his death and that book were bound together in my mind. He had chosen his vanity and pride over his family, over me. He would rather leave me fatherless, surrounded by what-else-to-call-them-but-nitwits, than let that leg go. But as I grew older, I began slowly to unpack his decision. I no longer took it personally. He had used the leg as a vehicle for revenge, I concluded. He seemed to be telling mother, 'You want to be rid of me anyhow, so I will rid myself of you before you have the chance. You think you can hide your disrespect of me, but my death will announce your loathing loud and clear. I will widow you (a second time), and leave you tormented.' The logic was as flawless as it was diabolical, and yet, how feebly it all worked out. My mother was never tormented; she saw quite clearly that his stubbornness and vanity, and nothing she had done, much less thought, had led to his death. Still, before I knew it, my father's logic got into my system without me even knowing it had, such was its flawlessness. It was running in my blood, so to speak, and one never questions the wholesomeness of one's blood until one becomes gravely ill. You see, an assumption will carry you to a conclusion, and no matter how ghastly that conclusion is, we cannot say that it doesn't have its own logical, diabolical motor force. Quite unconsciously, because he had used that leg as a vehicle for revenge against my my mother, I decided, with the very same inviolable logic, to seek my revenge by ignoring his magnum opus.

"It was easy enough to ignore, beginning with: how could a book titled *Magnum Opus* possibly *be* a magnum opus? No serious thinker, indeed, only a delusional thinker, one toiling away in an attic for twenty years, could possibly hold such a ridiculously self-congratulating opinion of something he'd written that no one had ever read. Magnum Opus! 'A great work.' Not only, as it turned out, did he mean 'A Great Work,' but when I ventured to look at it for the first, and as it turned out, the only time—oh, I must've been in my mid-twenties doing my doctoral work—as I flipped through it it became painfully obvious that what he meant by 'Magnum Opus' was *Magnum Opus* quite literally, *The* Great Work! You see, the term originated in the alchemists' workshops. It wasn't only the title of the work that led me to this conclusion: the man had divided the work into four sections: *nigrido, albido, citrinitis,* and *rubedo,* the

178

four stages alchemists believe matter must pass through before
it resolves into the one, essential, unifying element. Even to this
day, I'm ashamed to speak of it. Can you imagine, then, what
this discovery meant at the time when I was sharpening my
sword and filling my quiver as a doctoral student at Harvard?
What irony, that I was studying to be a medievalist, already
well versed in alchemical thinking and its place in the history of
thought. But that place was 500 years before in Paris or Oxford,
not in Missouri, year 1920. The whole immigrant self-flattery
depressed me to no end. He imagined that within him lay a
learned man, ready to turn the world inside out; a simple mer-
chant's son from Bialystock. He married my mother, you know,
because he believed she was a woman of means, a landowner—
which she was. He believed that her landed wealth—along
with a small remittance his father had left him—might give
him the chance to write and think his alchemical thoughts in
luxury. Having arrived in America just two years earlier, what
he understood a landowner to be was not the same as what she
understood. He saw a man, himself, with a walking stick stroll-
ing down a wide pebble path, deep in thought, with blossoming
oleanders on either side. Green pastures where horses maybe
grazed in the distance. What she saw was trees that needed to
be planted and pruned and ditches that needed to be dug and
bark diseases that needed to be healed. Even after he saw that by
"landowners," what she meant was ten acres of fruit trees with
a two-story clapboard home, he still saw Chenonceaux with its
paths and benches and swans.

"The reason she married him was understandable. Her
first husband was gathering supplies in Kansas City and was
run over by one of those newfangled contraptions called a car.
Widowed, with three children, what were her options?

"In any case, that is the back-story, as they call it. I knew
he believed it was a work of great import, his Magnum Opus.
Sometimes I would find him staring at a wall or at the ceiling,
deep in thought, and I'd ask him what are you thinking Father,
and he'd say, 'I am looking at the beauty of an idea I had last evening. Someday someone will discover how beautiful my ideas are.'

"Wherever I went and however I turned, that book would

orient me away from my father; indeed, I always knew where I stood vis-à-vis my father by where I stood in relation to that book, at first ignoring it, and later, loathing it. And now, presumably, having all but forgotten about it.

"But I would be dishonest If I didn't also admit that I felt guilt; and herein lies the last turn of the screw: I felt guilty because I had all the tools that he did not have, and who knows what he would have accomplished if he'd had those same tools. I was also stubborn and vain, but my stubbornness and vanity were exercised in an environment rich in tools. Moreover, my father was the very one, indeed the only one, who saw that I needed that environment. Before he died, he called his brother, my uncle Anson, who lived in Kansas City, out to the farm, and charged him with my education. This is how I ended up at the one of the most important boarding schools in all of Europe. This is where my so-called high-class education began. I was sent off while my siblings were left behind. He was self-taught, and I was blessed with some of the best teachers around. He had no one to talk to, and I had the best minds around to pick from. And it was all due to him."

"That's some story," Adam said.

"Let's leave the game to finish later," The Wizard said. "You've quite tired me out. I haven't spoken of these things in years."

"Thanks for taking me into your confidence."

"It's not that I was hiding anything. It's just that after a while one grows comfortable living alone with these things."

"I think I know what you mean."

"I dare say you do."

Adam wanted to get back to the book: where was it?

"Around here somewhere," The Wizard said, "in one of those big leather trunks in the basement. You're welcome to dig it up, but please don't make a mess of things like you always do. I don't know. Perhaps you'll find something of value in it. It's possible that if I were to read it now I'd see it in a different light."

When The Wizard had moved to California he'd taken the contents of a storage unit and stuffed them into trunks and had them shipped to Los Angeles, where he deposited it all in the "basement," that one reached by way of an exterior staircase. Inside the only source of light was a single bulb that revealed a small room, at the back of which was the very hillside that had been carved away to make room for the house.

There were several filing cabinets stuffed with lectures, drafts, and correspondences, dozens of cardboard boxes filled with odd books, and six leather trunks stacked into a single sagging column.

In the second trunk from the bottom Adam found the *Magnum Opus*. Adam imagined from its name, and from the god-only-knew how long its author had worked on it, that it would be a massive tome, but it barely exceeded 300 pages. The Wizard's father had taken great care binding it in what looked to be very old leather, much older than even fifty years, well worn, chocolate brown, and creased like an old ranchero's face. Dust had gathered on it, but with a single swipe of Adam's sleeve the cover shined.

Adam took the book upstairs and showed it to The Wizard. "Yes, that's it," he said, but he refused to take it in his hands. Adam felt The Wizard's feelings for that book boiling up again (after so many years, still?) and so he quietly went downstairs, got into bed, and started to read.

The manuscript was typed in old-fashioned Helvetica on what was now watermarked and yellowish onionskin paper. Adam started in out of curiosity, but also with a quiet hope. The Wizard's story about his father saddened Adam because he knew firsthand that between father and son there is nothing so sweet as high regard and nothing so crushing as contempt. Adam simply could not accept that The Wizard should live the rest of his life and go to the grave with so contemptuous an image of his father. There was no way Adam could possibly heal that big a wound, but perhaps a less emotionally loaded reading of the *Magnum Opus* would reveal something of value, something worthy of redemption, that might cast The Wizard's father in a slightly more favorable light for The Wizard.

That early hope was quickly dimmed. It was easy to see why The Wizard cringed at his father's magnum opus, what little of it he perused. He might've described it as a lowbrow notion of what highbrow sounded like. The self-conscious linguistic styles, from the medieval to the modern, the motley mix of religion and philosophy and alchemy, all meant to lend the book *gravitas*, was sure to be a turn off to The Wizard, who reveled in the rich efficiency of slang, street talk, broadsides and pamphleteering (what he named "illiterature"). Adam guessed that The Wizard's father had drawn his inspiration from Oswald Spengler's long-winded *Decline of the West* (which he had once dipped into *until it made him dizzy*), and its puffed up know-it-all tone.

In spite of the tone, Adam stayed with it through nearly 100 pages in which The Wizard's father regurgitated the history of philosophy from the time of Aquinas to the end of the nineteenth century to make way for what he believed was his singular contribution. To a more sophisticated reader, all this prefacing for the main would have been insufferable; but Adam was not *that* sophisticated a reader, and he kept at it because much of it was in fact new and even useful, however Victorian the writing. He read thirty or forty pages at a stretch, The Wizard's father leading him through the labyrinths of Albertus Magnus (whom he'd never even heard of) and Spinoza and Leibniz until he reached the second section, what The Wizard's father called "Albido," which translates from the Latin as "whitening," and connotes a process of purification.

In summoning Darwin, Freud, and Nietzsche—the god-fathers of the modern age—all at once the tone changed, and The Wizard's father seemed to be writing in the heat of the moment. One after the other he showed how these great thinkers had rolled over and crushed the old religious idols. Before the century's end it would be impossible for an educated man to orient himself using God, the Bible, or any of its expositors and apologists. The fundamental tenet of the modern age was that reason and reason alone possessed the power to unify persons with different points of view; a sure-footed guide, it would lead humans away from the perils of superstition and religion to a clear sighted view of the horizon. But instead all the old liberators had only and perhaps inadvertently led man to the edge of an abyss. It was called 'the primordial soup'; 'the unconscious'; Nietzsche called it 'will to power.' This triumvirate had not only undermined the Western world's faith in God, but had also undermined the Western world's faith in REASON as a guiding principle. Humans were too much at the mercy of impulses beyond reason's reach, and perhaps even the reach of consciousness; there was no lasso strong enough to rein the irrational in.

By the beginning of the twentieth century, The Wizard's father wrote, the question was not only what will we do without God, but also what will we do with ourselves? Man, defined up until then as the "rational animal," was now dying a slow and painful death. Reason did not have what its many high-minded advocates believed it had to get to the root: and what was left was a solipsism, a fractional, blunted way of seeing that wasn't so much interested in knowledge, or getting to the bottom of things, as in coloring, shaping the world to meet its darkly prejudicial needs. As Nietzsche put it in his Genealogy of Morals, "there is only perspective seeing, only a perspective knowing."

Thinking, far from discovering the world as it stood, was usually guilty of the opposite: Nietszche wrote, "The essential feature of our thought is fitting new material into old schema… making equal what is new. The entire apparatus of knowing is an apparatus for abstraction and simplification, directed not at knowledge but at taking possession of things." We do not will to know, we will to possess reality, and in possessing it, we shrink it into deformity. We believed we had been fighting to win reality over to our side for a least two hundred years, when in fact we, the West, had turned reality into a little beggar over there in the corner ensnared by our wills. If the entire apparatus of knowing is devised toward this end, it is only one short step to the question: "Is there a reality out there at all?" Is there anything beyond subjectivity, in other words?

Nihilism—the attitude that there is no God, no absolute point of reference, nothing beyond appearance and subjectivity, that man is left to fend for himself in a universe that remains aloof—was born as the only possible response, and all the isms that sprung from that era were a convulsive reaction to it. Into nihilism's vacuum rushed communism, egotism, what The Wizard's father called "scientism," and Nationalism.

Across the Atlantic an alternative to all these isms was in

the making. But before turning there, to America, that is, The Wizard's father returned to Nietzsche in his section "Citrinitis," or "Yellowing," for how to philosophically navigate around nihilism's dire straits. The Wizard's father took great pains, drawing both from Nietzsche's books and from his biographical details to explain how the philosopher had actually opened the gateway of hope. Nietzsche had observed that the West foundered from the death of God, and in his absence those who wanted to take his place fought tooth and nail. But rather than substitute one crown for another, Nietzsche looked for a radically different form of triumph. The Wizard's father discovered Nietzsche's discovery right alongside the passage cited above. Nietzsche said, "The more affects we allow to speak about one thing, the more eyes, different eyes, we can use to observe things the more complete will our concept of this thing, our 'objectivity' be."

Although Nietzsche poses this as a remedy to nihilism, what he had actually done was to expose the nature of reality per se, or as The Wizard's father called it, THE REAL. Western culture is not plagued by the absence of meaning leading to the abyss of Nihilisms, but by the proliferation of meanings to the point of madness and disintegration. Reality was not cut off at the head; it had turned into a hydra with an endless number of eyes. We had wanted to line perspectives up behind a single point of view (The Wizard's father spent ten pages covering the evolution of "optics"; the bottom line, the West hadn't moved a single iota from the time of Newton), but in the end it was too big for any single line of sight to contain.

All of this, for The Wizard's father, was not an abstract discussion. Faced with the proliferation of perspectives to the blistering point, a society with an infinitely more radical structure than any previous known needed to be born. THE REAL was unfolding in real time and a real place, America, passing a kind of threshold of no return during the Civil War, with Lincoln a central figure, even a kind of Messiah. He had presided over the battle for six years, and in that six years his own soul had been torn nearly asunder. At near stake of course were the abolition of slavery and the integrity of the Union, but at far stake, something Lincoln could only just barely register, was the integrity of THE REAL itself. As he stood near the finish line of the bloody battle, he observed that both North and South were convinced that God was on their side. In great contests of the past, The Wizard's father wrote, the victors had roundly claimed the crown, but in this one, Lincoln demurred: "Both read the same Bible, and pray to the same God; and each invokes His aid against the other," Lincoln told the thousands crowded in to receive his second inaugural address. At the very moment when Lincoln might have claimed victory, he reflected instead on the suffering paradox that America had become. The Civil War had laid bare the furthest limits of the old way of being and the old way of seeing. Because Lincoln was ultimately charged with embracing all sides, he was pushed into a new conception of reality, although at the time he could only indistinctly perceive its contours.

Its full shape would only take form after Lincoln's war. The Civil War brought THE REAL to blush, but it was during the great immigrations that followed in the late 19th and 20th centuries that THE REAL began to ripen. For the first time in human history, countless immigrants and their countless facets onto reality gathered in a single indivisible realm. Anglo-Saxons did not form America; they merely established the conditions for its birth; far from being outsiders, the foreigners who made there way here brought American into fruition. And America's destiny would be the destiny of reality itself, according to The Wizard's father.

The Princes of the earth, who had fought tooth and nail over the same piece of turf, were now in a position to recognize not only that the fight was unwinnable, but also that that turf wasn't turf at all. It was something else entirely. It was what The Wizard's father called THE PLETHORA, and here is how he described its appearance:

"...let us imagine, heretofore, an orb. From a distance, its surface appearance is smooth, glassy and luminous, but as we near upon it we notice it possesses a less homogeneous structure, resembling more a great faceted jewel lit from within. Closer still we see that these facets are windows, so many it would require an eternity to count."

This, The Wizard's father wrote, was what the mystic poet William Blake, standing at the edge of the Atlantic, prophetically saw rising from the crucible of the American Revolutionary War:

"And so the princes fade from earth, scarce seen by souls of men," Blake had written. "But tho' obscured, this is the form of the Angelic Land."

And that form mirrors precisely the very mind of God. On the surface this image contradicts the stern and myopic Old Testament God, to be sure, but a deeper reading of the Bible, according to The Wizard's Father, reveals that from the start God was actually a reluctant overlord: The giver of the laws and commandments, indeed of every structure and stricture, would have preferred the Jews simply trust and enjoy him, but out of a need to be like the surrounding tribes they begged for the security of not only the laws, but also of a King, a Temple, an Army. In exile from Eden, *trembling man petitions God for a compass to orient his skiff in creation's tossing seas.*

The coming into fruition of The Real, then, is also a kind of return to the original plan. It is what God had wanted all along. It is also a return to innocence. Plato claimed that when we are born humans forfeit knowledge of The Real, and that only slowly, by earnest and rigorous interrogation, might we retrieve what we had lost at birth. But for The Wizard's father, it was precisely the opposite: We come into the world with perfect comprehension of The Real. The infant's mind sees the Plethora completely, in all its shifting splendor, but slowly it is coaxed away from this splendor and made to fix its gaze and make static only the smallest fraction; its vision is diminished; in The Wizard's father's very words, *Its luxury dimmed.* From the perspective of an infant it is preposterous to ask whose point of view is right and whose point of view is wrong. This becomes a human necessity when we take possession of reality in exchange for enjoying it, when we *covet the divining rods instead of drinking from the jumping springs.*

The Wizard's father titled the fourth and last part of the book "Rubedo," or in English, "Reddening," the last phase of the alchemical process. In this part he shows how in every era, a few people are born whose luxury is not dimmed, who drink from those "jumping springs." They are capable of moving with uncanny facility from one window to the next, mystics via startling flashes and sudden jumps, and artists by working out of what they see in sensuous form. Shakespeare, as one might guess, worked according to The Wizard's father at the highest possible level: he is able to see through an infinite number of articulated windows onto a world of endless play. Hamlet is not stuck in grayness, made insane by ambiguity, The Wizard's father writes; he is overcome by sight of the Plethora, the maddening magnitude of The Real.

Hamlets, those that indulge countless points of view, are the artist's dangerous joy. But a time will come when the danger will fade away, and only the joy will remain. That will happen when there is a whole society of healthy Hamlets. Then The Grand Sum, the Mind of God itself, an endlessly faceted jewel on a hill will glow to be the light for the world. America, in its very evolving and radical structure, was on the threshold of becoming just that.

It took Adam three days to move through the book, three days during which he hardly came out of his room. Outside, the National Guard had "restored order." The convulsions had stopped; volunteers from every walk of life were cleaning up; people were holding candlelight vigils instead of lobbing bombs. He read and then wrote about what he'd read, all very quietly, cut off from everything, almost by willful dereliction, away from all of it.

Adam took breaks upstairs, and when The Wizard asked how Adam was doing, what he was doing downstairs, Adam only told him, "I'm making my way through your father's book." He did not ask what Adam had found—and Adam never told him. Although he was happy to work a problem out with anyone who conversed in good faith, if Adam rushed forward with an idea claiming it was marvelous, or stunning, or unique, short of proving it, The Wizard would finish him off. "Your Dad's Magnum Opus is pretty amazing!" Or "The man was a serious thinker with a fantastic imagination." None of that would work. Adam could just see The Wizard rolling his eyes at the first mention of "God." He saw himself dishing up his father's book, and saw The Wizard staring at it like half-cooked chicken. "Perhaps you should put it back in the oven," he might say, if his mood was generous.

The truth of the matter was, Adam frankly didn't know if what he was reading amounted to a philosophical revolution, plagiarism, or perhaps a more evolved or decorated version of some other philosopher's thoughts. Adam didn't know enough to say, but what he could say, and could even write about, was this: Since arriving, he'd felt one of three things about his place in America: either that it was made for him, or that it would reject him precisely like a body rejects a foreign object, or that it would take time for him to settle in. But if The Wizard's father was correct, Adam had been thinking about it the wrong way. For him, people who'd come from abroad were necessary; America wasn't just making room for him, it was waiting for him, it was waiting for Adam and others just like him to come so that it could come to completion!

The Wizard's father's idea was "beautiful, generous-hearted, but also one that seemed impossible to square with what was happening out there," Adam wrote. In three days he had witnessed up close and personal the willful destruction of the city. It wasn't even us versus them; in the end it was us against us; it was even me against me.

In any case, The Wizard's father was hardly a ridiculous little man. What he'd written had filled Adam, at least, with a sense of wonder, even a degree of peace. Yes, it was like the fruit had come to fruition and was putrefying on the tree, but who was to say that the tree was dead, that it wouldn't bloom again. But before Adam went to The Wizard with any of this, he vowed to himself to read the *Magnum Opus* at least two more times. He'd really do his homework before taking the test, so to speak. Adam packed the *Magnum Opus* in his duffel bag, along with his journal, clothes and toiletries, and headed upstairs. The Wizard had switched from Bach to Schubert's *Trout Quintet,* a piece of music they both loved. Adam listened to it for a spell and then told The Wizard that he was going outside for an *old-fashioned walk* before heading home. The Wizard nodded his head kindly and put a hand up in acknowledgement. Yes, Adam would digest his father's book as best he could, and then he'd feed it to The Wizard. Like a bird. *Turchoon.*

Adam made his way down the craggy road until he reached the bottom, a place called Deep Dell. Except for the stars, a billion billion flashing shards, the darkness there was nearly absolute, tucked so far away that not even the city lights could reach it. Adam heard something, an engine growling, but he ignored it and headed back up. It was inconceivable that someone would be driving down that narrow go-nowhere road so late at night.

Then he saw it, like two lanterns weaving through the trees and high brush. It turned the bend and was right on top of him; by this point the effulgence must've been nearly blinding.

PART 4

THE KURD AND I were set to meet at 8:00 for a drink, but I
had arrived an hour earlier so that I could be alone for a spell.
Two days after we'd all first met at the opening night of The
Kurd's one-man show in Santa Monica, my brother had bought
a 7 x 7 oil of a grand piano perched on the lip of a crumbling
cliff and hung it on the only wall in his apartment large enough
to hang it. I would later learn that it was the only painting Ari,
the owner, had sold from that show, and six months later he'd
closed the gallery and returned to Israel.

Within a month, my brother and The Kurd had become
friends. "The Kurd is heading to New York," he told me "I want
you to hang out with him." I put aside my work and we toured a
dozen galleries, and over dinner I introduced him to my middle-
eastern friends, artists all.

The Kurd could be whimsical, wildly funny, generous, and
even solicitous of others' points of view; but at regular intervals
he'd pull up in a tractor-trailer brimming with cynicism, chau-
vinism, and fatalism, laughing at the top his chest as he dumped
it at your feet. When The Kurd left, one of my friends, Ana, a
Palestinian poet-in-exile, summed it up for all of us: "Where did
he come from?"

That was the last I saw of The Kurd before Adam's funeral.
Afterwards, he came to the *hokee jash*, the meal for the soul,
as we call it, at my parents'. One by one, friends and relatives
drifted home teary eyed, but The Kurd wasn't going anywhere.

Hunkered down in mourning, we sat on the patio, until at least 2:00 a.m. talking—or rather, I listened to him tell what he and my brother had been through during the riots, and both of us speculated until we were strung out with exhaustion about what had actually happened the night he died.

What we know is that by around midnight he had probably started back up the road from the bottom at Deep Dell. On one side was a steep hill, so steep the owners of the house above used an elevator to lift them from garage level to their front door. On the other side was a canyon that dropped just as steeply as the hill rose. Two hundred yards or so from The Wizard's home he was stopped in his tracks by an oncoming car. Two neighbors, both sleeping, were woken by the sound of scrabbling tires and the engine's ferocious roar. They both assumed it was robbers or arsonists cruising the hills. The first neighbor had lived in the hills for twenty years, and knew how the dips and curves and sheer walls made for a wild echo chamber, so that a chain saw that sounded like it was just next door might be coming from half a mile away. This neighbor went back to sleep. This was probably what my brother figured when he heard the engine as well. It was also true, The Wizard told me, that sound in that section of the hills could get lost just as easily as it could carry.

Sharon, the second neighbor, startled, got up from bed and looked out her window. She saw the chrome back fender of a late-model truck flash as it barreled past her house and wildly careened down the road that led to the bottom, what they called Deep Dell. She checked to make sure her doors were locked and called a friend, who told her to turn the TV on and crank the volume up.

That is probably when the truck came upon Adam. He climbed over a short fence into an empty lot, but it was terribly steep and chock full of boulders and gopher holes, and not ten yards down he twisted his ankle, the shock and pain stopping him in his tracks. That's when, with God only knows what resolve, he scrambled further down the slope.

The Wizard was nodding off to sleep when he looked over at the clock; it was 1:48. He had been waiting to hear the door open and close to make sure "the boy," as he called my brother, had gotten back in okay. He checked his room and went upstairs and called his name, and then he stepped outside to see if his car was still parked in front of the driveway; it was. Back inside, he called 911. The 911 operator told him to call the non-emergency number and file a "missing persons" report. In the meantime, she advised him to stay in his home. The Wizard called the neighbor, Sharon, who was still watching TV with the sound on full blast and only heard the phone ring because she was holding it, and asked if she would accompany him to search for my brother. The Wizard was in no position to tramp down a raggedy road in the pitch dark. Sharon herself felt it was "too dangerous," and told The Wizard she'd call the neighbor below her, Tim, who was an avid hiker and see if he might go with them. Tim was up; he'd been woken by gunshots.

Those three gathered in front of The Wizard's house around 2:15 a.m., Tim with a high-power lantern, and the others with standard flashlights. Tim had been deliberating whether to tell the others that he'd heard gunshots. He decided to keep that information to himself so as to not alarm "an elderly man." They walked to the bottom and then made left and walked another hundred yards down Deep Dell before turning back, their lights combing the road. On the way Tim suggested the other two search the hillside and he would probe the canyon below.

About fifty yards from the bottom of Deep Dell, Tim saw a body lying face down in the brush. Sharon ran uphill, back up to her house, to call 911 again. Tim carefully wended down the hill, The Wizard repeating where he stood, 'oh my god, poor boy.'"

My brother might've survived if he'd gotten to the hospital, but as it turned out he'd choked on his own blood from a bullet that pierced his left lung. When I pushed the detective assigned to the case, he said, "It was probably just a pot shot." As Adam hobbled with a sprained ankle down a hill, they'd just for the fun of it emptied a chamber on him. "I doubt they intended to kill him; but bullets have ways of finding their mark; sometimes they have minds of their own."

I was in the skies somewhere over Pennsylvania, I later determined, when my brother took that bullet. The guilt of leaving my parents stranded, and my brother short-handed, and suddenly all of them reliving the horror of Beirut, had finally overtaken me. Los Angeles International had reopened, and so I hadn't any longer that excuse. Adam didn't want to put me out: "You just got off a plane a few days ago. Don't worry about us." I was able to book a flight departing at 9 p.m. from JFK, with a long layover in Denver.

It was just after 5 a.m. when I stepped into the terminal at LAX. I expected to take a taxi to my parents' apartment, and so I was surprised to find Hovig waiting for me at the gate, his eyes bloodshot, his quivering cheeks glistening with tears. My first thought was: while I was in route my father's shop had been set aflame. From the shock, he'd suffered a heart attack or stroke.

There are so few of us left, a friend of my mother's told me, that when a young one dies it is like a whole village burning down: Bitlis, Van, Erezoum. The funeral was almost a village itself; a thousand people, friends later estimated, had come. My mother and aunt hardly noticed; they were like stroke victims. I led them, one on each arm, to the front of the church. I knew the liturgy well, but enacted that afternoon over my brother's body and for the benefit of his soul, it felt like a half-dream.

The night before, at the viewing, I had put my arm around my father, and he reached over and took my hand in his. We sat together. My brother looked too handsome to be buried, I thought. He is too young to leave for good. A part of me wanted to shout out to him, "How dare you!"

"You are left now, the only one," Dad said. Because I had effectively abandoned them, a part of me expected something else—but what else was there?

By the time we reached the burial ground, a line of cars had trailed us for what seemed like twenty minutes. Beneath a canopy at Forest Lawn we gathered for the priest to consecrate my brother's body and deliver it to the care of his creator. He'd always loved the church; for him it was an authentic place of contemplation and refuge. If anyone was going to heaven, if there ever was a heaven, he was heading there, I thought. The family stayed until nothing was left but the workers and the box. The canopy came down and the skirt was undone and the coffin, naked on its supports, was lowered into the ground. Before any of us could stop him, my Dad had lowered himself into the ground as well. Everyone was now filled with hysterical grief. The two men working there, one on a backhoe the other with a shovel, ran up to pull him out of the hole. They had never seen anything like it. He'll never come out, I thought. Never.

I remember a day in Beirut, after my uncle's funeral, when my father led me, Adam, and Hovig to the front steps of our apartment building. Death is not the end, he said. To show us, he reached into his pocket, lifted out square of tissue paper and flicked a lighter beneath it. We watched it catch, a flame grow and the tissue blacken and curl up. Pointing to the rising smoke, "That is his spirit," he told us. "See it go to heaven. His body is gone but his spirit lives." End of story, he patted our heads. We returned inside, but I felt an empty space behind me, and when I looked back my brother was sweeping the ashes off the steps into a hand. He dropped them into a potted plant next to where we had sat, and put his arm around Hovig. His salvaging of those ashes was a small gesture, but one that captured his essential thoughtfulness, his peripheral-vision kindness.

I write this passage in memoriam, obviously, but also to express the following dark irony: the day after we'd all celebrated in word and song that singular attribute of his, we—that is me, my cousin, and the top tier of Hye (Armenian) Power—had gathered on the balcony of my parents' apartment to plan our brutal revenge—fuck the police.

Simply put, for us Adam was victim number one-and-a-half-million-and-one. It had only been a little more than a week since April 24, when we'd honored our martyrs. Sarkis, the putative leader of Hye Power, vowed to scour the streets for clues and squeeze whomever, however hard was necessary. If needed, he swore, he'd light up the city again. The usual interlocutors, the cool state-sponsored voices I heard in my head, the ones that urged us to make a reasonable distinction between his death in the Hollywood Hills and the genocide of our people, were wasting their breaths. Those paper-mâchés, those plodding bluesuits who had abandoned us in our time of need, needed to stay out the way; the new, virtually post-apocalyptic face of justice was Levon, Shant, Sarkis, and Bedros, these boiling-limbed fools, these sweaty Fresh-off-the-Boaters. Hovig, who'd never amounted to anything, embodied all the diabolic, heroic virtue that had kept Armenians, however few of us remained, from being reduced to dust and scattered to history.

By week's end, I found myself in the backseat of an '85 Lincoln Town Car, crammed with Hye Power, pistols at their sides. As we trolled the streets, again and again they seethed, "Kheyma gunenk!" ("We will make steak tartar out of him!") How good those two words tasted in Armenian, a dark ejaculation, a kind of exultation.

Next we were in the firebombed heart of South Central, where Sarkis claimed to have friends among the Crips. A car, sparkly metallic, chrome-rimmed, burbled in the parking lot of what had once been a block-long complex whose identity had been erased, and from which a thick bituminous smell still hung in the air.

No one got out, and there were no introductions, only an idling car full of blacks abreast an idling car full of Armenians, at some mind-twisting equilibrium. In the three years since he'd arrived, Sarkis knew more about what made the city tick than many who'd lived here for three generations. Sarkis made his case for their help in rooting out the mother-fuckers as calmly and capably as any businessman would make his case for funding from venture capitalists. "We just want the fuck who pulled the trigger. I don't want to ruin what we got going over that one punk. He's not worth it. We're serious about this. My boys won't play unless he pays." As we peeled out of there, I was sure they wouldn't want to jeopardize what-ever dark commerce was at stake.

Back at my parent's apartment we did punishing shots of vodka. The means were there, but now we needed to consider the ways: I liked best pulling him out of his rabbit hole and skinning him alive; I liked with spectacular relish dragging him hog-tied though the streets of Little Armenia before deposit-ing his excoriated body at the very bottom of Deep Dell, a note nailed into his forehead: AP.

"Just imagine," I told Sarkis, "what the cops are going to think when they see those letters carved into his fucking forehead: Associated Press?"

I was drunk on the thought for a week, then two, and still no word from Sarkis' black brothers. "Don't worry, don't worry, the name is coming." The more Sarkis protested our protest, the more I was convinced that there was nothing to worry about because the whole thing was a delusion; another example of our people's perennial mirage-making, our perennial sucking up to über forces that left us in the lurch. I was back staring at the trompe l'oeil they'd always been. I was back staring at myself. Is revenge always a detour from grief?

When Grandma died, Dad and I returned to Beirut to settle her meager estate—the contents of her apartment and a small savings account. Sitting in her tiny living room, everything was suddenly bolted in place. Everything that seemed disposable my Dad would reach out for, a sudden memory sparked, and want to keep. "Be careful with that," he'd tell me. "It's only a hand mirror, Dad." I was ready to tote home a few mementos, but I didn't share my father's unwillingness to let them go. For me her soul had already moved beyond these things, but I was only sixteen, too young to perceive their aura. Now, sitting in my brother's apartment, I felt to a numbing degree what my Dad had felt that day.

When the old die, what is left behind may amount to setpieces used to enact their daily rituals; but everything in a young person's life points to a tomorrow, a plan thwarted, a ritual less enacted than in the process of being born. CDs he was considering for setting a mood at the bar; a stack of books he'd hoped to get to; the recipe for a new cocktail sitting on his kitchen counter; even the post-it-note on his computer: "The world is full of enormous lights and mysteries, and man shuts them from himself with one small hand–Bal Shem Tov." They were all suddenly hovering in some purgatory. I couldn't possibly seal their fate; it was as though he hadn't died so much as gone missing.

So I did nothing, or rather I picked up where he left off. I inhabited his world, slept in his bed, and haunted his haunts. In

the morning I tramped two blocks to Holy Mud for breakfast.
I picked up cigarettes at Mel's along the way. There was a bookstore on Melrose he liked; I visited it twice a week. I listened
to those CDs, and friends, and neighbors, dropped by to listen
to them with me. It is a truism that when someone dear to you
dies, you are keen to conjure their memory; but also many mere
acquaintances pulled me aside to tell (in the black girl's case, it
amounted to a touching confession), of bump-ins and coversa-
tions they had with Adam before he was whisked away.

After forty days, and the *hokee hankeest* ceremony, returning home began to feel less a question of "when" than "if."
Alongside my desire to stay as close to him as possible, the
responsibility of "taking care" of my family had fallen squarely
on my shoulders.

Since I'd left Los Angeles, I'd let nearly all my contacts drop
away. When I did venture a trip out, twice a year or so, after
only a few days crisscrossing the city, I couldn't help but feel that
the vast majority of Los Angelenos lived as refugees, people in
exile who had arrived to a kind of encampment.

This was not only the case for its true refugees, who came
from every corner of the globe, but also for people born there:
the car you drove, the size of the house you lived in, the parties you were invited to, who you knew and who you didn't,
the quality of wine your drank or the purity of the coke you
snorted—these were the indices of your belonging.

With enough cash on hand, it was the only the place
where you could feel more at home after living there two months
than people who had lived there twenty years.

With that said, it wasn't the city itself; it was the suffocating influence of our family, the choking, depressing immigrant
mentality that kept me most at bay. I wanted to take Adam
with me, but he refused to leave—or rather, he didn't have what
it took to leave, I told myself. So twice a year I'd coax him to
New York, where we'd spend time together, among my friends,
going to museums, walking the Brooklyn Bridge, biking around
Central Park. After a week or two of what amounted to a kind of
cultural boot camp, I'd send him home buffed up.

I was sad seeing him leave, but if I'd paid more attention, I would've taken notice of my relief. One of us needed to be in LA to take care of our parents. Year after year I attributed his reluctance to move to weakness. He'd stayed behind because of his own lack of resolve. I was the brave one of the family, the artist forging a future; his goals were more modest, conservative; could there be any better proof than that he allowed himself to major in business at USC?

If I hadn't turned my back on the family, would he have had the liberty to turn his? A question I'd asked myself in passing before, it began to throb in my head. Was his desire to stay in LA genuine, or did it amount to a sacrifice he made for me? Had we, even more deeply, unconsciously, made a compact to that effect? I couldn't shake the thought, and I shared it with The Wizard one afternoon sitting across from him in my brother's chair.

It was near the end of an entire day we spent together. We talked as we took the dogs for a walk, had lunch at Norm's, and visited a couple of bookstores in Hollywood. He was a remarkably sophisticated man, highly cultured, a nuanced thinker, but also rough and tumble, just as my brother had described him to me a dozen times.

We were back at his house when I confessed, "I had this thought the other day. That my brother and I had unconsciously struck a deal. Someone had to be here for my parents, and so the deal was, I would go and he would stay. Now I wonder, what if Adam had gone and I had stayed? I ask, would he would have had a different life?"

The Wizard chuckled, and it wasn't the funny kind. Maybe I hadn't said it right, so I merely put it to him another way. "Yes, yes," he said, shooing it aside with a hand. "I heard you the first time just fine." He stroked the whippet's long arching back, and said, "What condescending nonsense."

I was taken aback; I tried to backtrack. He gently lifted the whippet off his lap and set it on its legs and excused himself, walked across the big room and disappeared down the stairs. I frankly had no idea he'd return. My brother had lived with that for years, apparently, undaunted. I had a picture in my mind of a puppy dog resting at his master's feet, but I was wrong—what a rude awakening. He returned in a short while with a backpack, Adam's backpack. "Please," he said "feel free to look me up when you're next in Los Angeles." He handed it to me, and showed me the door.

Driving home, I felt sick. Had I demolished one of the only human connections back to my brother? Why had a few carelessly chosen words offended The Wizard so deeply? I could see it, and I couldn't see it.

Back at his apartment, I unzipped his duffle back and poured the contents out on his bed: an old leather-bound book, reading glasses, a toothbrush, a pair of pants, a t-shirt. And in the side pocket, a simple-lined spiral notebook, the kind college kids use. I opened it to discover, written in Adam's rickety cursive, a daily log of the medications he had taken under Hartstein's supervision, along with detailed descriptions of his mental states and sleep patterns, and even a few dreams. Then, on page twenty-two, the writing turned a corner.

The balance of the book, about a hundred pages or so, was a personal journal full of observations, speculations, meditations, and conversations, on everything from philosophy to art to spirituality, penned over a two-year period up until the very night he died. He'd even hastily scribbled down a few thoughts on the riots.

I gobbled up his every word, his every thought—tough, kind, asinine, sublime—nearly as precious to me as his physical existence. It was like I'd stumbled from out of nowhere onto a bridge, a beautiful bridge back to him that I felt I could spend a lifetime crossing and re-crossing. And what he didn't say I filled in with what I knew. I ended his thoughts with my own. Almost from the first page, it was a conversation. But then the dialogue stopped: slipped between pages 103 and 104, I found a sheet of paper, folded twice, as though he intended to mail it: a suicide note, or maybe a draft.

About a hundred words long, its main purpose was to absolve us of responsibility for his decision, to preempt any feeling of guilt. "My place is no longer here," he wrote, "maybe it is somewhere else." As I read it, my heart was crushed bit by bit.

How could he have been suicidal without my having the slight-est clue? Why didn't he tell me? I could've helped him. I would have helped him! How did I let him slip so far away from me! You overplayed the older brother shtick! He might've come to you if you hadn't thrown your moralizing onto him. I wanted to bring him back and ask his forgiveness.

It felt like a second death. The death this time of what I believed we shared, the death of what I believed we'd built together. The reality that I'd abandoned him, my entire family, the first chance I could, now overwhelmed me.

My brother was thrilled to leave Lebanon, but I was sixteen years old, with friends I'd had since I was old enough to walk, and for me it was the worst possible time to go, to let go. I'd never lost hope that my crew would soon again be launching footballs into that beautiful Mediterranean blue, but once my parents had made the decision, I began making my own right alongside it. They had set us a sail, thinking we would stake a place in a new world while retaining all the old ways, but I had determined to journey into America so deeply that they would lose sight of me, or at least I'd lose sight of them, even if somewhere in the back of my mind I always intended to plot a route back.

Adam was just entering junior high school when I left for New York and Columbia University, where with a full scholar-ship in hand, I decided on a five year degree in Architecture.

I called back home every week the first semester, every month the second, and, using their ignorance to my advantage, I trumped up a dozen different "important" reasons for staying in New York during breaks. In any case, my parents were so proud of me ("They call it 'Full Ride'! Ivy League, Ivy League!"), they hardly protested. By the start of my junior year, Adam was the only person in my family who I regularly spoke to.

The second semester of that year I spent abroad in England, with twenty other students. From our base in London we'd tour cities and places of architectural significance, and one week, as we made our way through the West Midlands on our way to Scotland, we stopped for a half a day in Coventry, where we were told one of England's great Cathedrals was located.

I'd been to towering York, and Bath, and eerie Eli Cathedral, but even upon approach to Coventry, I felt I was nearing something cosmically different. The original sixteenth-century sandstone cathedral had been bombed by the Luftwaffe in WWII and reduced to vestiges. Rather than raze them, the architect, Basel Spence, decided to leave the ruins in state: apses and arches and bombed-out windows, like cobwebs spun in stone, and an impossibly preserved spire that still stood vigil over these skeletal remains. All this was physically joined at the hip, as it were, to the new cathedral, a structure in itself majestic, elegant and soaring.

Before the school year was over, I trekked back to Coventry three times on my own, trying to better fathom both the cathedral and my deep feelings about it, trying to understand what made the building, and my own heart, tick.

It would be too facile, perhaps, to say that that cathedral became a metaphor for my life, the presence or even absence of a bridge spanning Lebanon and America, but neither was there an honest way for me to avoid that metaphor.

Back in New York, the friends I'd collected, a kind of second family, understood what I was feeling all too well: a Palestinian poet, a Persian museum curator, an Iraqi composer, a Syrian stand-up comedian, and others, all of us exiles from historically rich cultures that were in tatters. We would meet three nights a week for kebobs, and hummus, and taboule, pounding our fists in outrage at the latest caricature of the Middle East. Every week we watched the cradle of civilization wheeled into the psych-ward. They showed our wars, internal strife, corrupt leaders and terrorists and jihadists and self-immolating pilgrims, but they never once let it be known that our birthplace was also the birthplace of agriculture, writing, and the fucking wheel!

Of course, the psych-ward was precisely where the current regimes of those lands belonged, and where each of us too belonged if we were ever stupid enough to venture back there to live, but still, from the outpost of America, we could salvage those great lands' historical image, all that lost richness buried under a 600-year pile of colonial shit, first the Turks, then the Brits, then the French, and now the Americans, by means of what we called "The Virtual Colonization." But who was there to hear? How were we to tell the world?

Architecture was the medium I was determined to use. But, as I was ginning up for my senior thesis, ironically, a single piece of architecture drove a wedge between me and my ambition. Across the street from my Newark apartment a beautiful, streamlined, modernist office complex, which had been built circa 1935, was getting razed to make room for a mini-mall. I decided rather than design a building, for my thesis, I'd film a building's demolition—from the sight of its body in states of evolving wreckage, to the dust that gathered over it like a lid, to its eerie graveyard stillness at dusk.

The other thesis students thought I'd cheated, but the professors praised the project for its originality. It was enough to set my artistic direction, if not obsession, in motion, and there was no shortage of subject matter. Before I knew it, I had a dozen leads on architectural gems on the verge of teardown in New York City alone. If at first I hoped to simply document their destruction, over the next few years I would film three shorts and one medium-length film that also showed the arrogance of the builders and how under a tide of greed they were washing history itself into the gutter.

Then, about a year ago, I got wind of a Master Plan in the making for a section of downtown Beirut, which was mostly left to waste after the war. I was able to attain the conceptual drawings from a childhood friend. I found what I suspected I'd find: the new design, covering several blocks, was a Beaux Arts whitewash. Using the most hackneyed architectural language, the very vernacular of the French colonial powers that had set the time bomb ticking, the designers were obliterating any memory of the past. It was Coventry Cathedral turned on its head, and of course, on a much larger and more consequential scale.

It occurred to me that that all my prior projects were stepping-stones to taking up this one. Still, it felt like a leap. Up until then I'd been documenting destruction, but now I'd be documenting an architectural urban plan whose materialization I was trying to preempt. Sasha gave me the last little push I needed: "You need to save the ruins from ruin!"

Within four months I'd drummed up a cracker-jack crew, secured a few thousand in funding, and set up interviews with the designers. By mid-April, we were on a plane headed for Beirut.

The last time I'd been there had been to help my dad with my grandmother's estate. The city was in a shambles, and I couldn't wait to leave, so raw was the destruction, but what surprised me now was how little I felt, like running a finger across a decades-old scar. The Beirut design team greeted us with demitasses of Turkish coffee and cookies and wide, warm embraces. Please, please, make yourself at home. In their airy studio a mile up from the beach we set up our cameras, and over a period of three days we did make ourselves at home. They explained in proud particulars their training, the genesis of their concept; the general thrust of the design, and then turned to the models themselves.

We studied them, and then I sat them down.

"Do you believe it is the architect's job to develop a language that takes into account the history of a place? By using the Beaux arts vernacular, aren't you repeating the very history and power relations that brought Beirut to its knees? Do you believe architects have a responsibility to account for the past, as violent as that past may be?"

But it is a universal language, they demurred, one that everyone recognizes. It stands for stability, perseverance; the language not only of the past, but of the future too. They hadn't gotten to it yet, but somewhere, along a certain path, they hoped to find room for a memorial.

As I waited for The Kurd, a few more customers took seats at the bar. I hadn't announced myself as Adam's brother, and none of the staff seemed to notice me, even though I'd seen them at his "Irish Wake" just about three weeks before when Nick opened up the bar to one and all. Sasha was my date. Nearly everyone from Holy Mud, even the wiry Asian, showed up. Michelle and Nikki laid their heavy heads on my shoulders and dabbed their eyes as they gushed with stories about him, full of affection.

"He was such a good guy; the stuff I told him!"

"Me too."

"He was just that way. So open. So accepting."

It was a kind of mourning I hadn't really gotten around to, quiet and tender, so different from the massive anchor-weight of my family's grief.

At eleven, David Garcia, my brother's favorite crooner, who covered songs from the Rat Pack era, came on board. He announced that he was going to sing "Come Fly With Me," which I discovered was my brother's all-time favorite song. The way he sunk his feelings into those few last notes made me cry into my glass, literally.

It was getting near Midnight when the evening started to take a strange turn. People were starting to get a little too drunk, laugh a little too loud, flirt a little too much. Nick, who was sitting right across from us, an arm tossed around a stunningly beautiful blonde whose neck he'd been shamelessly nibbling on for going on an hour, suddenly came to, stumbled out of the booth, and stepped up to the microphone and slurred, "Here is to my best friend, and manager. He was something. He was something special. You know people say it all the time: it's not going to be the same without him. It's true. The world changed when he left. The world changed."

"MANAGER!" How about partner? And you might've helped change his world, but instead you questioned his faithful running of the bar. My brother had held out hope until so dim did that hope turn that he'd written, "don't care anymore; only wondering whether I should care that I don't." Did Nick know he'd come to that? I doubted it. I only myself discovered the full extent of Adam's disappointment when reading his journal, how his plans of helping Dad, which he'd kept secret from me, had been crushed. Two long years of entries by the last guy on earth to complain, complaining in painful detail about Nick, and here I was drinking his twenty-four-year-old scotch "on the house." Without even thanking him, Sasha and I left, deciding to go for a late night dinner at Canter's.

I "slept" on her couch that evening, tossing and turning, until a little after 2:00 a.m. I sat up, shot through with a deep carnal need—for Sasha. Attracted to each other for years, we'd cherished our flirtation, but for reasons that never were clear to me it also felt too delicate, too dangerous to consummate. I might've said we kept it a safe distance because we didn't want to spoil our friendship, or that she was still too residually Muslim and I still too residually Christian for it ever to work out, but deep down I believe we shied away from the foreignness in each other, the residual otherness that still adhered to our persons.

I went into her room, trembling, and called her name and came up to her bed and put out an unsure hand; she hesitated, and then made room for me to lie down. She stroked my hair, and I turned and cried in the crook of her neck, and in the hot fog of those tears we kissed. I'd had sex a dozen different ways for dozens of reasons, but I'd never had it to keep from drowning in sorrow. The sound and feel of her breath reached deep inside me, and with each thrust it seemed we were affirming the fact of our living flesh, affirming that the past didn't matter. We fucked like true Americans.

We each wanted something to wet our throats afterwards, so hand in hand we went to her living room. On her couch, she pointed to a statue of Mary just to the side of her fireplace. I hadn't thought much of it, or maybe I'd suppressed my curiosity because, let's face it, how weird was it that a once-upon-a-time-Muslim-currently-atheist decorated her home with the Virgin?

Mary wore a white nun's habit with blue sleeves; a long gold chain with a crucifix hung from her neck; her face was turned pensively away, her hands opened at her sides. Sasha told me she'd picked up for near nothing at a flea market on Melrose. It was probably made in a workshop right here in LA in the mid-1950s. "A bit of local history, piety, and beauty, all rolled into one for twenty-five bucks," she said. "Okay. I also wanted something to block the front of the faux fireplace."

My brother, she told me, didn't understand why she had bought it, much less accorded it such a prominent place in her living room. "I told him I liked it, that was all. Her naked feet in those sandals were pretty.

"My answer got under his skin," she said. "No way he believed me; he kept nagging each time he'd come over, 'Why the hell do you keep that Mary there?'

'Why don't you believe me when I tell you it's because I think she's pretty,' I'd say."

In Los Angeles, unlike in New York, you met people all the time whose innocence was strategic. "They're ashamed to admit they're here for power and fame," Sasha said, "and so they put on this, 'Oh, I'm from Scranton, we don't act like that there,' front. So my knee-jerk thought was oh sure, another Los Angeleno pretending to be an innocent abroad. But obviously, he was hardly from Scranton, and so he got me thinking, okay, why did I put Mary there? Why did I buy her in the first place? Maybe it isn't just about how pretty she is. The next time I saw him I told him that he was right, that it wasn't just about ornamentation. I told him that I bought her to free her, free her from the chokehold of the cross, prayers, incense, the whole thing. It was about her beauty, but not about her beauty per se, but the way it shined when brought out of the gloom of the church.

"I thought that was pretty clever," she said, sitting up. "Anyway, he made me laugh."

"He'd fallen away from the faith during college, for all the obvious reasons, but a single encounter had brought him back into the fold," I told her. "The family was at an Armenian picnic and happened to sit right beside the archbishop of our diocese. When they were finished eating, they got to talking about this and that. 'You are in college then,' the Priest says, 'How goes your faith?' My brother answers that it wasn't going, not well at all, and explained to the priest that anthropology and psychology and philosophy and political science, and even economics, had led him to the conclusion that God didn't exist, or if He did, not anywhere it might matter. He listened to my brother and then said, 'Well, that is okay. If that is where you are, that is where God wants you. You were baptized in the church, no? Then you are part of our family. You take your time and ask all the questions that you need. Maybe God put those questions in your heart. The church will always be there for you.'

"That one conversation had the effect of releasing him from his suspicions of the church. Not of his intellectual doubts, but of his suspicions, which were even deeper than his doubts.

I remember telling him, 'Can't you see how condescending that is?' I mean to me it's obvious. The priest just sidestepped my brother's doubts with this drivel. But Adam didn't see it that way; he didn't feel it that way at all. He hardly became a church-goer again, but in his own way, he loved the church; he loved that about the church."

"What was that—'that'?" Sasha asked.

"That 'that,' I suppose, is what they call grace."

I'd been sipping scotch for a little over an hour when The Kurd walked in. He was wearing a big leather jacket over a collarless shirt. I watched him from the booth while he made small talk with the bouncer, and then I stood and waved him over. He approached with his arms extended for a hug. "I'm sorry I'm late," he said, slapping me on the back. "I was looking for book on southern California birds, and I lost track of the time."

He scooted into the booth, and a waitress, fair-skinned, redheaded, rosy, and plump, stepped up.

"What are you drinking?" she asked.

"I drink the vodka after dinner," he told her. "In the morning I only feel tired. Whisky, rum, even the gin it makes me miserable. On ice, please."

The Kurd asked the waitress where she was from; just out-side of Chicago, she said. The Kurd smiled and watched her go. "For me these milk-fed Midwestern girls, they are pure American woman." The Kurd shook his head. "That drink will hit me like a truth potion, I tell you, this Noble Barn, Barn Noble, its like some Aztec built it, so many levels, What, are they tearing out hearts on the roof? Books how to get sick the right way, how to live to cry, how to feed your chicken, books how to die. It mind-boggles the mind. Oh," he sighed, fixing his big gray eyes on mine. "What a forty days and forty nights."

"It's felt like that," I told him. "That sort of wilderness. I've discovered some new things about my brother, and some new things about myself. Not all of them flattering," I confessed.

"It is always this way," The Kurd said. "A brother or sister or good friend is the mirror we are most afraid of looking into

208

while they are alive. But don't torture yourself too much. It is the masses. The masses are a dark force. From day one they are dragging the world into their Mickey the Mouse oblivion. But I need that drink; then we can toast to My Buddy, our brother. You can tell from the bartender service alone that this city has reached an exhaustion point past exhaustion."

"You moved here from Chicago, no?" I said.

"I went from the Chicago to San Francisco and then Los Angeles," he replied. "I was born and raised in heat and dust, and as much as I loved the Chicago, let's face it, it is made for Igloo people. But it was a great city in the sixties, I will tell you that. That was some city, the Chicago. For ten dollars you could go into hibernation for two months, what they served you these Italians restaurants. Here, I don't know what: on a plate the size of a sewer cap they put a slice of this, a curlicue of that, tied, pinched, tucked with a flower on top—are they making food or objects for Zen meditation? Enough! Just give me the food and take my appetite as a man seriously, I want to tell them."

"You've been to some pretty fancy restaurants lately," I told The Kurd.

The Kurd continued, "And the girls there in the Chicago. This Polish and that Irish would come to my little apartment, and we'd pour the wine and go to Halstead Street and move from Kingston Mine to twenty different blues and jazz clubs. You didn't have to pay a penny; the music poured into the street, like that, like honey. And these little Catholic girls, after a night of wine and saxophone, were lions in bed. I swear by the time they through with me I was ready for the confession." He shook his head.

"I feel sorry for women these days. Their sex is so wound up, so complicated. In struggle for justice, marching and chanting and burning the bras, the fire got out of control, and now look, their own house is burning down."

"Maybe women have to burn their houses down," I said, "before they can build them back up."

"Okay, but in the meantime, it is tragic watching it go up in smoke."

The waitress returned. She put a cocktail napkin down and set the drink on it. "Sorry it took so long," she said.

"As long as it comes from you, let it take until Jesus comes," The Kurd said. She smiled curiously, and left.

"No," he said, "nothing like sinking your teeth into a good Midwestern lamb chop." He picked the drink up and turned it in his hand. "People make love to wine, flirt with cocktails, but Vodka is a handshake between common people, between peasants." He took a serious gulp.

"Armenians call it arakh," I said. "It means sweat. Greeks ouzo. The Italians grappa. I suppose the Turks call it rakki."

"Please, don't tell me anything Turkish. The Turk has never had its own anything; its entire culture is a mongrel falsehood."

"Sorry," I told him. "I should've known."

"Yes, you, of all people, should have known. Oppression and torture is the only contributions the Turks have made to culture. At this they are Raphaelos."

"To my brother," I said.

"To Adam." We clinked glasses. The Kurd closed his eyes, tucking his pain in. We both did, in remembrance, for a minute or so.

When we looked up, a trio of gorgeous Persian girls had just scooted into a booth across from us.

The Kurd said, "Let us face the fact; no city in the world has beautiful women the way this city does. Even ugly girls here have odd good looks. True, in a place like Kurdistan, out of the dust and oil and stones all of the sudden a true beauty will appear so exquisite there is no way for the American moonscape to produce something like that. But what you must wait a whole year to bubble up in that part of the world bubbles up here every two minutes."

"Persian woman really are beautiful," I said, thinking of Sasha.

"Persian," he laughed. "Please. Were they Persian when they fled Iran like cockroaches? Did they use Persian money to build a thousand Taj Majals in Beverly Hills? They are ashamed of naming the dirty little place they come from, but they weren't ashamed of stealing the wealth from that dirty little place."

It was time to change the subject. I'd always wondered his age, and now had a chance to ask him.

"I am almost exactly twice your brother's age," he said. "Fifty-five, and I don't mind telling. No, I ran off a hundred cliffs before I was thirty years old. Only now am I beginning to hug the road."

"And have you ever been married?" I asked.

"Yes. My wife was a hippie, a true lotus-sitting, tofu-eating flower-child. We met in San Francisco in 1970, a great city then, San Francisco, a great time. Getting sex, I tell you, was back then nothing. Read a few wobbly lines of poetry or strum a ten-dollar guitar, and you were good to go for a week. Now all you find are peacocks in pastry shops reading self-help and I don't know what. Everybody in San Francisco these days, they're beyond revolution, beyond sex. They are in preservation mode, ready to last ten thousand years, like some Egyptian. I was married for only a year, so why even call it married. She wanted to sip chamomile tea and hold hands and read the stars, and all I wanted to do was screw her like one of those passionate apes, Sonny Bonos or bonobos or hobos, I don't know the name. I devoured her completely, and then I left. When I say goodbye, I say goodbye to everything. One day I am there, and the next day I don't know where I am, with only my paintings and the pants I wear. The same way I left my home country."

"Iraq," I said.

"Kurdistan," he replied. "There has never been an Iraq; Iraq is a fantasy invention of the British Mongols. [The way he pronounced it sounded like Moguls, as in *British Moguls*; I didn't bother to clear it up] When I got this scholarship to study in America at the Art Institute, I packed up and got on a bus to visit my family one last time. We had traveled half a day north from Baghdad when our bus was stopped at a checkpoint. Two soldiers stepped up, Saddam's men, and they began to ask questions. 'What do you do? Where are you going? An artist? Get your art and come outside!' I had a dozen small paintings rolled up by my leg. I stepped off the bus into the heat and dust and one by one they made me unroll my canvases, right there, on the hot, dusty, good-for-lizards road.

"'What is this?' they shouted at me. 'Who do you think you are?'

"It was a kind of naïve impressionism, nothing avant-garde, but it boiled their cold-hearted blood that anyone should do his own thing, as the Americans say. One of the big shots took his cigarette and dropped it on the canvas and crushed it out with his boot, laughing, and in the end they snatched all my paintings up—to humiliate me."

"That's some story," I said.

"But they did not humiliate me. I laughed at their laughter: in a few weeks I would be in America and they would still be smoking their cheap cigarettes and guarding their dusty, angry, nationalistic road to nothingness. I breathed free; the breath of freedom, there is nothing, I tell you, like it. But now look, now look at what has happened this country. The way this city shit in its own nest. But this is how it always look as you near the end."

It was the kind of doomsday rhetoric I expected of him, but still I was curious to know, In what way? "In what way are we nearing the end?"

"In every way. Turn on the TV. Every week, a new soda or toaster or shampoo or toothbrush or dog food, a three-blade razor now, didn't two do? In my village once or twice year gyp-sies would roll up in their crazy carts to sell this love potion and that secret balm, but here they stand day and night waiting for what stupid, throwaway booble the gypsies are peddling next. I need the detox clinic after stepping into this Ralph's or Vons: chemicals and steel carts and down a hundred glossy aisles the smell of decadent sadness and exhaustion. What a difference from these old-world bazaars, where humans have been rubbing shoulders for five thousand years, squeezing tomatoes, gather-ing gossip, getting a recipe for how to treat the baby's cough. We have traded this for a hundred different sausages and the simple potato mashed, hashed, bashed, curly and country style." The Kurd laughed.

He continued: "We have traded this for a woman with sore bloated feet standing in front of silly machine, 'Cash or Credit?' I tell you, we have substituted the bazaar for the bizarre.

Look at this fatness, what do they call it, morbid, morbod, morbody, obesity, obscenity, I don't know what. There are whole towns in the middle of this US where half the people look like they were bred to win the blue ribbon at the county fair."

Sounding professorial, even to my own ears, I told him, "Researchers say their diet is all off balance; these people eat little enough, but they eat the wrong things; because they don't have the money to eat good food, they eat what is cheap and convenient."

The Kurd scoffed: "It isn't the first time I've heard this nonsense. Please. What is cheaper than a head of cauliflower a pot of beans or a sturdy loaf of bread? No, they eat these chips and fries and dips and candy and soda for one simple reason: because it tastes good, because it brings a crazy sexy feeling in the mouth. Let us not complicate our brains with this Daffty Duck logic. When I came here, the sixties, the bodies of black women were slim, beautiful toned, strong as cables tested to 2,000 pounds. Now they are so horrible fat, the pressure on their bodies like waiting for a barrel of gunpowder to explode. The human body is in some kind of sadistic shock treatment from what they shovel into it. What we are doing to evolution's greatest masterpiece, like pissing everyday on a million Leonardos. The same way we gunk and fill with junk this planet, a glorious gem, one of a kind among a billion billion drifting stones. This, this exhausted animal orgy that is America killed your brother, if you want to know the truth the whole truth and nothing but it."

Instinctively, I looked around, maybe someone was listening in.

"Who is hearing you hold your tongue anymore?" said The Kurd. "Why should we care what anybody thinks after what they did to Adam? We are two birds on the verge of extinction singing. Let it be enough." He thought about it, and laughed, then picked up his drink and guzzled as though he'd just toasted the matter. "I'm sorry," The Kurd said, "I make you nervous."

"No," I told him, "I was thinking of my brother, too."

The Kurd said, "Let's go for a smoke."

The weather had grown a little balmy. There must've been

a cloud cover because I saw no stars.

"What sad, trashy corners we've left to them, poor things." He was speaking of the few prostitutes who had gathered at the corner of the boulevard.

I told him, "A friend of mine just finished a documentary following three prostitutes for over a year. All had been raped at an early age by a family member. A lot of these girls have been sexually molested."

"Then why hold their faces in the sewer with an SS boot too? We should honor them, because from the beginning of time, these prostitutes have been there, just like the artists have been there, to remind us that there is more to life than gnawing on the dried-up bones the Mongols throw us." No question now, he'd said Mongols, not Moguls.

"What is this anyway," The Kurd said, "that you photograph sex and pay the girl fifty dollars and show it on video and that is not prostitution."

"In that case, it is entertainment," I said.

"I tell you, this country and its hypocrisy is reminding me more and more of Islam," said The Kurd. "Where everything is paved over with religion and morality you will find in the tiniest cracks the most extreme hypocrisy and decadence. Look at these shahs and princes and whatever, these wicked little Muslim god-trembling playboys from Dubai and The Emirates and Kuwait and Saudi Arabia, all these disgusting oil slicks; they buy girls from around the world and do to them things the American Cup of Joe can't even imagine. I tell you, America is turning this way too."

I said, "Hardly. Just the opposite. If anything, we're on the other extreme. Sometimes I wonder if there are any boundaries left. Not that I'm terribly worried about losing them."

"Religion has many faces," he said. "Ours is not about sex, you are right, it is beyond the sex, beyond even the sweating, bustling, crumbling human flesh. It is about the self. No, not even the self, but the fantasy of it. Self-worth and self-esteem and the inner self and the voice within and the child inside and I don't know what. We've gone from living the life of quiet desperation to living the life of noisy emptiness. We've gone from greasy industrial machines built to last five lifetimes to some cheap made-in-Taiwan gadget that breaks down every six months. Look at the Jews, a people who never looked to anyone for a shekel, the way they have become crybabies. Every third millionaire is a Jew and half the nations on earth are shoving billions to cover their loss and he acts like some poor orphan still stuck in the ghetto, whining and pounding fists and jumping up and down, making the world believe that behind every corner a giant waits to stomp him to death when in fact there is nothing more than a neurotic little midget. It's gotten to the point if a Jew runs you over you're an anti-Semite for denting his car. They've turned this Holocaust into another Burning Bush." The Kurd crushed his cigarette out with a foot and announced, "Enough Already!" The bouncer opened the door. "Efharisto," The Kurd said. The bouncer smiled and nodded.

"He is Greek," The Kurd told me as we scooted back into the booth. "I could tell when I first came in. As soon as the American waters turn stale and stinky, a fresh wave of ethnics always float up on the shores to build new castles in the sand. The beauty of this place, but even this has changed. I know the first hand. Every birthday, every Christmas, a thousand different holidays, my little niece and nephew they demand from my poor brother and his wife a Rose Bowl Float parade. In Kurdistan you would have to bring running water to a village to get such cakes and whistles and balloons. This program and that program, safety nets and jungle gyms and learning ladders and trampolines and still kids throw the tantrum and drop out and shoot up and zone out, I don't know what. Before a boy is ten years old here there is no dragon that isn't slain for him. Our kids have no muscle. They're all Jell-O, ready to explode Jell-Os, sniffling-shuffling-'whatever-man'-napalm bombs. The Imams create the same jiggle-wiggle-boom: men watching over themselves like vultures, flinching and ducking, what sickness. But these same flinchers are the ones I tell you who will not flinch an inch to blow up a plane if given the chance."

"I always thought," I told The Kurd, "that all that had to do with the economic dead-end of the Muslim world." It was a point of view that all my middle-eastern friends shared.

The Kurd said, "It is beyond question. Islam turns men, lions just dying for a juicy rib eye, into weed-eating goats. Islam demands this crazy fanatic religious devotion at the same time that it demands a fattened, dead, submissive fatalism. But let us just say it *it is*, they have their zombies and we have ours. Look at these CEO's, these fanatical ayatollahs who praise you for coming to work when you are sick, for flogging your overtime flesh, until your body, mind, and soul, your wife, your family, until your humanity is *totally completely* crushed under, what do they call it, your *work load*? What was it it said that sign they hung over the door at Auschwitz: "Work Will Set You Free!" Anyway, the days of fighting back of setting traps circling the wagons the way the Indians did are over. There is nothing left but the wagon trains, heading for the cliff edge of oblivion."

"You mean the Native Americans," I said.

"Okay, please; so now with our Nikes and Reeboks and Adidas we shoot hoops on the bones of ten million American Native whatever-they-call-them, Indians. But look," The Kurd laughed, "they've made a comeback as cheesy Las Vegas MCs; setting traps for a billion burrito-shape retirees with sparkly lights and velvet rugs. My heart bleeds to see the dignity of this magnificent culture, its ancient respect for the wild, the ways of the river, the spirit of trees, to see all this traded in for Kung Pao Poker and ten cent slots? A world-class disaster. Still, to the Indians and Blacks this country should put up a memorial, an immense memorial in the center of Washington DC that twenty-four hours a day is running blood. Not another Disney museum where tourists can come and take their silly pictures—cheese!"

"You've got it against Disneyland, don't you," I said.

"I went to this human catastrophe a few years ago, with my brother and his kids, and I'm still chugging the pepto-*dismol*. This character and that in their big bloated suits; like corpses left to rot in the sun. It felt like these retirement convolution constipation homes, you know, where they cart Grandma to die her lonely American death. Old people slumped in wheelchairs like banana peels, some Filipino girls smiling "open wide" and shoving the microwave lasagna into their mouths. Forcing this into their ass and that down their throat, and then pushing them in front of the TV to watch the Wheel of Fortune or The Price it is Right. The Mongols have found a way of sucking the marrow from even these bones. No, it is the duty of the shepherd to protect the sheep against these Mongols that come in the name of compassion, quality of life, or progress or free-enterprise, free market or what is they now call it, the new word, globule-ization, I don't know what."

"'Globalization.' It's the term they're using to describe the way the world is interconnected, economic and information-wise. No boundaries between countries any longer."

"It is a nice tummy-warming concept," he said, "holding hands singing 'We are the World.'"

I said, "Some say that in a few years all the economies of the world will be linked up in such a way that war will become obsolete."

"Don't worry," he replied, "these Genghis Khans will use it to do what they've always done, raping the earth and every life form on the earth in the name of their unholy Mecca."

The Kurd smiled broadly and said, "I loved to watch this Star Trek when I first came to America: Kirk and Scotty and Zulu and Chekov and Orooroo and McCoy, zipping to galaxies in the blink of an eye, light speed warp speed, I don't know what speed, reading minds and healing with a wand, but with their simple humanity shining bright. For me, the starship Enterprise was like a giant lantern these brave men and women carried through the darkest of dark ignorance galaxies. The essence of America, what the future was so supposed to bring, but with each step forward in technology our simple humanity has taken ten steps back. Yes, you will find scrawny pot-smoking anarchists protesting, but what chance do these tattooed billy-goats have of reaching the Average America Cup of Joe when Joe is a stray dog whose eyes are plucked and whose ears are chewed? I used to think that women might lead the way out, that maybe men were the stumbling-block problem, but for all their talk about softer-gentler, they are just as quick to drop the babies down the village well and join the invasion. Please, leave these slogans at the door."

He excused himself to the bathroom.

This was not the way I had hoped the evening would go. I had come with the expectation of getting to know him better, and maybe, if the opening was there, to ask him whether he knew of my brother's suicide attempt. But instead I'd invited a dark carpet-bombing of America. I wondered about the source of it, aside from my brother's death, which no doubt provided the bulk of the fuel. He was fifty years old, unmarried with no significant other, working as a scenic artist for a movie studio, when he dreamed of being a fine artist working in his personal studio. He'd had some shows, a modicum of success, but it was certain that no serious collector knew of his work. Without youth, beauty, wealth, or fame, and without the shelter of a family, I wondered how his ego fared in a city like Los Angeles. Not very well, I imagined.

And then I recalled that I had actually met The Kurd on three occasions, not two. The third, very briefly, had been just months earlier, while on my way to vacation in Hawaii. It was a red-eye flight with a two-hour layover at LAX. I wanted to see my brother, but that night he was having cocktails with The Kurd. He said he'd cancel that date, but I told him, let's the three of us have a drink then.

To make it easy, we agreed to meet at the top of the Theme Building, what we called The Spider, at LAX. My flight was about an hour late, and I distinctly remember walking into the bar, sure that they'd be waiting quietly for my arrival. Then I saw them at a booth: The Kurd was waving his arms in the air, as my brother pounded the table with his fists, doubled over in hilarity, coming up for a breather before doubling over again. They were like two kids whooping it up at the empty bleachers at school. Watching them, I felt envy corroding me. I knew I hadn't had that with my brother since Lebanon—but I hadn't realized the degree to which he had it without me. Now, I was grateful for their friendship. Alongside my feelings of guilt, I was deeply grateful to anyone who had loved my brother, especially if they were there in his time of need when I was not.

I looked up from my thoughts. The bar was getting busier, and a band was winding up. I called over the waitress. When

The Kurd returned, I told him the drinks were on me and I was ready to go. Next time I will buy, he said. I hope there is a next time, I said. Of course there will be, he said. I asked him if he was up for a walk. He put a hand out for me to lead the way.

He fired up a cigarette and we walked in silence down La Brea. I had just determined that he'd burnt himself out, when he said, "Last year, I went to Kurdistan. One evening, I was with one of my favorite cousins; older than me, like a big brother. We had a pasha's meal and then they brought from I don't know where this cognac. Oh, what cognac that was! The dirt and wind and sun and even the farmer's leather boots was in it. With this bottle, we toasted to the Kurds, to Ocalan, to freedom, and then to his son, Ahmed, who sat quietly, almost dumb, on the other side of the table. He was only twenty-eight year old, Ahmed. He limped and his speech was slow, but people treated him with deep respect, because his body was torn on the battlefield, fighting for a free Kurdistan. Then Ahmed's son, four years old, who had been playing outside, came in and sat on his grandpa's lap. My cousin kissed him, and then he poured another round of that cognac and raised his glass: 'To the next generation that will fight for a homeland.' My God, I thought. Here, his son was made lame from war, and he was toasting his grandson who was next in line. I look at that and then I look at this."

And as though teeing it up, he paused, just outside an art gallery, and looked in: a series of photos of a single woman's face, each roughly eight by nine inches in size, running in a line across three walls of the room.

The Kurd said, "I don't know what has happened. Really, is art today anything more than a Toy Poodle competition?"

"The shows I go to are nothing like toy poodle competitions," I told him.

"I'm sure you are right," The Kurd said. "Every real artist is really in communion with every other real artist. But our communion table might as well be on the Neptune, so far from this Mickey-D culture that not even the Judases bother to show up."

"True enough," I said, "it can feel that lonely sometimes."

"Critics used to guide people away from this dark riddle nonsense, toward beauty and truth, but now they are like timid serfs following the cow with their milk buckets. When the cow comes to a stop, they pull out their stools and begin pumping. When no milk comes, they claim the absence of milk is the cows' greatest genius."

The Kurd laughed so loudly the laughter bounced off the storefronts, dimly echoing. "Maybe there is no room left to dreams our dreams," he said, starting back toward the bar. "We turn on the television and there it is. The brain collapses like some Cowardly Lion before this new Wizard of Oz. When I was a child we used to all sit around the tonir. You know what this is, no?"

"Yes," I told him. "A hole, a kind of fireplace, in the ground in the middle of the home."

"We bake our bread in it way the Hindus do in those, what do they call them?"

"Tandoori ovens," I said.

"At night," he continued, "a large blanket was placed over the tonir, and we'd stick our feet under it for warmth and listen to stories the old people told. When I look back I see that my whole inside life rose from that hole. Now we sit on our triple-stuffed super-size couches listening to stories told by idiotic, emotionally dwarfed people in Hollywood. Our new wisdoms, our new heroes carrying epic stories of greatness and caution back from distant lands, come from the brains of the neurotic, idiotic, emotionally dwarfed. There is no space left for the imagination to heat up, rise and wander. It thinks it is wandering, but it's wandering like these *alkazheimer* people wander through the K-Mart looking for their shopping carts. These Hollywood Mongol Madonnas talk about this aborigines and that tribe and whales and dolphins and little jungle frogs, about a million different extinctions, but what about the human imagination, each the equal of a hundred Byzantium, they've extinguished with their oblivion.

"Let us face it *it is*; we have entered a new kind of spirituality. Those desert people who fasted and poured ashes on their heads, those first Christians who drove their bodies to the cliff edge of nothingness waiting for the Messiah to come, we are not much different from them. Look what happened when the crazy, rampaging, uncontrollable mob reached the gates of Beverly Hills? Like pilgrims, they dropped to their knees and sang their Hail Marys and Allahu Akbars and Barukh ata Adanoais. They broke out the beads and holy books and spun the prayer wheels. The clouds of black smoke floating to the Mongols nostrils, I tell you, it was incense, I tell you, it was their frankincense and myrrh. When it was all said and done the 1,000-dollar-a-square-foot shrines needed a little Windex, about it."

We'd rounded back to the bar where we both parked. It was getting on 1:00 a.m., but I wasn't ready to turn in—there was no way I could sleep. So when The Kurd asked if I'd like to come to his place for a drink, I agreed.

We took our separate cars. As I turned right on Beverly, on the side of a large electrical box someone had glued a poster that read IT'S TIME TO HEAL. People were rising in unison to say it again and again. In good faith, they were coming out with shovels and brooms and mops and sponges. I both admired and resented them. I couldn't help feeling that they were sweeping away my brother, sweeping away his memory. Maybe not in a month, nor even a year, but if Beirut, club-footed Beirut could rise from its ashes, Los Angeles would also rise and in a tenth of the time.

The Kurd had converted his one bedroom apartment into a studio. Paintings and found objects—a dish, a rag, a doll—hung here and there between the paintings. A single bed was in what looked to be the kitchen nook. "I have no garage," he explained, "so I had to sacrifice the bedroom for storage."

"I want to show you these," he said, and broke out a short stack of photographs. Photos of buildings transfigured by the fires, of a long brick wall that was left standing while everything else to which it had once been connected had fallen. "Pure poetry," he said. He'd shot them over a period of a single week, right after the burning, but they contained enough information for a lifetime of meditation.

The photos seemed to have inspired a painting that stood on a large easel, maybe 7 x 7, fixed against the largest wall. There had been a fire, a great fire that had consumed a landscape, probably a forest, and what remained were a few scorched areas, and a single tree and single bird on that tree, or rather, their shadows. And a dreamy, beautiful blue was slowly washing over this fire-stormed world, like the mind slowly washes over a terrible memory until that memory is all but gone. All in all, it was the portrait of a kind of amnesia, violent and rapturous in its beauty, the very definition of sublime.

The Kurd turned on the dining room light, which he'd converted into a separate workspace, and against one wall hung a portrait of a woman, dressed in traditional peasant-like clothing. Her eyes, like The Kurd's, were large, brown, and intense, her face hardened but handsome. She stood cut off at the waist, in front of a bombed-out brick building through which fire poured from a window, with one hand reaching out to the viewer, to give her last offering.

"It is my mother," he told me. "I painted it after she died. It is also for The Kurdish people."

I looked at the painting again and told him, "I can see my own people in it. My own grandmother."

"It is a picture of survival, and few people in history know survival like your people do. 'What is the big deal,' they say, 'it happened seventy-five years, so long ago.' But for a people three thousand years old, this is a drop in the bucket of time. Let me tell you, if America should ever feel the thundering drive of an invading army, ever see the heads of their young rolling in front of their eyes, two thirds of their population gone, not for two thousand years would they forget. The whole world would be brought to their knees for the killing of a thousand innocent Americans, I guarantee you."

He left for the kitchen, and returned with a Mason jar in one hand and three small glasses stacked in the other. The Kurd said, "He loved this stuff. Let's drink some together, in memory of that first time we met, me, you, and our brother." He emptied an even amount of the brew into each of the three glasses, and set one glass to the side. There was only one place to sit, really, and so we sat there, fifteen feet or so in front of the painting, he in his painting chair, an old leather lounger, and I in a simple wooden chair next to it. The anise smell rose like the sweetest memory of my brother as I brought the glass to my lips.

The Kurd said, "Maybe I just have to get over it, or get on with it or accept it for the way it is; or be at peace or love the one you're with. Leave it or love it. Maybe it is just me, as the Americans say."

"But we are American," I told The Kurd.

The Kurd said, "Yes, you are Armenian-American, I am Kurdish-American, there is Italian-, Swedish-, and Mexican-America. That little hypen, hyphen, whatever they call it, that little bridge sturdy as the Golden Gate, held worlds together. But now look, the hyphen has crumbled, snapped. This country has become one of these Greek medusas with a thousand tribes on her head all biting and poisoning each other. America," he laughed, "what does this mean anymore?"

I said, "It's obvious. We're here; we're in America; so we are Americans."

He said, "We are in the place, of course, but the concept has always been separate from the place."

"The concept is elastic," I said. "What it means is for us to decide; for each generation to decide for its own. Just the way you decide for yourself what each painting will look like."

The Kurd lit up a cigarette. He slid one out for me.

He took a puff and said, "The summer after I came to Chicago, I went to New York City and visited all the places I'd only seen pictures of. I wanted to see it all, but Statue of Liberty is what I wanted to see most, so I took the ferry out to the little island there. In reality, there is no picture that can do her justice: her monumentality is beyond the puny human brain. That lantern she holds, an invitation, but also a kind of challenge. She lighted the way here for generations, but now, I think she is lighting the way out of here; watching over America's passage away from America. If the concept is plastic, elastic, as you say, what fixes it to this wasteland? It has migrated beyond and it will survive beyond. The same way that Alexander took the Greeks to the beyond. Maybe in a little tent in a Syrian refugee camp, or a studio apartment in Tbilisi, or a hillside village in Bangladesh, you will find Americans. And maybe these Americans will rise up from that hut or tent, enough of them will rise and a new America in a place we would never expected will be born."

"And maybe it can be reborn here. Look at what this country has survived. The Civil War; slavery; suffrage, two world wars, McCarthyism, Vietnam."

The Kurd replied, "Maybe was too much for human kind this experiment, and always will be. Maybe the great irony is unfolding before our eyes: the Mongols, the Americans-in-name, are snuffing any tiny human hope-lantern that turns on any-where in the world, just like they snuffed out our brother. But I am going nowhere. I will stay. When I was a boy I was in love with America. I can only call it love for this brave knight, his heroic adventure in the face of ten thousand ogres, dragons, and evil sorcerers of history. I admit, I am like a little boy who guards the castle even if the castle is empty."

From the peripheries I could see that he'd been weaving my brother's fate into this damning portrait of America.

"Are you saying that America died with these riots; that America died when my brother died?"

The Kurd said, "Let us not make it into some metaphys-ics. It would make cheap his death."

"I agree."

"But he was a victim; the noisy spinning tops on the way to their oblivion cut him down. Of that I am sure. One hundred percent sure! There is no other explanation."

The Kurd sighed and shook his head.

"But if there was another explanation," The Kurd said, "our brother would find it. He was always finding in the most ridiculous things something to ponder, to wonder about. Someone would say something stupid and I'd want to crush it, put it out of its misery, and he would reach down and try to save it, feed it honey like he was feeding an injured bird."

"He didn't have it in him to hold grudges," I said, "except maybe against himself. Did you know he tried to commit suicide?"

"Yes."

"I found out about it when reading his journal. He never told me."

"He didn't want his family to know. He was afraid it would cause you too much pain and worry."

"Now it's causing me a different kind of pain. That he would keep it from me."

"I'm so sorry," The Kurd said.

"This is what I was talking about when I said that I was discovering things about us that were hard to deal with."

"Don't punish yourself," he said. "He might have told you in time, but they took his time away."

"While he was going through it! He didn't tell me when he was going through it!"

I buried my head in my hands.

The Kurd let me cry. For several minutes he let my cry before he said, "It is one of many deaths you will go through. You must cry your heart out over each and every one. Even if there are a hundred, and even if they last your whole life. With each tear you shed you are watering his memory. You are keeping it alive."

"I could have loved him better when he was alive. I could have nurtured him better."

"This is the number one sign of love; that we recognize that we have fallen short and that we wish we could have done better. Do not confuse completion of love for loving."

"When did he talk to you about it?"

"He called me from the hospital where they jailed him up. I went and visited him there. I remember that I told him this story, because I thought it would help. When I lived in Chicago, I made friends with an older man, a painter, one of these social realists, Ashcan school or something. He was wonderful and youthful, in his mid-seventies when we met. I visited him two, three times a month and we'd talk about art and poetry and music. I was going through some hard time, and to help he told me this wonderful story: he said that when he was in thirties he was forced to move into a basement, no windows and a low, low

225

ceiling, where he painted with one stupid bulb hanging above his head. No matter how he painted, no matter the luster of his washes, all of his paintings turned out sad, gloomy. He thought he'd lost his touch as an artist, and when he finally left that place, he picked through his paintings and decided only a handful was worth keeping. As he brought the others outside for the dumpster, he was stunned. The darkness of his basement had led him to overcompensate for color, and now, in the fullness of the sun, the paintings were vibrant, trembling with color. He thought he'd lost the touch, but the absence of good light had led him to some of his most amazing work."

"That's a beautiful story," I told him.

"I loved that man. He was to me what The Wizard was to your brother. A substitute grandfather for me. Since I left Kurdistan, I have always been looking for substitutes. A family. Your brother was a substitute brother for me too," he said.

"I hope," I told The Kurd, "that that makes us brothers as well." I told him that though I did not—could not—agree with all he'd said, I respected his honest reckoning with the world. "That honesty," I told him, "is probably what my brother loved about you."

"And what I loved about him," The Kurd said.

I asked him, "What keeps you working, what keeps you painting?"

"There was one time," he said, "when I wanted it all. But now my painting has become like a ritual, something I do, just do, like the cavemen went into the caves and did what they did."

"But who are you painting for?"

"You," he said; "people like you, and your brother. Those who carry the torch into the cave."

I'd asked him this, because I felt, in the middle of that darkness, something spark inside me; a strong conviction that I should complete my project about Lebanon, and then immediately start another one.

"I want to write a book about what happened here. What happened to my brother? I can't just let him go, not without saying or doing something."

"Maybe it is only in the artist's mind that if we write it or paint it we have stopped it from falling into oblivion. That we have snatched it from the mouths of the Mongol horde. And you are the perfect person," he told me, "to write that book too: only someone with half a foot in this country and half a foot out can write a book that tells it the way it happened here. Once you are in with both feet it is already too late; they have already swallowed you up."

With that said, he tacked toward the painting in front of him. "I cannot stop thinking of the problem hidden in this painting," he said. "Each canvas has its own personality. Sometimes is like the wise fool that is ridiculing you; other times it takes hold of you like a world-class whore. This canvas, sometimes it happens, is doing both."

The Kurd used a big table to store his paints, a hundred different colors that he prepared in the old-fashioned way from pigments and linseed oil. He enjoyed painting with acrylic, he said, but the process of painting with oil—like, he imagined, the process of writing in long hand—slowed the act down and created depth in the painting that was impossible to get otherwise. Something of a purely material nature happened on the canvas, he said, that had nothing to do with the intent of the artist, an alchemical thing. The Kurd rose from his lounger and stepped up to his painting table and lifted in one hand his palette and in the other a brush. He backed up, and studied his work-in-progress.

I was studying it too, in particular the unearthly and beautiful blue that was slowly eating away at everything. Only a few apertures onto the fire remained, and through them you could see the shadows of the bird and the tree.

The Kurd said, "There is a brutal truth and beauty in the ruins, no? Their broken bodies reveal something fundamental."

It was a point of view, of course, that I'd been making my own for years. From Lebanon, or even before I was born, to Armenia, to New York, to Los Angeles, and now the body of my brother, I had been following a virtual trail of ruins for the better part of my life.

227

He came up to the painting , dabbed his brush on the palette and made a few strokes on the canvas, and then dabbed again and made a few more strokes. Finally, he stepped back for me to see. "That," he said, "is for you; for you and Adam." On the left and halfway up, he'd painted a horizontal band of sunlight. Still wet, the oil was golden and glistening. But whether the light it provided was coming or going was impossible to say; whether it was breaking on the horizon, or draining away from beneath a door.